W9-CEN-195

NON SANZ DROICT

William Shakespeare

MEASURE
for
MEASURE

Edited by S. Nagarajan

The Signet Classic Shakespeare
GENERAL EDITOR: SYLVAN BARNET

*Revised and Updated
Bibliography*

A SIGNET CLASSIC

NEW AMERICAN LIBRARY

NEW YORK AND SCARBOROUGH, ONTARIO

COPYRIGHT © 1964 BY S. NAGARAJAN
COPYRIGHT © 1963 BY SYLVAN BARNET
ALL RIGHTS RESERVED

©

SIGNET CLASSIC TRADEMARK REG. U.S. PAT. OFF. AND FOREIGN COUNTRIES
REGISTERED TRADEMARK—MARCA REGISTRADA
HECHO EN CHICAGO, U.S.A.

SIGNET, SIGNET CLASSIC, MENTOR, PLUME, MERIDIAN AND NAL
BOOKS are published in the United States by
New American Library,
1633 Broadway, New York, New York 10019,
in Canada by The New American Library of Canada Limited,
81 Mack Avenue, Scarborough, Ontario M1L 1M8

FIRST PRINTING, JUNE, 1964

13   14   15   16   17   18   19   20

PRINTED IN THE UNITED STATES OF AMERICA

Contents

Shakespeare: Prefatory Remarks

Between the record of his baptism in Stratford on 26 April 1564 and the record of his burial in Stratford on 25 April 1616, some forty documents name Shakespeare, and many others name his parents, his children, and his grandchildren. More facts are known about William Shakespeare than about any other playwright of the period except Ben Jonson. The facts should, however, be distinguished from the legends. The latter, inevitably more engaging and better known, tell us that the Stratford boy killed a calf in high style, poached deer and rabbits, and was forced to flee to London, where he held horses outside a playhouse. These traditions are only traditions; they may be true, but no evidence supports them, and it is well to stick to the facts.

Mary Arden, the dramatist's mother, was the daughter of a substantial landowner; about 1557 she married John Shakespeare, who was a glove-maker and trader in various farm commodities. In 1557 John Shakespeare was a member of the Council (the governing body of Stratford), in 1558 a constable of the borough, in 1561 one of the two town chamberlains, in 1565 an alderman (entitling him to the appellation "Mr."), in 1568 high bailiff—the town's highest political office, equivalent to mayor. After 1577, for an unknown reason he drops out of local politics. The birthday of William Shakespeare, the eldest son of this locally prominent man, is unrecorded; but the Stratford parish register records that the infant was baptized on 26 April 1564. (It is quite possible that he was born on 23 April, but this date has probably been assigned by tradition because it is the date on which, fifty-two years later, he died.) The attendance records of the Stratford grammar school of the period are not extant, but it is reasonable to assume that the son of a local official attended the school and received substantial training in Latin. The masters of the school from Shakespeare's seventh to fifteenth years held Oxford degrees; the Elizabethan curriculum excluded mathematics and the natural sciences but taught a good deal of Latin rhetoric, logic, and literature. On 27 November 1582 a marriage license was issued to Shakespeare and Anne Hathaway, eight years his senior. The couple had a child in May, 1583. Perhaps the marriage was necessary, but perhaps the couple had earlier engaged in a formal "troth plight" which would render their children legitimate even if no further ceremony were performed. In 1585 Anne Hathaway bore Shakespeare twins.

That Shakespeare was born is excellent; that he married and had children is pleasant; but that we know nothing about his departure from Stratford to London, or about the beginning of his theatrical career, is lamentable and must be admitted. We would gladly sacrifice details about his children's baptism for details about his earliest days on the stage. Perhaps the poaching episode is true (but it is first reported almost a century after Shakespeare's death), or perhaps he first left Stratford to be a schoolteacher, as another tradition holds; perhaps he was moved by

> Such wind as scatters young men through the world,
> To seek their fortunes further than at home
> Where small experience grows.

In 1592, thanks to the cantankerousness of Robert Greene, a rival playwright and a pamphleteer, we have our first reference, a snarling one, to Shakespeare as an actor and playwright. Greene warns those of his own educated friends who wrote for the theater against an actor who has presumed to turn playwright:

> There is an upstart crow, beautified with our feathers, that with his *tiger's heart wrapped in a player's hide*

supposes he is as well able to bombast out a blank verse as the best of you, and being an absolute Johannes-factotum is in his own conceit the only Shake-scene in a country.

The reference to the player, as well as the allusion to Aesop's crow (who strutted in borrowed plumage, as an actor struts in fine words not his own), makes it clear that by this date Shakespeare had both acted and written. That Shakespeare is meant is indicated not only by "Shake-scene" but by the parody of a line from one of Shakespeare's plays, *3 Henry VI:* "O, tiger's heart wrapped in a woman's hide." If Shakespeare in 1592 was prominent enough to be attacked by an envious dramatist, he probably had served an apprenticeship in the theater for at least a few years.

In any case, by 1592 Shakespeare had acted and written, and there are a number of subsequent references to him as an actor: documents indicate that in 1598 he is a "principal comedian," in 1603 a "principal tragedian," in 1608 he is one of the "men players." The profession of actor was not for a gentleman, and it occasionally drew the scorn of university men who resented writing speeches for persons less educated than themselves, but it was respectable enough: players, if prosperous, were in effect members of the bourgeoisie, and there is nothing to suggest that Stratford considered William Shakespeare less than a solid citizen. When, in 1596, the Shakespeares were granted a coat of arms, the grant was made to Shakespeare's father, but probably William Shakespeare (who the next year bought the second-largest house in town) had arranged the matter on his own behalf. In subsequent transactions he is occasionally styled a gentleman.

Although in 1593 and 1594 Shakespeare published two narrative poems dedicated to the Earl of Southampton, *Venus and Adonis* and *The Rape of Lucrece,* and may well have written most or all of his sonnets in the middle nineties, Shakespeare's literary activity seems to have been almost entirely devoted to the theater. (It may be significant that the two narrative poems were written in years when the plague closed the theaters for several months.) In 1594 he was a charter member of a theatrical company called the Chamberlain's Men (which in 1603 changed its name to the King's Men); until he retired to Stratford (about 1611, apparently), he was with this remarkably stable company. From 1599 the company acted primarily at the Globe Theatre, in which Shakespeare held a one-tenth interest. Other Elizabethan dramatists are known to have acted, but no other is known also to have been entitled to a share in the profits of the playhouse.

Shakespeare's first eight published plays did not have his name on them, but this is not remarkable; the most popular play of the sixteenth century, Thomas Kyd's *The Spanish Tragedy,* went through many editions without naming Kyd, and Kyd's authorship is known only because a book on the profession of acting happens to quote (and attribute to Kyd) some lines on the interest of Roman emperors in the drama. What is remarkable is that after 1598 Shakespeare's name commonly appears on printed plays—some of which are not his. Another indication of his popularity comes from Francis Meres, author of *Palladis Tamia: Wit's Treasury* (1598): in this anthology of snippets accompanied by an essay on literature, many playwrights are mentioned, but Shakespeare's name occurs more often than any other, and Shakespeare is the only playwright whose plays are listed.

From his acting, playwriting, and share in a theater, Shakespeare seems to have made considerable money. He put it to work, making substantial investments in Stratford real estate. When he made his will (less than a month before he died), he sought to leave his property intact to his descendants. Of small bequests to relatives and to friends (including three actors, Richard Burbage, John Heminges, and Henry Condell), that to his wife of the second-best bed has provoked the most comment; perhaps it was the bed the couple had slept in, the best being reserved for visitors. In any case, had Shakespeare not excepted it, the bed would have gone (with the rest of his household possessions) to his daughter and her husband. On 25 April 1616 he was buried within the chancel of the church at Stratford. An unattractive monument to his memory, placed on a wall near the grave, says he died on 23 April. Over the grave itself are the lines, perhaps by Shakespeare, that (more than his literary fame) have kept his bones undisturbed in the crowded burial ground where old bones were often dislodged to make way for new:

> Good friend, for Jesus' sake forbear
> To dig the dust enclosèd here.
> Bless be the man that spares these stones
> And cursed be he that moves my bones.

Thirty-seven plays, as well as some nondramatic poems, are held to constitute the Shakespeare canon. The dates of composition of most of the works are highly uncertain, but there is often evidence of a *terminus a quo* (starting point) and/or a *terminus ad quem* (terminal point) that provides a framework for intelligent guessing. For example, *Richard II* cannot be earlier than 1595, the publication date of some material to which it is indebted; *The Merchant of Venice* cannot be later than 1598, the year Francis Meres mentioned it. Sometimes arguments for a date hang on an alleged topical allusion, such as the lines about the unseasonable weather in *A Midsummer Night's Dream,* II.i.81–117, but such an allusion (if indeed it is an allusion) can be variously interpreted, and in any case there is always the possibility that a topical allusion was inserted during a revision, years after the composition of a play. Dates are often attributed on the basis of style, and although conjectures about style usually rest on other conjectures, sooner or later one must rely on one's literary sense. There is no real proof, for example, that *Othello* is not as early as *Romeo and Juliet,* but one feels *Othello* is later, and because the first record of its performance is 1604, one is glad enough to set its composition at that date and not push it back into Shakespeare's early years. The following chronology, then, is as much indebted to informed guesswork and sensitivity as it is to fact. The dates, necessarily imprecise, indicate something like a scholarly consensus.

PLAYS

1588–93	*The Comedy of Errors*
1588–94	*Love's Labor's Lost*
1590–91	*2 Henry VI*
1590–91	*3 Henry VI*
1591–92	*1 Henry VI*
1592–93	*Richard III*
1592–94	*Titus Andronicus*
1593–94	*The Taming of the Shrew*
1593–95	*The Two Gentlemen of Verona*
1594–96	*Romeo and Juliet*
1595	*Richard II*
1594–96	*A Midsummer Night's Dream*
1596–97	*King John*
1596–97	*The Merchant of Venice*
1597	*1 Henry IV*
1597–98	*2 Henry IV*
1598–99	*Henry V*
1598–1600	*Much Ado About Nothing*
1599	*Julius Caesar*
1599–1600	*As You Like It*
1599–1600	*Twelfth Night*
1600–01	*Hamlet*
1597–1601	*The Merry Wives of Windsor*
1601–02	*Troilus and Cressida*
1602–04	*All's Well That Ends Well*
1603–04	*Othello*
1604	*Measure for Measure*
1605–06	*King Lear*
1605–06	*Macbeth*
1606–07	*Antony and Cleopatra*
1605–08	*Timon of Athens*
1607–09	*Coriolanus*
1608–09	*Pericles*
1609–10	*Cymbeline*
1610–11	*The Winter's Tale*
1611	*The Tempest*
1612–13	*Henry VIII*

POEMS

1592	*Venus and Adonis*
1593–94	*The Rape of Lucrece*
1593–1600	*Sonnets*
1600–01	*The Phoenix and the Turtle*

Shakespeare's Theater

In Shakespeare's infancy, Elizabethan actors performed wherever they could—in great halls, at court, in the courtyards of inns. The innyards must have made rather unsatisfactory theaters: on some days they were unavailable because carters bringing goods to London used them as depots; when available, they had to be rented from the innkeeper; perhaps most important, London inns were subject to the Common Council of London, which was not well disposed toward theatricals. In 1574 the Common Council required that plays and playing places in London be licensed. It asserted that

> sundry great disorders and inconveniences have been found to ensue to this city by the inordinate haunting of great multitudes of people, specially youth, to plays, interludes, and shows, namely occasion of frays and quarrels, evil practices of incontinency in great inns having chambers and secret places adjoining to their open stages and galleries,

and ordered that innkeepers who wished licenses to hold performances put up a bond and make contributions to the poor.

The requirement that plays and innyard theaters be licensed, along with the other drawbacks of playing at inns, probably drove James Burbage (a carpenter-turned-actor) to rent in 1576 a plot of land northeast of the city walls and to build here—on property outside the jurisdiction of the city—England's first permanent construction designed for plays. He called it simply the Theatre. About all that is known of its construction is that it was wood.

It soon had imitators, the most famous being the Globe (1599), built across the Thames (again outside the city's jurisdiction), out of timbers of the Theatre, which had been dismantled when Burbage's lease ran out.

There are three important sources of information about the structure of Elizabethan playhouses—drawings, a contract, and stage directions in plays. Of drawings, only the so-called De Witt drawing (c. 1596) of the Swan—really a friend's copy of De Witt's drawing—is of much significance. It shows a building of three tiers, with a stage jutting from a wall into the yard or center of the building. The tiers are roofed, and part of the stage is covered by a roof that projects from the rear and is supported at its front on two posts, but the groundlings, who paid a penny to stand in front of the stage, were exposed to the sky. (Performances in such a playhouse were held only in the daytime; artificial illumination was not used.) At the rear of the stage are two doors; above the stage is a gallery. The second major source of information, the contract for the Fortune, specifies that although the Globe is to be the model, the Fortune is to be square, eighty feet outside and fifty-five inside. The stage is to be forty-three feet broad, and is to extend into the middle of the yard (i.e., it is twenty-seven and a half feet deep). For patrons willing to pay more than the general admission charged of the groundlings, there were to be three galleries provided with seats. From the third chief source, stage directions, one learns that entrance to the stage was by doors, presumably spaced widely apart at the rear ("Enter one citizen at one door, and another at the other"), and that in addition to the platform stage there was occasionally some sort of curtained booth or alcove allowing for "discovery" scenes, and some sort of playing space "aloft" or "above" to represent (for example) the top of a city's walls or a room above the street. Doubtless each theater had its own peculiarities, but perhaps we can talk about a "typical" Elizabethan theater if we realize that no theater need exactly have fit the description, just as no father is the typical father with 3.7 children. This hypothetical theater is wooden, round or polygonal (in *Henry V* Shake-

speare calls it a "wooden *O*"), capable of holding some
eight hundred spectators standing in the yard around the
projecting elevated stage and some fifteen hundred additional spectators seated in the three roofed galleries. The
stage, protected by a "shadow" or "heavens" or roof, is
entered by two doors; behind the doors is the "tiring
house" (attiring house, i.e., dressing room), and above the
doors is some sort of gallery that may sometimes hold
spectators but that can be used (for example) as the
bedroom from which Romeo—according to a stage direction in one text—"goeth down." Some evidence suggests
that a throne can be lowered onto the platform stage,
perhaps from the "shadow"; certainly characters can descend from the stage through a trap or traps into the
cellar or "hell." Sometimes this space beneath the platform accommodates a sound-effects man or musician (in
Antony and Cleopatra "music of the hautboys is under the
stage") or an actor (in *Hamlet* the "Ghost cries under the
stage"). Most characters simply walk on and off, but because there is no curtain in front of the platform, corpses
will have to be carried off (Hamlet must lug Polonius' guts
into the neighbor room), or will have to fall at the rear,
where the curtain on the alcove or booth can be drawn
to conceal them.

   Such may have been the so-called "public theater." Another kind of theater, called the "private theater" because
its much greater admission charge limited its audience to
the wealthy or the prodigal, must be briefly mentioned.
The private theater was basically a large room, entirely
roofed and therefore artificially illuminated, with a stage
at one end. In 1576 one such theater was established in
Blackfriars, a Dominican priory in London that had been
suppressed in 1538 and confiscated by the Crown and
thus was not under the city's jurisdiction. All the actors
in the Blackfriars theater were boys about eight to thirteen
years old (in the public theaters similar boys played female
parts; a boy Lady Macbeth played to a man Macbeth).
This private theater had a precarious existence, and ceased
operations in 1584. In 1596 James Burbage, who had
already made theatrical history by building the Theatre,

began to construct a second Blackfriars theater. He died in 1597, and for several years this second Blackfriars theater was used by a troupe of boys, but in 1608 two of Burbage's sons and five other actors (including Shakespeare) became joint operators of the theater, using it in the winter when the open-air Globe was unsuitable. Perhaps such a smaller theater, roofed, artificially illuminated, and with a tradition of a courtly audience, exerted an influence on Shakespeare's late plays.

Performances in the private theaters may well have had intermissions during which music was played, but in the public theaters the action was probably uninterrupted, flowing from scene to scene almost without a break. Actors would enter, speak, exit, and others would immediately enter and establish (if necessary) the new locale by a few properties and by words and gestures. Here are some samples of Shakespeare's scene painting:

> This is Illyria, lady.

> Well, this is the Forest of Arden.

> This castle hath a pleasant seat; the air
> Nimbly and sweetly recommends itself
> Unto our gentle senses.

On the other hand, it is a mistake to conceive of the Elizabethan stage as bare. Although Shakespeare's Chorus in *Henry V* calls the stage an "unworthy scaffold" and urges the spectators to "eke out our performance with your mind," there was considerable spectacle. The last act of *Macbeth,* for example, has five stage directions calling for "drum and colors," and another sort of appeal to the eye is indicated by the stage direction "Enter Macduff, with Macbeth's head." Some scenery and properties may have been substantial; doubtless a throne was used, and in one play of the period we encounter this direction: "Hector takes up a great piece of rock and casts at Ajax, who tears up a young tree by the roots and assails Hector." The matter is of some importance, and will be glanced at again in the next section.

The Texts of Shakespeare

Though eighteen of his plays were published during his lifetime, Shakespeare seems never to have supervised their publication. There is nothing unusual here; when a playwright sold a play to a theatrical company he surrendered his ownership of it. Normally a company would not publish the play, because to publish it meant to allow competitors to acquire the piece. Some plays, however, did get published: apparently treacherous actors sometimes pieced together a play for a publisher, sometimes a company in need of money sold a play, and sometimes a company allowed a play to be published that no longer drew audiences. That Shakespeare did not concern himself with publication, then, is scarcely remarkable; of his contemporaries only Ben Jonson carefully supervised the publication of his own plays. In 1623, seven years after Shakespeare's death, John Heminges and Henry Condell (two senior members of Shakespeare's company, who had performed with him for about twenty years) collected his plays—published and unpublished—into a large volume, commonly called the First Folio. (A folio is a volume consisting of sheets that have been folded once, each sheet thus making two leaves, or four pages. The eighteen plays published during Shakespeare's lifetime had been issued one play per volume in small books called quartos. Each sheet in a quarto has been folded twice, making four leaves, or eight pages.) The First Folio contains thirty-six plays; a thirty-seventh, *Pericles,* though not in the Folio, is regarded as canonical. Heminges and Condell suggest in an address "To the great variety of readers" that the republished plays are presented in better form than in the quartos: "Before you were abused with diverse stolen and surreptitious copies, maimed and deformed by the frauds and stealths of injurious impostors that exposed them; even those, are now offered to your view cured and perfect of their limbs, and all the rest absolute in their numbers, as he [i.e., Shakespeare] conceived them."

Whoever was assigned to prepare the texts for publication in the First Folio seems to have taken his job seriously and yet not to have performed it with uniform care. The sources of the texts seem to have been, in general, good unpublished copies or the best published copies. The first play in the collection, *The Tempest,* is divided into acts and scenes, has unusually full stage directions and descriptions of spectacle, and concludes with a list of the characters, but the editor was not able (or willing) to present all of the succeeding texts so fully dressed. Later texts occasionally show signs of carelessness: in one scene of *Much Ado About Nothing* the names of actors, instead of characters, appear as speech prefixes, as they had in the quarto, which the Folio reprints; proofreading throughout the Folio is spotty and apparently was done without reference to the printer's copy; the pagination of *Hamlet* jumps from 156 to 257.

A modern editor of Shakespeare must first select his copy; no problem if the play exists only in the Folio, but a considerable problem if the relationship between a quarto and the Folio—or an early quarto and a later one —is unclear. When an editor has chosen what seems to him to be the most authoritative text or texts for his copy, he has not done with making decisions. First of all, he must reckon with Elizabethan spelling. If he is not producing a facsimile, he probably modernizes it, but ought he to preserve the old form of words that apparently were pronounced quite unlike their modern forms—"lanthorn" "alablaster"? If he preserves these forms, is he really preserving Shakespeare's forms or perhaps those of a compositor in the printing house? What is one to do when one finds "lanthorn" and "lantern" in adjacent lines? (The editors of this series in general, but not invariably, assume that words should be spelled in their modern form.) Elizabethan punctuation, too, presents problems. For example in the First Folio, the only text for the play, Macbeth rejects his wife's idea that he can wash the blood from his hand:

> no: this my Hand will rather
> The multitudinous Seas incarnardine,
> Making the Greene one, Red.

Obviously an editor will remove the superfluous capitals, and he will probably alter the spelling to "incarnadine," but will he leave the comma before "red," letting Macbeth speak of the sea as "the green one," or will he (like most modern editors) remove the comma and thus have Macbeth say that his hand will make the ocean *uniformly* red?

An editor will sometimes have to change more than spelling or punctuation. Macbeth says to his wife:

> I dare do all that may become a man,
> Who dares no more, is none.

For two centuries editors have agreed that the second line is unsatisfactory, and have emended "no" to "do": "Who dares do more is none." But when in the same play Ross says that fearful persons

> floate vpon a wilde and violent Sea
> Each way, and moue,

need "move" be emended to "none," as it often is, on the hunch that the compositor misread the manuscript? The editors of the Signet Classic Shakespeare have restrained themselves from making abundant emendations. In their minds they hear Dr. Johnson on the dangers of emending: "I have adopted the Roman sentiment, that it is more honorable to save a citizen than to kill an enemy." Some departures (in addition to spelling, punctuation, and lineation) from the copy text have of course been made, but the original readings are listed in a note following the play, so that the reader can evaluate them for himself.

The editors of the Signet Classic Shakespeare, following tradition, have added line numbers and in many cases act and scene divisions as well as indications of locale at the beginning of scenes. The Folio divided most of the plays into acts and some into scenes. Early eighteenth-century editors increased the divisions. These divisions, which provide a convenient way of referring to passages in the plays, have been retained, but when not in the text chosen as the basis for the Signet Classic text they are enclosed in square brackets [ ] to indicate that they are editorial additions. Similarly, although no play of Shakespeare's published during his lifetime was equipped with indications of locale at the heads of scene divisions, locales have here been added in square brackets for the convenience of the reader, who lacks the information afforded to spectators by costumes, properties, and gestures. The spectator can tell at a glance he is in the throne room, but without an editorial indication the reader may be puzzled for a while. It should be mentioned, incidentally, that there are a few authentic stage directions—perhaps Shakespeare's, perhaps a prompter's—that suggest locales; for example, "Enter Brutus in his orchard," and "They go up into the Senate house." It is hoped that the bracketed additions provide the reader with the sort of help provided in these two authentic directions, but it is equally hoped that the reader will remember that the stage was not loaded with scenery.

No editor during the course of his work can fail to recollect some words Heminges and Condell prefixed to the Folio:

> It had been a thing, we confess, worthy to have been wished, that the author himself had lived to have set forth and overseen his own writings. But since it hath been ordained otherwise, and he by death departed from that right, we pray you do not envy his friends the office of their care and pain to have collected and published them.

Nor can an editor, after he has done his best, forget Heminges and Condell's final words: "And so we leave you to other of his friends, whom if you need can be your guides. If you need them not, you can lead yourselves, and others. And such readers we wish him."

SYLVAN BARNET
Tufts University

Introduction

Measure for Measure was first published in 1623 in the Folio of Shakespeare's works. It was probably written in 1604, for it is on record that a play called *Mesure for Mesure,* by "Shaxberd," was performed before King James I on 26 December of that year, when it was presumably a new play. It was thus composed just before the writing of the great tragedies in which Shakespeare's powers were at their height. It does not seem to have been performed again till 1662, and in fact, till recently, it was not popular on the stage in spite of its theatrical craftsmanship.

It was not popular with the older critics, either. Coleridge, to whom we owe some of our most penetrating Shakespeare criticism, found it "a hateful work," indeed "the only painful play" that Shakespeare ever wrote. Its comedy disgusted him and its tragedy seemed merely horrible. His sense of justice was also revolted by the pardon of Angelo, the corrupt deputy who is virtually guilty of both rape and murder. The heroine, Isabella, was to Coleridge an unamiable character who primly preferred her own chastity to her brother's life. That brother himself, Claudio, was a weak, vacillating youth who expected his sister to save him from the consequences of his own immorality. The play slithered through to an unearned happy ending which was entirely unconvincing. In general, the opinion of the nineteenth century was that *Measure for Measure* was essentially a dark comedy, full of bitter satire and cynicism, reflecting some obscure

phase of tragedy or disillusionment in the personal life
of Shakespeare himself.

In our own day a far different view of the play has
been favored. The twin myths of Shakespeare's personal
sorrows and of a general gloom during the early years
of the sixteenth century are no longer seriously held. It is
urged that the play should be read not as a picture of
normal human affairs with naturalistic character and
action, but as a dramatic parable, embodying some of
the noblest precepts of the Christian religion. The new
interpretation may now and then claim a consistency of
impression not quite warranted by the play itself, but it
seems more coherent than the old view which implicitly
accused Shakespeare of confusing art with life. While this
is the majority view of *Measure for Measure* today, there
are some modern critics who feel that the play is uneven,
though great. They think that Shakespeare's artistic experience has raised questions that cannot properly be
answered, sometimes even asked, in a tragicomedy; the
medium is inhibiting. As for the play's religious significance, they feel that the action and characterization are
more intimately inspired by Shakespeare's immediate
sources in drama and folklore than by Christianity. The
Italian storybook which probably gave him his plot contains several tales on the theme of a woman's forgiving
an enemy who has done her an irreparable wrong, and
the folklore of Shakespeare's day had popularized the
legend of the good monarch who, like the Duke in the
play, moves among his people in disguise to find out the
truth for himself and to protect the good and punish the
bad.

To help us toward a plausible interpretation of the play,
we may briefly look at its sources, and what Shakespeare
made of them. The chief one is almost certainly George
Whetstone's *Promos and Cassandra* (1578), a tedious,
though earnest, play in two parts of five acts each. Whetstone made a prose version of the story for his collection
of stories called the *Heptameron of Civil Discourses*
(1582). In addition to these works, Shakespeare very
probably knew the Italian source of Whetstone, the

Hecatommithi (1565) of Giraldi Cinthio, and Cinthio's dramatized version of the story, *Epitia* (1583). In Whetstone's play, Cassandra pleads with Promos for the life of her brother, Andrugio, who has been condemned to death for fornication. Promos agrees to pardon Andrugio if Cassandra will lie with him. She refuses, but ultimately consents when her brother appeals to her sisterly affection. After she has kept her side of the bargain, Promos goes back on his word, and commands the jailer to behead Andrugio and present the head to Cassandra. The compassionate jailer happens to know the truth and conceals Andrugio, presenting Cassandra with the head of a recently executed felon. Cassandra wants to commit suicide, but decides to appeal to the King first and to seek vengeance on Promos. The King finds that the complaint is true and orders that Promos should marry her and then be put to death. But as soon as the marriage is solemnized, Cassandra finds herself "tied in the greatest bonds of affection to her husband." She now becomes "an earnest suitor for his life" with the King, but in vain. In the meanwhile, her brother, who has been living under a disguise, comes to know of her predicament and reveals himself to the King. Promos is pardoned, and everything ends happily.

When Shakespeare took up this tale for dramatic treatment, he made certain far-reaching changes. In the first place, Cassandra's compelled acceptance of the loathsome and virtually illusory choice thrust on her by Promos hurts the moral feelings of the reader beyond healing, and her last-minute marriage, by royal fiat, to the violator of her honor merely adds insult to injury. Even in Shakespeare's day, Puritan moralists, to specify a single group, held that there were wrongs which no marriage could redress. The sudden change of Cassandra's affections from hatred to love as soon as she is married to Promos is also rather incredible. Very properly, therefore, Shakespeare made his heroine refuse to yield to Angelo. But since the story required that Angelo's condition should somehow be met, he created the character of Mariana and substituted her for Isabella by means of an old folktale device which was presumably acceptable to the original audience. He had already used "the bed trick," as it is usually called, in what is very likely an earlier play, *All's Well That Ends Well*. The "bed trick" does not commend itself to modern taste, and does not also quite agree with the realistic context of the play, but we must remember that Mariana is deeply in love with Angelo, and the consummation of her love leads to her marriage with him at the end. Our sympathies are so fully engaged in her behalf that we want her to be happy, and wink at this otherwise dubious mode of securing her happiness.

Shakespeare also altered the significance of the brother's offense. In Whetstone's play, Andrugio is guilty of fornication, committed, as in Shakespeare's play, with the voluntary consent of the girl. Cassandra attributes her brother's offense partly to the irresistible force of love and partly to his youth. In *Measure for Measure,* however, Claudio explains the reason for his arrest differently:

> From too much liberty, my Lucio, liberty.
> As surfeit is the father of much fast,
> So every scope by the immoderate use
> Turns to restraint. Our natures do pursue,
> Like rats that ravin down their proper bane,
> A thirsty evil, and when we drink, we die. (I.ii.128–33)

In our very nature there is something that drives us into acts of too much liberty, which we loathe even while we indulge in them.

> For that which I do, I allow not: for what I would, that do I not; but what I hate, that do I. . . . For I know that in me (that is, in my flesh) dwelleth no good thing: for to will is present with me; but how to perform that which is good I find not. For the good that I would, I do not: but the evil which I would not, that I do. . . . I find then a law, that, when I would do good, evil is present with me. For I delight in the law of God after the inward man. But I see another law in my members, warring against the law of my mind and

bringing me into captivity to the law of sin which is in
my members.

                              (Romans 7:15, 18, 19, 21–23)

Claudio is angry and disgusted with himself. But he
does not know what to do with this problem. His friend
Lucio, described in the original list of actors as a "fantastic," does not see that there is a problem. Lucio's view
of the matter is reflected in the imagery of his speech when
he describes Claudio's offense:

> Your brother and his lover have embraced;
> As those that feed grow full, as blossoming time
> That from the seedness the bare fallow brings
> To teeming foison, even so her plenteous womb
> Expresseth his full tilth and husbandry.
>
>   (I.iv.40–44)

Juliet's "fertility" was realized by Claudio's "tilth." *Not*
to do as Claudio did is to be guilty of a lack of "husbandry." There is enough truth in this view of human sex
to make it superficially attractive, but we are put on our
guard by being shown its consequences. Lucio has se-
duced Mistress Kate Keepdown and has abandoned her
and the child. (Incidentally, the child has been looked
after by a bawd, a fact which should make us distrust
theories of Shakespeare's cynicism in *Measure for Measure*.) He has degenerated into a coarse sensualist, bent
on his own pleasures and reckless of all the essential ob-
ligations of a decent life in society. Even his interest in
Claudio's pardon is not quite disinterested. "I pray she
may"—that is, Isabella may persuade Angelo—he tells
Claudio, "as well for the encouragement of the like,
which else would stand under grievous imposition, as for
the enjoying of thy life, who I would be sorry should be
thus foolishly lost at a game of tick-tack." (I.ii.191–95.)

Shakespeare enlarged the role of the overlord in the
story to make him a disguised spectator of and later an
active participant in the action of the play. Duke Vincentio has been rather slack in his princely duties, loving his subjects not wisely but too well, but otherwise

he is a scholar, a statesman, and a soldier. We are told further that his supreme concern has always been to know himself. When he contributes, in his indirect way, to the debate initiated by Claudio, he implies that self-restraint is both essential and possible. When he goes to the prison, disguised as a friar, to console "the afflicted spirits" there, he requests the provost to inform him of the nature of the crimes committed by the condemned prisoners so that he may "minister to them accordingly." With Claudio the ministration takes the form of setting him free from "the deceiving promises of life" and of creating in him a calm resolution to face the approaching end. Sir Thomas More, the Tudor statesman and saint about whom Shakespeare perhaps helped to write a play, declares in his little treatise, *The Four Last Things,* which he wrote to teach "the art of dying well," that nothing can more effectively withdraw the human soul from the wretched affections of the body than a sincere remembrance of death. "The thirsty evil" which Claudio bemoans is the consequence of an excessive attachment to life, itself the result of our forgetfulness of our "glassy essence."

Shakespeare made Isabella a novice of Saint Clare. Why he did so is not quite obvious, for his young women do not need any "motivation" to justify their preference for chastity. Chastity is an absolute value with them. Isabella's novitiate should perhaps be regarded as her answer to the problem of the "prompture of the blood," of which she seems to have some personal knowledge if one may judge from the accents of her admission to Angelo that women, no less than men, are frail:

> Ay, as the glasses where they view themselves,
> Which are as easy broke as they make forms.
> Women! Help heaven! Men their creation mar
> In profiting by them. Nay, call us ten times frail;
> For we are soft as our complexions are,
> And credulous to false prints.

(II.iv.125–30)

Her denunciation of her brother when he timidly suggests that she should yield to Angelo no doubt grates on our ears—Sir Arthur Quiller-Couch was moved to declare that there was something rancid in her chastity—but her harshness reflects her bitterness at being asked to abet the "prompture of the blood." It is significant that the only conventual rule that we hear of in the play relates to receiving male visitors, and that Isabella should desire a stricter restraint upon the votarists of Saint Clare though that order has the reputation of being the strictest women's order of the Roman Catholic Church. At the end of the play, the Duke makes her a proposal which, he says, "much imports her good," surely not a material good, for she is not presented as a girl with whom such frivolous considerations would weigh. Presumably she accepts the Duke's proposal; in Shakespeare's day, it was perfectly in order for a novice to go back to secular life. Though the play itself is ambiguous on the point, it is attractive to believe that Isabella made the discovery that the "prompture of the blood" could be resolved in the married state also.

Halfway through the play, Isabella meets Mariana. Mariana plays a small but significant part in the design of the drama. In spite of Angelo's "unjust unkindness" which should "in all reason" have quenched her love for him, she continues to cherish him. But she will not substitute herself for Isabella until "the friar" whose advice has often stilled her "brawling discontent" assures her that it is no sin. In the last act she pleads that her husband's evil is a passing cloud which will leave him purer than before. Her love is dedicated entirely to the welfare of the beloved's soul, and we may describe it, without undue exaggeration, as a humble human instance of the divine love which found out the remedy when all the souls that were, were forfeit. Mariana's love has transcended the problem of the "prompture of the blood." We know that Isabella is deeply moved by the story of Mariana's love, and it is her appeal that Angelo's very evil may be the cause of his regeneration which in the end wins Isabella over to plead for him. Perhaps Isabella learned the secret of a soul-centered love from Mariana.

Between Isabella and Angelo there is a curious superficial resemblance. Angelo has lived in retirement, and
evidently prefers it to the public office which he is summoned to. He has tried to "blunt his natural edge" with
"profits of the mind, study and fast." A due sincerity
governs his deeds till he looks on Isabella. But the
"prompture of the blood" finally overcomes him. Isabella's very virtue corrupts him, while the strumpet with
all her double vigor, art and nature, could never once stir
him. He has identified virtue wholly with a mode of external conduct. His seemingly virtuous conduct does not
represent a transformed will, but is a mere factitious creation, a state whereon he has studied, not a habit of the
soul. He himself points out that the problem of "we
would" and "we would not" arises when we forget our
"grace," a word which may well have a specific Christian
sense in view of Isabella's charge that he is not "new
made." It is characteristic of him that he should mistake
Mariana's love for levity. His ear, coarsened by the stri-
dent jazz of a code that is throttling the instincts, cannot
catch the quiet melody of an ethic that observes the very
rhythm of the blood. So "the natural guiltiness" lurks
within, subverting virtue itself to cause his fall. "Sin, taking occasion by the commandment, deceived me, and by
it slew me" (Romans 7:11). The sentence of death that
the Duke passes on him frees Angelo from an intolerable, meaningless existence, and he welcomes it. He is a
new-made man after he is pardoned. To detest him and
to disagree with his pardon is natural, for the process of
his contrition is rather hurried, but we must try to understand his predicament.

Angelo's ignorance of the inwardness of virtue is also
the cause of the excessive legalism of his rule. At bottom, the criticism of the rule of law as Angelo interprets
it is that it is ultimately futile. Its severity is aimless, and
its achievements are transitory. "There is so great a fever
on goodness that the dissolution of it must cure it," says
the disguised Duke to Escalus. The time has come when
nothing but a total dissolution of the fever that afflicts
goodness can restore it to its pristine health. The laws

are no doubt "the needful bits and curbs of headstrong weeds," but they can at best regulate conduct; they cannot change the "old man" in us. And as long as that change does not take place, sensuality will prevail in Vienna, openly or covertly.

The wise old Escalus, the most genial character in the play, tries to deal with the problem in his gentle, humanitarian way, but even he is shocked when he discovers that Mistress Overdone is still forfeit in the same kind after double and treble admonition. Pompey refuses to change at all. The Duke himself, as it happens, intervenes to save Claudio's life precisely at the moment when Claudio sues to be rid of it; that is, when Claudio is cured of his malady. In dealing with Barnardine again, the Duke reveals his essentially spiritual approach to the problem of law and justice. Barnardine is a murderer and has a stubborn soul that apprehends no further than this life, and he has squared his life accordingly. When the Duke pardons all his earthly faults, he entrusts him to a friar for advice.

With Angelo, however, he decides on "measure for measure." "Judge not, that ye be not judged. For with what judgment ye judge, ye shall be judged: and with what measure ye mete, it shall be measured to you again" (Matthew 7:1–2). He also reminds Isabella that her brother's ghost cries out for vengeance. In condemning Angelo, the Duke thus seems to observe the law of the Old Testament—an eye for an eye and a tooth for a tooth. But actually he is testing Isabella's adherence to the New Law, which commands that one's enemy shall be loved as a friend, and that good shall be returned for evil. How superbly she answers the test! She does not plead for Angelo's pardon, for she has seen that Mariana's plea for mercy has been disallowed. With a boldness that takes away one's breath, she asserts that Angelo is not guilty at all. There are three charges against him. His "salt imagination" wronged her honor; he violated sacred chastity; and he broke his promise that he would pardon Claudio if the foul ransom were paid. The first charge, the Duke himself has recommended should be pardoned because that "salt imagination" provided the opportunity of doing a service to Mariana. The second charge is not true because Mariana was Angelo's wife on a precontract. As for the "promise breach," it cannot be denied that Isabella did not in fact lie with Angelo or that her brother was guilty, after all, of the crime for which he was sentenced. The type of betrothal which Claudio and Juliet had entered upon did not in law give them any marital rights, whereas Mariana's contract with Angelo did, at least in law. Finally, it is true that Angelo intended to violate her, but the intention never became an act and law cannot take cognizance of thoughts. "Thoughts are no subjects, / Intents but merely thoughts." Counsel for the defense submits therefore that the accused is not guilty on any count, does not need a pardon, and much less can be punished with "measure for measure." The prosperous art which she shows in playing with reason and discourse could hardly be stretched further.

> Ye have heard that it hath been said, Thou shalt love thy neighbor, and hate thine enemy. But I say unto you, Love your enemies, bless them that curse you, do good to them that hurt you, and pray for them which despitefully use you and persecute you. That ye may be the children of your Father which is in heaven: for he maketh his sun to rise on the evil and on the good, and sendeth rain on the just and on the unjust. . . . Be ye therefore perfect, even as your Father which is in heaven is perfect.
>
> (Matthew 5:43–45, 48)

Such then are some of the themes and characters of the play before us. Shakespeare's contemporaries would have probably called it a tragicomedy, a new genre in those days. Tragicomedy is not a loose putting together of tragedy with comedy, but an independent form of dramatic composition with an aesthetic of its own. As the Italian playwright Giambattista Guarini, who had himself written a tragicomedy, set forth in his *Compendium of Tragicomic Poetry* (published in 1601): "He who makes a tragicomedy does not intend to compose separately either a tragedy or a comedy, but from the two a third thing that will be perfect of its kind, and may take from the others the parts that with most verisimilitude can stand together." From tragedy, said Guarini, tragicomedy takes the movement but not the disturbance of the feelings, the pleasure and not the sadness, the danger but not the death. From comedy, it takes laughter that is not excessive, modest amusement, feigned difficulty, happy reversal, and above all, the comic order. Speaking of the style proper to tragicomedy, Guarini said that the magnificent was its norm, combined not with the grave as in a tragedy, but with the polished. There is something in this description of tragicomedy that reminds us of *Measure for Measure*. For instance, our awareness of the immanence of the Duke, with his declared objective of testing whether power will change purpose effectively, prevents the first part of the play from the tragic course. The "intrigue" of the fourth act does not exist for its own sake, but serves to establish the control of the Duke over the action and to lead to a happy conclusion. The episode of Barnardine makes clear that the resolution to face death which "the friar" has preached to Claudio is far from the insensibility and desperateness of a Barnardine, who will not "wake." The style of the play ranges from the passionate conjurations of Isabella, the tortured self-examinations of Angelo, the exploratory dialectic of Angelo and Isabella, the meditative analysis of the Duke and the surging thrill of terror in Claudio as he stands at the brink of the grave to the irreverent bawdry of Lucio and the petty cunning of Pompey's coiled speech with Escalus. Coleridge was obliged to acknowledge that *Measure for Measure* was Shakespearean throughout. It is indeed one of Shakespeare's most impressive achievements whether we consider the seriousness of the issues it deals with, its characterization, or its construction.

S. NAGARAJAN
University of Poona

Measure for Measure

The Scene: Vienna

The names of all the actors:

Vincentio, the Duke
Angelo, the Deputy
Escalus, an ancient Lord
Claudio, a young gentleman
Lucio, a fantastic
Two Other Like Gentlemen
Provost
Thomas } two friars
Peter
[A Justice]
[Varrus]
Elbow, a simple constable
Froth, a foolish gentleman
Clown [Pompey, servant to Mistress Overdone]
Abhorson, an executioner
Barnardine, a dissolute prisoner
Isabella, sister to Claudio
Mariana, betrothed to Angelo
Juliet, beloved of Claudio
Francisca, a nun
Mistress Overdone, a bawd
[Lords, Officers, Citizens, Boy, and Attendants]

Measure for Measure

ACT I

Scene I. [*The Duke's palace.*]

Enter Duke, Escalus, Lords, [and Attendants].

Duke. Escalus.

Escalus. My lord.

Duke. Of government the properties°¹ to unfold,
Would seem in me t' affect speech and discourse,
Since I am put to know° that your own science°   5
Exceeds, in that, the lists° of all advice
My strength can give you. Then no more remains
But that, to your sufficiency as your worth is able,°
And let them work. The nature of our people,
Our city's institutions, and the terms   10
For common justice, y'are as pregnant in°
As art and practice hath enrichèd any
That we remember. There is our commission,
From which we would not have you warp.° Call
   hither,

---

¹ The degree sign° indicates a footnote, which is keyed to the text by
line number. Text references are printed in *italic* type; the annotation
follows in roman type.
I.1.3 *properties* characteristics 5 *put to know* given to understand
5 *science* knowledge 6 *lists* limits 8 *to your sufficiency. . . able* (perhaps a line is missing after this line) 11 *pregnant in* full of knowledge
14 *warp* deviate

15   I say, bid come before us Angelo.

                                              [*Exit an Attendant.*]

    What figure° of us, think you, he will bear?°
    For you must know, we have with special soul°
    Elected him our absence to supply;
    Lent him our terror, dressed him with our love,
20   And given his deputation all the organs°
    Of our own pow'r. What think you of it?

Escalus. If any in Vienna be of worth
    To undergo° such ample grace and honor,
    It is Lord Angelo.

                  Enter Angelo.

Duke.   Look where he comes.

25   *Angelo.* Always obedient to your Grace's will,
    I come to know your pleasure.

Duke.   Angelo,
    There is a kind of character° in thy life,
    That to th' observer doth thy history
    Fully unfold. Thyself and thy belongings°
30   Are not thine own so proper° as to waste
    Thyself upon thy virtues, they on thee.
    Heaven doth with us as we with torches do,°
    Not light them for themselves; for if our virtues
    Did not go forth of us, 'twere all alike
    As if we had them not. Spirits are not finely
35   touched
    But to fine issues,° nor Nature never lends
    The smallest scruple° of her excellence
    But like a thrifty goddess she determines

---

16 *figure* image   16 *bear* represent   17 *soul* thought   20 *organs*
means of action   23 *undergo* enjoy   27 *character* secret handwriting   29 *belongings* endowments   30 *proper* exclusively   32 *Heaven*
. . . *do* (see Luke 11:33: "No man, when he hath lighted a candle,
putteth it in a secret place, neither under a bushel, but on a candlestick that they which come in may see the light." Also Matthew 7:16:
"Ye shall know them by their fruits")   35–36 *Spirits . . . issues* i.e.,
great qualities are bestowed only so that they may lead to great
achievements   37 *scruple* 1/24 oz.

Herself the glory of a creditor,
Both thanks and use.° But I do bend° my speech   40
To one that can my part in him advertise.°
Hold therefore, Angelo:
In our remove° be thou at full ourself;
Mortality and mercy in Vienna
Live in thy tongue and heart. Old Escalus,   45
Though first in question,° is thy secondary.°
Take thy commission.

Angelo.   Now, good my lord,
Let there be some more test made of my mettle°
Before so noble and so great a figure
Be stamped upon it.

Duke.   No more evasion.   50
We have with a leavened° and preparèd choice
Proceeded to you; therefore take your honors.
Our haste from hence is of so quick condition
That it prefers itself,° and leaves unquestioned°
Matters of needful value. We shall write to you,   55
As time and our concernings shall importune,
How it goes with us, and do look to know
What doth befall you here. So fare you well.
To th' hopeful execution do I leave you
Of your commissions.

Angelo.   Yet give leave, my lord,   60
That we may bring° you something on the way.

Duke. My haste may not admit it;
Nor need you, on mine honor, have to do
With any scruple; your scope is as mine own,
So to enforce or qualify the laws   65
As to your soul seems good. Give me your hand.
I'll privily away; I love the people,
But do not like to stage me to their eyes.
Though it do well, I do not relish well

40 *use* interest   40 *bend* address   41 *advertise* display prominently
43 *remove* absence   46 *question* consideration   46 *secondary* sub-
ordinate   48 *mettle* (pun on "metal," i.e., material)   51 *leavened*
i.e., long-pondered   54 *prefers itself* takes precedence   54 *unques-
tioned* unexamined   61 *bring* escort

70   Their loud applause and aves° vehement.
      Nor do I think the man of safe discretion
      That does affect it. Once more, fare you well.

Angelo. The heavens give safety to your purposes.

Escalus. Lead forth and bring you back in happiness.

75   _Duke._ I thank you; fare you well.   _Exit._

Escalus. I shall desire you, sir, to give me leave
      To have free speech with you; and it concerns me
      To look into the bottom of my place.°
      A pow'r I have, but of what strength and nature,
80   I am not yet instructed.

Angelo. 'Tis so with me. Let us withdraw together,
      And we may soon our satisfaction have
      Touching that point.

Escalus.   I'll wait upon your honor.
                                        Exeunt.

Scene II. [_A street._]

Enter Lucio and two other Gentlemen.

Lucio. If the Duke, with the other dukes, come not
      to composition° with the King of Hungary,° why
      then all the dukes fall upon the King.

First Gentleman. Heaven grant us its peace, but not
5   the King of Hungary's!

Second Gentleman. Amen.

Lucio. Thou conclud'st like the sanctimonious pirate,
      that went to sea with the Ten Commandments, but
      scraped one out of the table.

70 _aves_ salutations   78 _To look . . . place_ i.e., to examine carefully
the range of my authority   I.ii.2 _composition_ agreement   2 _Hun-
gary_ (perhaps a pun on "hungry")

Second Gentleman. "Thou shalt not steal"?   10

Lucio. Ay, that he razed.

First Gentleman. Why, 'twas a commandment to command the captain and all the rest from their functions: they put forth to steal. There's not a soldier of us all that, in the thanksgiving before meat, do   15
relish the petition well that prays for peace.

Second Gentleman. I never heard any soldier dislike it.

Lucio. I believe thee, for I think thou never wast where grace was said.   20

Second Gentleman. No? A dozen times at least.

First Gentleman. What, in meter?

Lucio. In any proportion,° or in any language.

First Gentleman. I think, or in any religion.

Lucio. Ay, why not? Grace is grace, despite of all   25
controversy: as, for example, thou thyself art a wicked villain, despite of all grace.

First Gentleman. Well, there went but a pair of shears between us.°

Lucio. I grant; as there may between the lists° and   30
the velvet. Thou art the list.

First Gentleman. And thou the velvet. Thou art good velvet; thou'rt a three-piled° piece, I warrant thee. I had as lief be a list of an English kersey,° as be piled, as thou art piled, for a French velvet.° Do   35
I speak feelingly° now?

Lucio. I think thou dost; and, indeed, with most pain-

23 *proportion* length   28–29 *there . . . us* i.e., we are cut from the same cloth   30 *lists* selvage or border of a cloth (usually of a different material from the body)   33 *three-piled* (1) pile of a treble thickness (2) "piled" (bald) as a result of venereal disease   34 *kersey* coarse cloth (therefore "plain and honest")   35 *French velvet* (1) excellent velvet (2) French prostitute (syphilis was also known as "the French disease")   35–36 *Do . . . feelingly* i.e., do I touch you there?

ful feeling° of thy speech. I will, out of thine own
confession, learn to begin thy health; but, whilst I
40   live, forget to drink after thee.°

First Gentleman. I think I have done myself wrong,
have I not?

Second Gentleman. Yes, that thou hast, whether thou
art tainted or free.

Enter Bawd [Mistress Overdone].

45   *Lucio.* Behold, behold, where Madam Mitigation
comes! I have purchased as many diseases under
her roof as come to—

Second Gentleman. To what, I pray?

Lucio. Judge.

50   *Second Gentleman.* To three thousand dolors° a year.

First Gentleman. Ay, and more.

Lucio. A French crown° more.

First Gentleman. Thou art always figuring diseases in
me, but thou art full of error. I am sound.

55   *Lucio.* Nay, not as one would say, healthy, but so
sound as things that are hollow. Thy bones are
hollow; impiety° has made a feast of thee.

First Gentleman. How now! Which of your hips has
the most profound sciatica?

60   *Mistress Overdone.* Well, well; there's one yonder arrested and carried to prison was worth five thousand of you all.

Second Gentleman. Who's that, I pray thee?

Mistress Overdone. Marry,° sir, that's Claudio,
65   Signior Claudio.

38 *feeling* personal experience   39–40 *learn . . . thee* drink to your
health but not after you from the same cup (to avoid the infection)
50 *dolors* (pun on "dollars")   52 *French crown* (1) *écu* (2) head
that has gone bald from venereal disease   57 *impiety* immorality
64 *Marry* (a light oath, from "by the Virgin Mary")

First Gentleman. Claudio to prison? 'Tis not so.

Mistress Overdone. Nay, but I know 'tis so. I saw him arrested; saw him carried away, and which is more, within these three days his head to be chopped off.   70

Lucio. But, after all this fooling, I would not have it so. Art thou sure of this?

Mistress Overdone. I am too sure of it; and it is for getting Madam Julietta with child.

Lucio. Believe me, this may be. He promised to meet   75
me two hours since, and he was ever precise in promise-keeping.

Second Gentleman. Besides, you know, it draws something near to the speech we had to such a purpose.   80

First Gentleman. But, most of all, agreeing with the proclamation.

Lucio. Away! Let's go learn the truth of it.
                    Exit [Lucio with Gentlemen].

Mistress Overdone. Thus, what with the war, what with the sweat,° what with the gallows, and what   85
with poverty, I am custom-shrunk.

                Enter Clown [Pompey].

How now? What's the news with you?

Pompey. Yonder man is carried to prison.

Mistress Overdone. Well; what has he done?

Pompey. A woman.   90

Mistress Overdone. But what's his offense?

Pompey. Groping for trouts in a peculiar° river.

Mistress Overdone. What? Is there a maid with child by him?

85 *sweat* sweating sickness, plague   92 *peculiar* private

95 *Pompey.* No, but there's a woman with maid by him.
    You have not heard of the proclamation, have you?

Mistress Overdone. What proclamation, man?

Pompey. All houses in the suburbs° of Vienna must
    be plucked down.

100 *Mistress Overdone.* And what shall become of those
    in the city?

Pompey. They shall stand for seed: they had gone
    down too, but that a wise burgher put in for them.

Mistress Overdone. But shall all our houses of resort
105 in the suburbs be pulled down?

Pompey. To the ground, mistress.

Mistress Overdone. Why, here's a change indeed in
    the commonwealth! What shall become of me?

Pompey. Come, fear not you; good counselors lack
110 no clients. Though you change your place, you
    need not change your trade; I'll be your tapster°
    still. Courage, there will be pity taken on you; you
    that have worn your eyes almost out in the service,
    you will be considered.

115 *Mistress Overdone.* What's to do here, Thomas
    Tapster? Let's withdraw.

Pompey. Here comes Signior Claudio, led by the
    provost to prison; and there's Madam Juliet.
                                              Exeunt.

    *Enter Provost, Claudio, Juliet, Officers, Lucio,
                and two Gentlemen.*

Claudio. Fellow, why dost thou show me thus to th'
    world?
120 Bear me to prison, where I am committed.

Provost. I do it not in evil disposition,

98 *suburbs* (in Shakespeare's London, the area of the brothels)
111 *tapster* bartender, waiter (here, pimp)

But from Lord Angelo, by special charge.

Claudio. Thus can the demigod Authority
Make us pay down for our offense by weight.
The words of heaven: on whom it will, it will;   *125*
On whom it will not, so. Yet still 'tis just.°

Lucio. Why, how now, Claudio! Whence comes this
restraint?

Claudio. From too much liberty, my Lucio, liberty.
As surfeit is the father of much fast,
So every scope by the immoderate use   *130*
Turns to restraint. Our natures do pursue,
Like rats that ravin down their proper bane,°
A thirsty evil, and when we drink, we die.

Lucio. If I could speak so wisely under an arrest, I
would send for certain of my creditors. And yet, to   *135*
say the truth, I had as lief have the foppery° of
freedom as the mortality of imprisonment. What's
thy offense, Claudio?

Claudio. What but to speak of would offend again.

Lucio. What, is't murder?   *140*

Claudio. No.

Lucio. Lechery?

Claudio. Call it so.

Provost. Away, sir, you must go.

Claudio. One word, good friend. Lucio, a word with
you.   *145*

Lucio. A hundred, if they'll do you any good.
Is lechery so looked after?

Claudio. Thus stands it with me: upon a true contract

125–26 *The words . . . just* (see Romans 9:15,18: "For he saith to
Moses, I will have mercy on whom I will have mercy, and I will
have compassion on whom I will have compassion. . . . Therefore
hath he mercy on whom he will have mercy, and whóm he will he
hardeneth")   132 *ravin . . . bane* greedily devour what is poisonous
to them   136 *foppery* foolishness

I got possession of Julietta's bed.
150 You know the lady, she is fast my wife,
Save that we do the denunciation° lack
Of outward order. This we came not to,
Only for propagation° of a dower
Remaining in the coffer of her friends,°
155 From whom we thought it meet to hide our love
Till time had made them for us. But it chances
The stealth of our most mutual entertainment
With character too gross is writ on Juliet.

Lucio. With child, perhaps?

Claudio.   Unhappily, even so.
160 And the new deputy now for the Duke—
Whether it be the fault and glimpse of newness,°
Or whether that the body public be
A horse whereon the governor doth ride,
Who, newly in the seat, that it may know
165 He can command, lets it straight feel the spur;
Whether the tyranny be in his place,
Or in his eminence that fills it up,
I stagger in°—but this new governor
Awakes me all the enrollèd° penalties
170 Which have, like unscoured armor, hung by th' wall
So long, that nineteen zodiacs° have gone round,
And none of them been worn; and, for a name,
Now puts the drowsy and neglected act
Freshly on me. 'Tis surely for a name.

175 *Lucio.* I warrant it is, and thy head stands so tickle°
on thy shoulders, that a milkmaid, if she be in love,
may sigh it off. Send after the Duke, and appeal
to him.

Claudio. I have done so, but he's not to be found.
180 I prithee, Lucio, do me this kind service:
This day my sister should the cloister enter,

---

151 *denunciation* formal announcement   153 *propagation* increase
154 *friends* relatives   161 *fault and glimpse of newness* i.e., weakness arising from the sudden vision of new authority   168 *stagger in* am not sure   169 *enrollèd* inscribed in the rolls of the laws
171 *zodiacs* i.e., years   175 *tickle* insecure

And there receive her approbation.°
Acquaint her with the danger of my state;
Implore her, in my voice, that she make friends
To the strict deputy; bid herself assay° him.   185
I have great hope in that; for in her youth
There is a prone° and speechless dialect,
Such as move men; beside, she hath prosperous art
When she will play with reason and discourse,
And well she can persuade.   190

Lucio. I pray she may; as well for the encouragement
of the like, which else would stand under grievous
imposition, as for the enjoying of thy life, who I
would be sorry should be thus foolishly lost at a
game of tick-tack.° I'll to her.   195

Claudio. I thank you, good friend Lucio.

Lucio. Within two hours.

Claudio.   Come, officer, away!

Exeunt.

Scene III. [*A monastery.*]

Enter Duke and Friar Thomas.

Duke. No, holy father; throw away that thought;
Believe not that the dribbling dart° of love
Can pierce a complete° bosom. Why I desire thee
To give me secret harbor, hath a purpose
More grave and wrinkled° than the aims and ends   5
Of burning youth.

---

182 *approbation* novitiate   185 *assay* test, i.e., attempt to persuade
187 *prone* winning   195 *tick-tack* (literally, a game using a board
into which pegs were fitted)   I.iii.2 *dribbling dart* arrow feebly shot
3 *complete* protected, independent   5 *wrinkled* mature, aged

Friar Thomas.   May your Grace speak of it?

Duke. My holy sir, none better knows than you
    How I have ever loved the life removed,
    And held in idle price to haunt assemblies
10   Where youth and cost, witless bravery° keeps.
    I have delivered to Lord Angelo,
    A man of stricture° and firm abstinence,
    My absolute power and place here in Vienna,
    And he supposes me traveled to Poland;
15   For so I have strewed it in the common ear,°
    And so it is received. Now, pious sir,
    You will demand of me why I do this.

Friar Thomas. Gladly, my lord.

Duke. We have strict statutes and most biting laws,
20   The needful bits and curbs to headstrong weeds,
    Which for this fourteen° years we have let slip,
    Even like an o'ergrown lion in a cave,
    That goes not out to prey. Now, as fond fathers,
    Having bound up the threat'ning twigs of birch,
25   Only to stick it in their children's sight
    For terror, not to use; in time the rod
    Becomes more mocked than feared; so our decrees,
    Dead to infliction,° to themselves are dead,
    And Liberty° plucks Justice by the nose;
30   The baby beats the nurse, and quite athwart
    Goes all decorum.

Friar Thomas.   It rested in your Grace
    To unloose this tied-up Justice when you pleased,
    And it in you more dreadful would have seemed
    Than in Lord Angelo.

Duke.   I do fear, too dreadful:
35   Sith° 'twas my fault to give the people scope,
    'Twould be my tyranny to strike and gall them

---

10 *witless bravery* senseless show   12 *stricture* strictness   15 *common ear* the ear of the people   21 *fourteen* (in I.ii.171 the time has been "nineteen" years. Doubtless the printer's copy in both lines had either xiv or xix and in one line was misread)   28 *Dead to infliction* utterly unenforced   29 *Liberty* license   35 *Sith* since

For what I bid them do; for we bid this be done
When evil deeds have their permissive pass,
And not the punishment. Therefore, indeed, my
    father,
I have on Angelo imposed the office,   40
Who may, in th' ambush° of my name, strike home,
And yet my nature never in the fight
To do it slander. And to behold his sway,
I will, as 'twere a brother of your order,
Visit both prince and people. Therefore, I prithee,
Supply me with the habit° and instruct me
How I may formally in person bear
Like a true friar. Moe° reasons for this action
At our more leisure shall I render you;
Only, this one: Lord Angelo is precise,°   50
Stands at a guard with envy;° scarce confesses
That his blood flows, or that his appetite
Is more to bread than stone. Hence shall we see,
If power change purpose, what our seemers be.

                              Exit [with Friar].

Scene IV. [*A nunnery.*]

    Enter Isabella and Francisca, a nun.

Isabella. And have you nuns no farther privileges?

Francisca. Are not these large enough?

Isabella. Yes, truly. I speak not as desiring more,
    But rather wishing a more strict restraint
    Upon the sisterhood, the votarists of Saint Clare.°   5

Lucio. (*Within*) Ho! Peace be in this place!

41 *in th' ambush* under cover 46 *habit* garment 48 *Moe* more
50 *precise* fastidiously strict   51 *Stands . . . envy* defies all malicious
criticism I.iv.5 *Saint Clare* (a notably strict order)

Isabella.   Who's that which calls?

Francisca. It is a man's voice. Gentle Isabella,
　　Turn you the key, and know his business of him.
　　You may, I may not: you are yet unsworn.
　　When you have vowed, you must not speak with
10　　　men
　　But in the presence of the prioress:
　　Then, if you speak, you must not show your face,
　　Or, if you show your face, you must not speak.
　　He calls again; I pray you, answer him.　　[*Exit.*]

15　*Isabella.* Peace and prosperity! Who is't that calls?

[*Enter Lucio.*]

Lucio. Hail, virgin—if you be, as those cheek-roses
　　Proclaim you are no less! Can you so stead° me
　　As bring me to the sight of Isabella,
　　A novice of this place and the fair sister
20　　To her unhappy brother, Claudio?

Isabella. Why "her unhappy brother"? Let me ask,
　　The rather for I now must make you know
　　I am that Isabella and his sister.

Lucio. Gentle and fair, your brother kindly greets you.
25　　Not to be weary with you, he's in prison.

Isabella. Woe me! For what?

Lucio. For that which, if myself might be his judge,
　　He should receive his punishment in thanks:
　　He hath got his friend with child.

Isabella. Sir! Make me not your story.°

30　*Lucio.*   'Tis true.
　　I would not, though 'tis my familiar sin
　　With maids to seem the lapwing,° and to jest,
　　Tongue far from heart, play with all virgins so.
　　I hold you as a thing enskied and sainted,
35　　By your renouncement, an immortal spirit;

17 *stead* help   30 *story* subject for mirth   32 *lapwing* pewit (a bird
which runs away from its nest to mislead intruders)

And to be talked with in sincerity,
As with a saint.

Isabella. You do blaspheme the good in mocking me.

Lucio. Do not believe it. Fewness and truth,° 'tis thus:
Your brother and his lover have embraced;   *40*
As those that feed grow full, as blossoming time
That from the seedness° the bare fallow brings
To teeming foison,° even so her plenteous womb
Expresseth his full tilth and husbandry.

Isabella. Someone with child by him? My cousin
Juliet?   *45*

Lucio. Is she your cousin?

Isabella. Adoptedly, as schoolmaids change their
names
By vain, though apt, affection.

Lucio.   She it is.

Isabella. O, let him marry her.

Lucio.   This is the point:
The Duke is very strangely gone from hence;   *50*
Bore many gentlemen, myself being one,
In hand and hope of action,° but we do learn
By those that know the very nerves of state,
His givings-out were of an infinite distance
From his true-meant design. Upon his place,   *55*
And with full line of his authority,
Governs Lord Angelo, a man whose blood
Is very snow-broth; one who never feels
The wanton stings and motions of the sense,
But doth rebate and blunt his natural edge   *60*
With profits of the mind, study and fast.
He—to give fear to use and liberty,°
Which have for long run by the hideous law,
As mice by lions—hath picked out an act,

---

39 *Fewness and truth* briefly and truly   42 *seedness* sowing   43
foison harvest   51–52 *Bore . . . action* deluded . . . with the hope
of military action   62 *use and liberty* habitual license

65 Under whose heavy sense° your brother's life
Falls into forfeit; he arrests him on it,
And follows close the rigor of the statute,
To make him an example. All hope is gone,
Unless you have the grace by your fair prayer
70 To soften Angelo. And that's my pith of business
'Twixt you and your poor brother.

Isabella. Doth he so? Seek his life?

Lucio.   Has censured° him
Already, and, as I hear, the provost hath
A warrant for's execution.

75 *Isabella.* Alas, what poor ability's in me
To do him good?

Lucio.   Assay the pow'r you have.

Isabella. My power? Alas, I doubt—

Lucio.   Our doubts are traitors,
And makes° us lose the good we oft might win,
By fearing to attempt. Go to Lord Angelo,
80 And let him learn to know, when maidens sue,
Men give like gods; but when they weep and kneel,
All their petitions are as freely theirs
As they themselves would owe° them.

Isabella. I'll see what I can do.

Lucio.   But speedily.

85 *Isabella.* I will about it straight,
No longer staying but to give the Mother
Notice of my affair. I humbly thank you;
Commend me to my brother; soon at night
I'll send him certain word of my success.°

Lucio. I take my leave of you.

90 *Isabella.*   Good sir, adieu.
                                   Exeunt.

---

65 *sense* interpretation   72 *censured* pronounced judgment on   78
makes (a plural subject sometimes takes a verb ending in -*s*)
83 *owe* own   89 *success* outcome

ACT II

Scene I. [*A room.*]

Enter Angelo, Escalus, and Servants, Justice.

Angelo. We must not make a scarecrow of the law,
Setting it up to fear the birds of prey,
And let it keep one shape, till custom make it
Their perch and not their terror.

Escalus.   Ay, but yet
Let us be keen, and rather cut a little,   5
Than fall,° and bruise to death. Alas, this gentleman
Whom I would save had a most noble father.
Let but your honor know,
Whom I believe to be most strait° in virtue,
That, in the working of your own affections,°   10
Had time cohered with place or place with wishing,
Or that the resolute acting of your blood
Could have attained th' effect of your own purpose,
Whether you had not sometime in your life
Erred in this point which now you censure him,   15
And pulled the law upon you.

Angelo. 'Tis one thing to be tempted, Escalus,
Another thing to fall. I not deny,

II.i.6 *fall* let fall   9 *strait* strict   10 *affections* passions

The jury, passing on the prisoner's life,

20 May in the sworn twelve have a thief or two
    Guiltier than him they try. What's open made to
        Justice,
    That Justice seizes. What knows the laws
    That thieves do pass on thieves? 'Tis very preg-
        nant,°
    The jewel that we find, we stoop and take't

25 Because we see it; but what we do not see
    We tread upon, and never think of it.
    You may not so extenuate his offense
    For I have had such faults; but rather tell me,
    When I, that censure him, do so offend,

30 Let mine own judgment pattern out my death,
    And nothing come in partial. Sir, he must die.

Escalus. Be it as your wisdom will.

Angelo.   Where is the provost?

Enter Provost.

Provost. Here, if it like your honor.

Angelo.   See that Claudio
    Be executed by nine tomorrow morning.

35 Bring him his confessor, let him be prepared,
    For that's the utmost of his pilgrimage.
                                    [*Exit Provost.*]

Escalus. Well, Heaven forgive him, and forgive us all.
    Some rise by sin, and some by virtue fall:
    Some run from breaks of ice,° and answer none;

40 And some condemnèd for a fault° alone.

Enter Elbow, Froth, Clown [Pompey], Officers.

Elbow. Come, bring them away. If these be good peo-
    ple in a commonweal that do nothing but use their
    abuses in common houses, I know no law. Bring
    them away.

---

23 *pregnant* clear   39 *Some . . . ice* i.e., some escape after gross
violations of chastity   40 *fault* (1) small crack in the ice (2) act
of sex

Angelo. How now, sir! What's your name? And what's   45
the matter?

Elbow. If it please your honor, I am the poor Duke's
constable, and my name is Elbow. I do lean upon
justice, sir, and do bring in here before your good
honor two notorious benefactors.   50

Angelo. Benefactors? Well, what benefactors are they?
Are they not malefactors?

Elbow. If it please your honor, I know not well what
they are, but precise villains they are, that I am
sure of, and void of all profanation in the world   55
that good Christians ought to have.

Escalus. This comes off well; here's a wise officer.

Angelo. Go to: what quality° are they of? Elbow is
your name? Why dost thou not speak, Elbow?

Pompey. He cannot, sir; he's out at elbow.°   60

Angelo. What are you, sir?

Elbow. He, sir! A tapster, sir, parcel-bawd,° one that
serves a bad woman whose house, sir, was, as they
say, plucked down in the suburbs, and now she
professes a hothouse,° which, I think, is a very ill   65
house too.

Escalus. How know you that?

Elbow. My wife, sir, whom I detest° before Heaven
and your honor—

Escalus. How! Thy wife?   70

Elbow. Ay, sir—whom, I thank Heaven, is an honest°
woman—

Escalus. Dost thou detest her therefore?

Elbow. I say, sir, I will detest myself also, as well as

58 *quality* profession   60 *out at elbow* somewhat seedy   62 *parcel-
bawd* partly a bawd   65 *hothouse* bathhouse   68 *detest* i.e., protest
71 *honest* chaste

75 she, that this house, if it be not a bawd's house, it
is pity of her life, for it is a naughty° house.

Escalus. How dost thou know that, constable?

Elbow. Marry, sir, by my wife, who, if she had been a
woman cardinally° given, might have been accused
80 in fornication, adultery, and all uncleanliness there.

Escalus. By the woman's means?

Elbow. Ay, sir, by Mistress Overdone's means; but as
she spit in his face, so she defied him.

Pompey. Sir, if it please your honor, this is not so.

85 *Elbow.* Prove it before these varlets here, thou honorable man; prove it.

Escalus. Do you hear how he misplaces?

Pompey. Sir, she came in great with child; and longing,
saving your honor's reverence, for stewed prunes.°
90 Sir, we had but two in the house, which at that very
distant time stood, as it were, in a fruit dish, a dish
of some threepence; your honors have seen such
dishes; they are not china dishes, but very good
dishes—

95 *Escalus.* Go to, go to; no matter for the dish, sir.

Pompey. No, indeed, sir, not of a pin; you are therein
in the right; but to the point. As I say, this Mistress
Elbow, being, as I say, with child, and being great-
bellied, and longing, as I said, for prunes; and hav-
100 ing but two in the dish, as I said, Master Froth here,
this very man, having eaten the rest, as I said, and,
as I say, paying for them very honestly; for, as you
know, Master Froth, I could not give you threepence again.

105 *Froth.* No, indeed.

Pompey. Very well, you being then, if you be remem-

76 *naughty* immoral   79 *cardinally* i.e., carnally   89 *stewed prunes*
(supposed to be a favorite dish among prostitutes)

b'red, cracking the stones of the foresaid prunes—

Froth. Ay, so I did indeed.

Pompey. Why, very well; I telling you then, if you be
remember'd, that such a one and such a one were   *110*
past cure of the thing you wot° of, unless they kept
very good diet, as I told you—

Froth. All this is true.

Pompey. Why, very well, then—

Escalus. Come, you are a tedious fool; to the purpose.   *115*
What was done to Elbow's wife, that he hath cause
to complain of? Come me to what was done to her.

Pompey. Sir, your honor cannot come to that yet.°

Escalus. No, sir, nor I mean it not.

Pompey. Sir, but you shall come to it, by your honor's   *120*
leave. And, I beseech you, look into Master Froth
here, sir, a man of fourscore pound a year, whose
father died at Hallowmas.° Was't not at Hallowmas, Master Froth?

Froth. All-hallond Eve.°   *125*

Pompey. Why, very well; I hope here be truths. He,
sir, sitting, as I say, in a lower chair, sir, 'twas in
the Bunch of Grapes, where, indeed, you have a
delight to sit, have you not?

Froth. I have so, because it is an open room, and   *130*
good for winter.

Pompey. Why, very well, then; I hope here be truths.

Angelo. This will last out a night in Russia,
When nights are longest there. I'll take my leave,
And leave you to the hearing of the cause,   *135*
Hoping you'll find good cause to whip them all.

---

111 *wot* know   117–18 *Come me . . . that yet* (the verbs carry a
sexual innuendo)   123 *Hallowmas* All Saints' Day, November 1st
125 *All-hallond Eve* October 31st

Escalus. I think no less. Good morrow to your lord-
    ship.   *Exit* [*Angelo*].
Now, sir, come on: what was done to Elbow's wife,
once more?

140 *Pompey.* Once, sir? There was nothing done to her
    once.

Elbow. I beseech you, sir, ask him what this man did
    to my wife.

Pompey. I beseech your honor, ask me.

145 *Escalus.* Well, sir; what did this gentleman to her?

Pompey. I beseech you, sir, look in this gentleman's
    face. Good Master Froth, look upon his honor;
    'tis for a good purpose. Doth your honor mark his
    face?

150 *Escalus.* Ay, sir, very well.

Pompey. Nay, I beseech you, mark it well.

Escalus. Well, I do so.

Pompey. Doth your honor see any harm in his face?

Escalus. Why, no.

155 *Pompey.* I'll be supposed° upon a book, his face is the
    worst thing about him. Good, then; if his face be
    the worst thing about him, how could Master Froth
    do the constable's wife any harm? I would know
    that of your honor.

160 *Escalus.* He's in the right. Constable, what say you
    to it?

Elbow. First, and° it like you, the house is a re-
    spected° house; next, this is a respected fellow;
    and his mistress is a respected woman.

165 *Pompey.* By this hand, sir, his wife is a more respected
    person than any of us all.

155 *supposed* i.e., deposed   162 *and* if   162–63 *respected* i.e., sus-
pected

Elbow. Varlet, thou liest; thou liest, wicked varlet! The
    time is yet to come that she was ever respected with
    man, woman, or child.

Pompey. Sir, she was respected with him before he   *170*
    married with her.

Escalus. Which is the wiser here, Justice or Iniquity?°
    Is this true?

Elbow. O thou caitiff! O thou varlet! O thou wicked
    Hannibal!° I respected with her before I was mar-   *175*
    ried to her! If ever I was respected with her, or she
    with me, let not your worship think me the poor
    Duke's officer. Prove this, thou wicked Hannibal,
    or I'll have mine action of batt'ry on thee.

Escalus. If he took you a box o' th' ear, you might   *180*
    have your action of slander too.

Elbow. Marry, I thank your good worship for it. What
    is't your worship's pleasure I shall do with this
    wicked caitiff?

Escalus. Truly, officer, because he hath some offenses   *185*
    in him that thou wouldst discover if thou couldst,
    let him continue in his courses till thou know'st
    what they are.

Elbow. Marry, I thank your worship for it. Thou seest,
    thou wicked varlet, now, what's come upon thee.   *190*
    Thou art to continue now, thou varlet; thou art to
    continue.

Escalus. Where were you born, friend?

Froth. Here in Vienna, sir.

Escalus. Are you of fourscore pounds a year?   *195*

Froth. Yes, and't please you, sir.

Escalus. So. [*To Pompey*] What trade are you of, sir?

Pompey. A tapster, a poor widow's tapster.

172 *Justice or Iniquity* (personified characters in morality plays)
175 *Hannibal* i.e., cannibal, fleshmonger (?)

Escalus. Your mistress' name?

200 *Pompey.* Mistress Overdone.

Escalus. Hath she had any more than one husband?

Pompey. Nine, sir; Overdone by the last.

Escalus. Nine! Come hither to me, Master Froth.
Master Froth, I would not have you acquainted
205 with tapsters: they will draw you,° Master Froth,
and you will hang them. Get you gone, and let me
hear no more of you.

Froth. I thank your worship. For mine own part, I
never come into any room in a taphouse, but I am
210 drawn in.

Escalus. Well, no more of it, Master Froth; farewell.
                                      [*Exit Froth.*]
Come you hither to me, Master Tapster. What's
your name, Master Tapster?

Pompey. Pompey.

215 *Escalus.* What else?

Pompey. Bum, sir.

Escalus. Troth, and your bum is the greatest thing
about you; so that, in the beastliest sense, you are
Pompey the Great. Pompey, you are partly a bawd,
220 Pompey, howsoever you color° it in being a tapster,
are you not? Come, tell me true; it shall be the
better for you.

Pompey. Truly, sir, I am a poor fellow that would live.

Escalus. How would you live, Pompey? By being a
225 bawd? What do you think of the trade, Pompey?
Is it a lawful trade?

Pompey. If the law would allow it, sir.

---

205 *draw you* (1) draw drinks for you (2) empty you, disembowel
you   220 *color* camouflage

Escalus. But the law will not allow, it, Pompey; nor it shall not be allowed in Vienna.

Pompey. Does your worship mean to geld and splay all the youth of the city? *230*

Escalus. No, Pompey.

Pompey. Truly, sir, in my poor opinion, they will to't, then. If your worship will take order for the drabs and the knaves, you need not to fear the bawds. *235*

Escalus. There is pretty orders beginning, I can tell you; it is but heading° and hanging.

Pompey. If you head and hang all that offend that way but for ten year together, you'll be glad to give out a commission for more heads; if this law hold *240* in Vienna ten year, I'll rent the fairest house in it after threepence a bay;° if you live to see this come to pass, say Pompey told you so.

Escalus. Thank you, good Pompey; and, in requital of your prophecy, hark you: I advise you, let me *245* not find you before me again upon any complaint whatsoever; no, not for dwelling where you do. If I do, Pompey, I shall beat you to your tent, and prove a shrewd Caesar to you; in plain dealing, Pompey, I shall have you whipped. So, for this *250* time, Pompey, fare you well.

Pompey. I thank your worship for your good counsel; [*aside*] but I shall follow it as the flesh and fortune shall better determine.
Whip me? No, no; let carman whip his jade.° *255*
The valiant heart's not whipped out of his trade.
                                              Exit.

Escalus. Come hither to me, Master Elbow; come hither, Master constable. How long have you been in this place of constable?

---

237 *heading* beheading 242 *bay* space under a single gable 255 *carman whip his jade* (the cartman whipped the whore after carting her through the streets; a "jade" is literally a nag)

260 *Elbow*. Seven year and a half, sir.

Escalus. I thought, by the readiness in the office, you
had continued in it some time. You say, seven years
together?

Elbow. And a half, sir.

265 *Escalus*. Alas, it hath been great pains to you. They
do you wrong to put you so oft upon't.° Are there
not men in your ward sufficient to serve it?

Elbow. Faith, sir, few of any wit in such matters. As
they are chosen, they are glad to choose me for
270 them; I do it for some piece of money, and go
through with all.

Escalus. Look you bring me in the names of some
six or seven, the most sufficient of your parish.

Elbow. To your worship's house, sir?

275 *Escalus*. To my house. Fare you well. [*Exit Elbow.*]
What's o'clock, think you?

Justice. Eleven, sir.

Escalus. I pray you home to dinner with me.

Justice. I humbly thank you.

280 *Escalus*. It grieves me for the death of Claudio,
But there's no remedy.

Justice. Lord Angelo is severe.

Escalus.   It is but needful:
Mercy is not itself, that oft looks so;
Pardon is still° the nurse of second woe.
285 But yet—poor Claudio! There is no remedy.
Come, sir.
                                        Exeunt.

266 *put you so oft upon't* i.e., impose on you the task of being
constable   284 *still* always

Scene II. [*A room.*]

Enter Provost, [and a] Servant.

Servant. He's hearing of a cause; he will come straight:
  I'll tell him of you.

Provost.   Pray you, do. [*Exit Servant.*] I'll know
  His pleasure; maybe he will relent. Alas,
  He hath but as offended in a dream.
  All sects,° all ages smack of this vice; and he   5
  To die for't!

Enter Angelo.

Angelo.   Now, what's the matter, provost?

Provost. Is it your will Claudio shall die tomorrow?

Angelo. Did not I tell thee yea? Hadst thou not order?
  Why dost thou ask again?

Provost.   Lest I might be too rash.
  Under your good correction, I have seen,   10
  When, after execution, judgment hath
  Repented o'er his doom.

Angelo.   Go to; let that be mine.°
  Do you your office, or give up your place,
  And you shall well be spared.

Provost.   I crave your honor's
  pardon.
  What shall be done, sir, with the groaning Juliet?   15
  She's very near her hour.

Angelo.   Dispose of her
  To some more fitter place, and that with speed.

II.ii.5 *sects* classes   12 *mine* i.e., my responsibility

[*Re-enter Servant.*]

Servant. Here is the sister of the man condemned
      Desires access to you.

Angelo.   Hath he a sister?

20 *Provost.* Ay, my good lord, a very virtuous maid
      And to be shortly of a sisterhood,
      If not already.

Angelo.   Well, let her be admitted.
                                    [*Exit Servant.*]
      See you the fornicatress be removed;
      Let her have needful, but not lavish, means;
      There shall be order for't.

                Enter Lucio and Isabella.

25 *Provost.*   'Save your honor.

Angelo. Stay a little while. [*To Isabella*] Y'are wel-
      come: what's your will?

Isabella. I am a woeful suitor to your honor,
      Please but your honor hear me.

Angelo.   Well; what's your suit?

Isabella. There is a vice that most I do abhor,
30   And most desire should meet the blow of justice,
      For which I would not plead, but that I must,
      For which I must not plead, but that I am
      At war 'twixt will and will not.

Angelo.   Well: the matter?

Isabella. I have a brother is condemned to die.
35   I do beseech you, let it be his fault,°
      And not my brother.

Provost.   [*Aside*] Heaven give thee moving graces.

Angelo. Condemn the fault, and not the actor of it?
      Why, every fault's condemned ere it be done.

35 *let it be his fault* i.e., condemn his fault, not him

Mine were the very cipher of a function,
To fine the faults whose fine stands in record,　　*40*
And let go by the actor.

Isabella.　　　　　　　　O just but severe law!
I had a brother, then. Heaven keep your honor.

Lucio. [*Aside to Isabella*] Give't not o'er so. To him
　　again, entreat him,
Kneel down before him, hang upon his gown;
You are too cold; if you should need a pin,　　　*45*
You could not with more tame a tongue desire it.
To him, I say!

Isabella. Must he needs die?

Angelo.　　　　　　　　　Maiden, no remedy.

Isabella. Yes; I do think that you might pardon him,
And neither heaven nor man grieve at the mercy.　*50*

Angelo. I will not do't.

Isabella.　　　　　　　But can you, if you would?

Angelo. Look what° I will not, that I cannot do.

Isabella. But might you do't, and do the world no
　　wrong,
If so your heart were touched with that remorse°
As mine is to him?

Angelo.　　　　　　He's sentenced; 'tis too late.　　*55*

Lucio. [*Aside to Isabella*] You are too cold.

Isabella. Too late? Why, no: I, that do speak a word,
May call it again. Well, believe this:
No ceremony° that to great ones 'longs,
Not the king's crown, nor the deputed sword,　　*60*
The marshal's truncheon, nor the judge's robe,
Become them with one half so good a grace
As mercy does.
If he had been as you, and you as he,

52 *Look what* whatever　54 *remorse* compassion　59 *ceremony* in-
signia of greatness

65 You would have slipped like him; but he, like you,
 Would not have been so stern.

Angelo.   Pray you, be gone.

Isabella. I would to heaven I had your potency,
 And you were Isabel; should it then be thus?
 No; I would tell what 'twere to be a judge,
 And what a prisoner.

Lucio. [*Aside to Isabella*] Ay, touch him; there's the
70 vein.

Angelo. Your brother is a forfeit of the law,
 And you but waste your words.

Isabella.   Alas, alas!
 Why, all the souls that were were forfeit once;
 And He that might the vantage best have took
75 Found out the remedy. How would you be,
 If He, which is the top of judgment, should
 But judge you as you are? O, think on that,
 And mercy then will breathe within your lips,
 Like man new made.

Angelo.   Be you content, fair maid;
80 ⎣It is the law, not I, condemn your brother.⎦
 Were he my kinsman, brother, or my son,
 It should be thus with him; he must die tomorrow

Isabella. Tomorrow! O, that's sudden! Spare him,
 spare him!
 He's not prepared for death. Even for our kitchens
85 We kill the fowl of season:° shall we serve heaven
 With less respect than we do minister
 To our gross selves? Good, good my lord, bethink
 you:
 Who is it that hath died for this offense?
 There's many have committed it.

Lucio. [*Aside to Isabella*]   Ay, well said.

Angelo. The law hath not been dead, though it hath
90 slept.

85 *of season* in season

Those many had not dared to do that evil,
If the first that did th' edict infringe
Had answered for his deed. Now 'tis awake,
Takes note of what is done, and, like a prophet,
Looks in a glass, that shows what future evils,   *95*
Either new, or by remissness new conceived,°
And so in progress to be hatched and born,
Are now to have no successive degrees,
But here they live, to end.

Isabella.   Yet show some pity.

Angelo. I show it most of all when I show justice,   *100*
For then I pity those I do not know,
Which a dismissed° offense would after gall;
And do him right that, answering one foul wrong,
Lives not to act another. Be satisfied;
Your brother dies tomorrow; be content.   *105*

Isabella. So you must be the first that gives this sen-
          tence,
And he, that suffers. O, it is excellent
To have a giant's strength; but it is tyrannous
To use it like a giant.

Lucio. [*Aside to Isabella*] That's well said.

Isabella. Could great men thunder   *110*
As Jove himself does, Jove would ne'er be quiet,
For every pelting,° petty officer
Would use his heaven for thunder.
Nothing but thunder. Merciful heaven,
Thou rather with thy sharp and sulfurous bolt   *115*
Splits the unwedgeable and gnarlèd oak
Than the soft myrtle. But man, proud man,
Dressed in a little brief authority,
Most ignorant of what he's most assured,

95–96 *future. . . conceived* i.e., evils that will take place in future,
but that are either now planned or may be planned later ("remissness": careless omission of duty)   102 *dismissed* forgiven   112 *pelting* paltry

120   His glassy essence,° like an angry ape,
Plays such fantastic tricks before high heaven
As makes the angels weep; who, with our spleens,°
Would all themselves laugh mortal.

Lucio. [*Aside to Isabella*] O, to him, to him, wench!
    He will relent;
He's coming; I perceive't.

125 *Provost.*   [*Aside*] Pray heaven she win him.

Isabella. We cannot weigh our brother with ourself:
Great men may jest with saints; 'tis wit in them;
But in the less, foul profanation.

Lucio. Thou'rt i' th' right, girl; more o' that.

130 *Isabella.* That in the captain's but a choleric word,
Which in the soldier is flat blasphemy.

Lucio. [*Aside to Isabella*] Art avised° o' that? More
on't.

Angelo. Why do you put these sayings upon me?

Isabella. Because authority, though it err like others,
135 Hath yet a kind of medicine in itself,
That skins the vice° o' th' top; go to your bosom,
Knock there, and ask your heart what it doth know
That's like my brother's fault; if it confess
A natural guiltiness such as is his,
140 Let it not sound a thought upon your tongue
Against my brother's life.

Angelo.   [*Aside*] She speaks, and 'tis
Such sense, that my sense breeds with it. [*Aloud*]
    Fare you well.

Isabella. Gentle my lord, turn back.

Angelo. I will bethink me; come again tomorrow.

120 *glassy essence* the rational soul which reveals to man, as in a
mirror, what constitutes him a human being (?) fragile nature (?)
122 *spleens* (the spleen was believed the seat of mirth and anger)
132 *avised* informed   136 *skins the vice* i.e., covers the sore of vice
with a skin, but does not heal it (or perhaps "skims off the visible
layer of vice")

Isabella. Hark how I'll bribe you; good my lord, turn
     back.   *145*

Angelo. How? Bribe me?

Isabella. Ay, with such gifts that heaven shall share
     with you.

Lucio. [*Aside to Isabella*] You had marred all else.

Isabella. Not with fond sicles° of the tested gold,
     Or stones whose rate are either rich or poor   *150*
     As fancy values them; but with true prayers
     That shall be up at heaven, and enter there
     Ere sunrise, prayers from preservèd souls,
     From fasting maids whose minds are dedicate
     To nothing temporal.

Angelo.   Well; come to me tomorrow.   *155*

Lucio. [*Aside to Isabella*] Go to; 'tis well; away.

Isabella. Heaven keep your honor safe.

Angelo.   [*Aside*] Amen:
     For I am that way going to temptation,
     Where prayers cross.°

Isabella.   At what hour tomorrow
     Shall I attend your lordship?

Angelo.   At any time 'fore noon.   *160*

Isabella. 'Save your honor.
          [*Exeunt Isabella, Lucio, and Provost.*]

Angelo.   From thee, even from thy virtue!
     What's this? What's this? Is this her fault or mine?
     The tempter or the tempted, who sins most?
     Ha, not she. Nor doth she tempt; but it is I
     That, lying by the violet in the sun,   *165*
     Do as the carrion does, not as the flow'r,
     Corrupt with virtuous season.° Can it be

149 *sicles* shekels   159 *cross* are at cross purposes   167 *Corrupt
with virtuous season* go bad in the season that blossoms the
flower

That modesty may more betray our sense
Than woman's lightness? Having waste ground
    enough,
170 Shall we desire to raze the sanctuary,
And pitch our evils° there? O fie, fie, fie!
What dost thou, or what art thou, Angelo?
Dost thou desire her foully for those things
That make her good? O, let her brother live:
175 Thieves for their robbery have authority
When judges steal themselves. What, do I love her,
That I desire to hear her speak again,
And feast upon her eyes? What is't I dream on?
O cunning enemy, that, to catch a saint,
180 With saints dost bait thy hook! Most dangerous
Is that temptation that doth goad us on
To sin in loving virtue. Never could the strumpet,
With all her double vigor, art and nature,
Once stir my temper; but this virtuous maid
185 Subdues me quite. Ever till now,
When men were fond,° I smiled, and wond'red
    how.   Exit.

Scene III. [*The prison.*]

Enter Duke [disguised as a friar] and Provost.

Duke. Hail to you, provost—so I think you are.

Provost. I am the provost. What's your will, good
    friar?

Duke. Bound by my charity and my blest order,
    I come to visit the afflicted spirits
5   Here in the prison. Do me the common right
    To let me see them, and to make me know

171 *evils* evil structures (e.g., perhaps whorehouses or privies)
186 *fond* infatuated

The nature of their crimes, that I may minister
To them accordingly.

Provost. I would do more than that, if more were
    needful.

Enter Juliet.

Look, here comes one: a gentlewoman of mine,   *10*
Who, falling in the flaws° of her own youth,
Hath blistered her report:° she is with child;
And he that got it, sentenced; a young man
More fit to do another such offense
Than die for this.   *15*

Duke. When must he die?

Provost.   As I do think, tomorrow.
  [*To Juliet*] I have provided for you; stay awhile,
And you shall be conducted.

Duke. Repent you, fair one, of the sin you carry?

Juliet. I do, and bear the shame most patiently.   *20*

Duke. I'll teach you how you shall arraign° your con-
    science,
And try your penitence, if it be sound
Or hollowly put on.

Juliet.   I'll gladly learn.

Duke. Love you the man that wronged you?

Juliet. Yes, as I love the woman that wronged him.   *25*

Duke. So, then, it seems your most offenseful act
Was mutually committed?

Juliet.   Mutually.

Duke. Then was your sin of heavier kind than his.

Juliet. I do confess it, and repent it, father.

Duke. 'Tis meet so, daughter. But lest you do repent   *30*

II.iii.11 *flaws* sudden gusts of wind 12 *report* reputation 21 *arraign* interrogate

As that the sin hath brought you to this shame—
Which sorrow is always toward ourselves, not
  heaven,
Showing we would not spare heaven as we love it,
But as we stand in fear—

35 *Juliet.* I do repent me, as it is an evil,
And take the shame with joy.

Duke.   There rest.
Your partner, as I hear, must die tomorrow,
And I am going with instruction to him.
Grace go with you, *Benedicite!*°   *Exit.*

40 *Juliet.* Must die tomorrow! O injurious love,
That respites° me a life, whose very comfort
Is still a dying horror.

Provost.   'Tis pity of him.   *Exeunt.*

Scene IV. [*A room.*]

Enter Angelo.

Angelo. When I would pray and think, I think and
  pray
To several° subjects: heaven hath my empty words,
Whilst my invention,° hearing not my tongue,
Anchors on Isabel: heaven in my mouth,
5 As if I did but only chew his name,
And in my heart the strong and swelling evil
Of my conception.° The state,° whereon I studied,
Is like a good thing, being often read,
Grown seared° and tedious; yea, my gravity,
10 Wherein, let no man hear me, I take pride,

39 *Benedicite* bless you 41 *respites* saves II.iv.2 *several* separate
3 *invention* imagination 7 *conception* thought 7 *state* attitude (?)
statecraft (?) 9 *seared* worn out

    Could I with boot° change for an idle plume
    Which the air beats for vain. O place, O form,
    How often dost thou with thy case,° thy habit,°
    Wrench awe from fools, and tie the wiser souls
    To thy false seeming! Blood, thou art blood.   *15*
    Let's write "good angel" on the devil's horn,°
    'Tis not the devil's crest. How now, who's there?

Enter Servant.

Servant. One Isabel, a sister, desires access to you.

Angelo. Teach her the way. [*Exit Servant.*] O heavens,
    Why does my blood thus muster to my heart,   *20*
    Making both it unable for itself,
    And dispossessing all my other parts
    Of necessary fitness?
    So play the foolish throngs with one that swounds,°
    Come all to help him, and so stop the air   *25*
    By which he should revive; and even so
    The general,° subject to a well-wished king,
    Quit their own part, and in obsequious fondness
    Crowd to his presence, where their untaught love
    Must needs appear offense.

Enter Isabella.

                       How now, fair maid?   *30*

Isabella. I am come to know your pleasure.

Angelo. That you might know it, would much better
    please me
    Than to demand what 'tis. Your brother cannot
    live.

Isabella. Even so. Heaven keep your honor.

Angelo. Yet may he live awhile, and it may be,   *35*
    As long as you or I; yet he must die.

Isabella. Under your sentence?

11 *with boot* with profit   13 *case* (either "chance" or "outside")
13 *habit* (either "behavior" or "garment")   16 *horn* phallus (?)
24 *swounds* swoons   27 *general* multitude

Angelo. Yea.

Isabella. When? I beseech you that in his reprieve,
40   Longer or shorter, he may be so fitted
        That his soul sicken not.

Angelo. Ha! Fie, these filthy vices! It were as good
        To pardon him that hath from nature stol'n
        A man already made, as to remit
45   Their saucy sweetness° that do coin heaven's image
        In stamps that are forbid: 'tis all as easy
        Falsely to take away a life true made,
        As to put metal in restrainèd° means
        To make a false one.

50 *Isabella.* 'Tis set down so in heaven, but not in earth.

Angelo. Say you so? Then I shall pose° you quickly.
        Which had you rather: that the most just law
        Now took your brother's life; or, to redeem him,
        Give up your body to such sweet uncleanness
        As she that he hath stained?

55 *Isabella.*   Sir, believe this:
        I had rather give my body than my soul.

Angelo. I talk not of your soul; our compelled sins
        Stand more for number than for accompt.°

Isabella.   How say you?

Angelo. Nay, I'll not warrant that; for I can speak
60   Against the thing I say. Answer to this:
        I, now the voice of the recorded law,
        Pronounce a sentence on your brother's life;
        Might there not be a charity in sin
        To save this brother's life?

Isabella.   Please you to do't,
65   I'll take it as a peril to my soul,
        It is no sin at all, but charity.

44–45 *to remit . . . sweetness* to pardon their lascivious pleasures
48 *restrainèd* forbidden   51 *pose* baffle (with a difficult question)
58 *Stand . . . accompt* are enumerated but not counted against us

Angelo. Pleased you to do't at peril of your soul,
　Were equal poise° of sin and charity.

Isabella. That I do beg his life, if it be sin,
　Heaven let me bear it. You granting of my suit,   *70*
　If that be sin, I'll make it my morn prayer
　To have it added to the faults of mine,
　And nothing of your answer.

Angelo.　　　　　　　Nay, but hear me.
　Your sense pursues not mine; either you are ig-
　　norant,
　Or seem so, crafty; and that's not good.   *75*

Isabella. Let me be ignorant, and in nothing good,
　But graciously to know I am no better.

Angelo. Thus wisdom wishes to appear most bright
　When it doth tax° itself, as these black masks
　Proclaim an enshield° beauty ten times louder   *80*
　Than beauty could, displayed. But mark me;
　To be receivèd plain, I'll speak more gross:
　Your brother is to die.

Isabella. So.

Angelo. And his offense is so, as it appears,   *85*
　Accountant° to the law upon that pain.°

Isabella. True.

Angelo. Admit no other way to save his life—
　As I subscribe° not that, nor any other,
　But in the loss of question°—that you, his sister,   *90*
　Finding yourself desired of such a person
　Whose credit with the judge, or own great place,
　Could fetch your brother from the manacles
　Of the all-binding law; and that there were
　No earthly mean to save him, but that either   *95*
　You must lay down the treasures of your body
　To this supposed, or else to let him suffer:

68 *poise* balance   79 *tax* censure   80 *enshield* concealed   86 *Accountant* accountable   86 *pain* punishment   89 *subscribe* assent to   90 *But . . . question* except to keep alive the argument

What would you do?

Isabella. As much for my poor brother as myself:
100 That is, were I under the terms of death,
Th' impression of keen whips I'd wear as rubies,
And strip myself to death as to a bed
That longing have been sick for, ere I'd yield
My body up to shame.

Angelo.   Then must your brother die.

105 *Isabella.* And 'twere the cheaper way.
Better it were a brother died at once
Than that a sister, by redeeming him,
Should die forever.

Angelo. Were not you, then, as cruel as the sentence
110 That you have slandered so?

Isabella. Ignomy in ransom and free pardon
Are of two houses; lawful mercy
Is nothing kin to foul redemption.

Angelo. You seemed of late to make the law a tyrant,
115 And rather proved the sliding of your brother
A merriment than a vice.

Isabella. O, pardon me, my lord. It oft falls out,
To have what we would have, we speak not what
we mean.
I something do excuse the thing I hate
120 For his advantage that I dearly love.

Angelo. We are all frail.

Isabella.   Else let my brother die,
If not a fedary, but only he
Owe and succeed thy weakness.°

Angelo. Nay, women are frail too.

Isabella. Ay, as the glasses where they view them-
125 selves,

122–23 *If . . . weakness* (probably a line has been omitted, but perhaps the meaning is: "Let my brother die if he is the only inheritor
of human frailty instead of being a mere vassal to it")

Which are as easy broke as they make forms.°
Women! Help heaven! Men their creation mar
In profiting by them. Nay, call us ten times frail;
For we are soft as our complexions are,
And credulous° to false prints.

Angelo.   I think it well,   130
And from this testimony of your own sex—
Since, I suppose, we are made to be no stronger
Than faults may shake our frames—let me be bold:
I do arrest your words.° Be that you are,
That is, a woman; if you be more, you're none;   135
If you be one, as you are well expressed°
By all external warrants, show it now,
By putting on the destined livery.°

Isabella. I have no tongue but one; gentle my lord,
Let me entreat you speak the former language.   140

Angelo. Plainly conceive, I love you.

Isabella. My brother did love Juliet,
And you tell me that he shall die for't.

Angelo. He shall not, Isabel, if you give me love.

Isabella. I know your virtue hath a license in't,   145
Which seems° a little fouler than it is,
To pluck on° others.

Angelo.   Believe me, on mine honor,
My words express my purpose.

Isabella. Ha! Little honor to be much believed,
And most pernicious purpose. Seeming, seeming!   150
I will proclaim thee, Angelo; look for't:
Sign me a present pardon for my brother,
Or with an outstretched throat I'll tell the world
    aloud
What man thou art.

---

126 *forms* images, appearances   130 *credulous* receptive   134 *I do
arrest your words* I take you at your word   136 *expressed* shown
to be   138 *the destined livery* the dress that it is the destiny of a
woman to wear   147 *pluck on* draw on

Angelo.   Who will believe thee, Isabel?
155 My unsoiled name, th' austereness of my life,
My vouch° against you, and my place i' th' state,
Will so your accusation overweigh,
That you shall stifle in your own report,
And smell of calumny. I have begun,
160 And now I give my sensual race the rein.
Fit thy consent to my sharp appetite,
Lay by all nicety and prolixious° blushes,
That banish what they sue for; redeem thy brother
By yielding up thy body to my will,°
165 Or else he must not only die the death,
But thy unkindness shall his death draw out
To ling'ring sufferance.° Answer me tomorrow,
Or, by the affection° that now guides me most,
I'll prove a tyrant to him. As for you,
170 Say what you can, my false o'erweighs your true.
             Exit.

Isabella. To whom should I complain? Did I tell this,
Who would believe me? O perilous mouths,
That bear in them one and the selfsame tongue,
Either of condemnation or approof;°
175 Bidding the law make curtsy to their will,
Hooking both right and wrong to th' appetite,
To follow as it draws. I'll to my brother.
Though he hath fall'n by prompture of the blood,
Yet hath he in him such a mind of honor,
180 That, had he twenty heads to tender down
On twenty bloody blocks, he'd yield them up,
Before his sister should her body stoop
To such abhorred pollution.
Then, Isabel, live chaste, and, brother, die:
185 "More than our brother is our chastity."
I'll tell him yet of Angelo's request,
And fit his mind to death, for his soul's rest. *Exit.*

156 *vouch* testimony 162 *prolixious* tediously drawn-out 164 *will*
carnal appetite 167 *sufferance* torture 168 *affection* passion
174 *approof* approval

ACT III

Scene I. [*The prison.*]

Enter Duke [as friar], Claudio, and Provost.

Duke. So then, you hope of pardon from Lord Angelo?

Claudio. The miserable have no other medicine
But only hope:
I have hope to live, and am prepared to die.

Duke. Be absolute° for death; either death or life   5
  Shall thereby be the sweeter. Reason thus with life:
  If I do lose thee, I do lose a thing
  That none but fools would keep; a breath thou art,
  Servile to all the skyey influences,°
  That dost this habitation, where thou keep'st,°   10
  Hourly afflict; merely, thou art death's fool,°
  For him thou labor'st by thy flight to shun,
  And yet run'st toward him still. Thou art not noble,
  For all th' accommodations° that thou bear'st
  Are nursed by baseness. Thou'rt by no means valiant,   15
  For thou dost fear the soft and tender fork°
  Of a poor worm. Thy best of rest is sleep,

III.i.5 *absolute* unconditionally prepared   9 *skyey influences* influence of the stars   10 *keep'st* dwellest   11 *fool* (the professional jester in a nobleman's household whose job was to keep his master amused)   14 *accommodations* necessities   16 *fork* forked tongue (of a snake)

And that thou oft provok'st;° yet grossly fear'st
Thy death, which is no more. Thou art not thyself;
20 For thou exists on many a thousand grains
That issue out of dust. Happy thou art not,
For what thou hast not, still thou striv'st to get,
And what thou hast, forget'st. Thou art not certain,°
For thy complexion shifts to strange effects,
25 After the moon.° If thou art rich, thou'rt poor.
For, like an ass whose back with ingots bows,
Thou bear'st thy heavy riches but a journey,
And death unloads thee. Friend hast thou none,
For thine own bowels,° which do call thee sire,
30 The mere effusion of thy proper loins,°
Do curse the gout, serpigo,° and the rheum,°
For ending thee no sooner. Thou hast nor youth
  nor age,
But, as it were, an after-dinner's sleep,
Dreaming on both; for all thy blessèd youth
35 Becomes as agèd, and doth beg the alms
Of palsied eld,° and when thou art old and rich,
Thou has neither heat, affection,° limb, nor beauty,
To make thy riches pleasant. What's yet in this
That bears° the name of life? Yet in this life
40 Lie hid moe thousand deaths; yet death we fear,
That makes these odds all even.

Claudio.   I humbly thank you.
  To sue to live, I find I seek to die,
  And seeking death, find life: let it come on.

Enter Isabella.

Isabella. What, ho! Peace here; grace and good company!

Provost. Who's there? Come in, the wish deserves a
45 welcome.

18 *provok'st* invokest   23 *certain* invariable   24–25 *For . . . moon*
your temperament (desire?) moves to numerous things, changeable
as (or "influenced by") the moon   29 *bowels* offspring   30 *The
mere . . . loins* the very issue of your own loins   31 *serpigo* a skin
disease   31 *rheum* catarrh   36 *eld* old age   37 *affection* feeling
39 *bears* deserves

Duke. Dear sir, ere long I'll visit you again.

Claudio. Most holy sir, I thank you.

Isabella. My business is a word or two with Claudio.

Provost. And very welcome. Look, signior, here's
   your sister.

Duke. Provost, a word with you.   50

Provost. As many as you please.

Duke. Bring me to hear them speak, where I may be
   concealed.   [*Duke and Provost withdraw.*]

Claudio. Now, sister, what's the comfort?

Isabella. Why,   55
   As all comforts are, most good, most good indeed.
   Lord Angelo, having affairs to heaven,
   Intends you for his swift ambassador,
   Where you shall be an everlasting leiger:°
   Therefore your best appointment° make with
      speed;   60
   Tomorrow you set on.

Claudio.   Is there no remedy?

Isabella. None, but such remedy as, to save a head,
   To cleave a heart in twain.

Claudio.   But is there any?

Isabella. Yes, brother, you may live;
   There is a devilish mercy in the judge,   65
   If you'll implore it, that will free your life,
   But fetter you till death.

Claudio.   Perpetual durance?°

Isabella. Ay, just; perpetual durance, a restraint,
   Though all the world's vastidity° you had,
   To a determined scope.°

59 *leiger* resident ambassador 60 *appointment* preparation 67
durance imprisonment 69 *vastidity* vast spaces 70 *determined
scope* fixed limit

70 *Claudio.*   But in what nature?

Isabella. In such a one as, you consenting to't,
    Would bark your honor from that trunk you bear,
    And leave you naked.

Claudio.   Let me know the point.

Isabella. O, I do fear thee, Claudio, and I quake,
75   Lest thou a feverous life shouldst entertain,
    And six or seven winters more respect
    Than a perpetual honor. Dar'st thou die?
    The sense° of death is most in apprehension,°
    And the poor beetle that we tread upon
80   In corporal sufferance finds a pang as great
    As when a giant dies.

Claudio.   Why give you me this shame?
    Think you I can a resolution fetch
    From flow'ry tenderness? If I must die,
    I will encounter darkness as a bride,
85   And hug it in mine arms.

Isabella. There spake my brother, there my father's
        grave
    Did utter forth a voice. Yes, thou must die,
    Thou art too noble to conserve a life
    In base appliances.° This outward-sainted deputy,
90   Whose settled visage and deliberate word
    Nips youth i' th' head, and follies doth enmew°
    As falcon doth the fowl, is yet a devil;
    His filth within being cast,° he would appear
    A pond as deep as hell.

Claudio.   The prenzie° Angelo!

95 *Isabella.* O, 'tis the cunning livery of hell,
    The damned'st body to invest and cover
    In prenzie guards.° Dost thou think, Claudio,
    If I would yield him my virginity,

---

78 *sense* feeling   78 *apprehension* imagination   89 *appliances* devices   91 *enmew* drive into the water (as a hawk drives a fowl)
93 *cast* vomited up   94 *prenzie* (meaning unknown; perhaps a slip for "princely")   97 *guards* trimmings

Thou mightst be freed?

Claudio.   O heavens, it cannot be.

Isabella. Yes, he would give't thee, from this rank
        offense,   *100*
    So to offend him still. This night's the time
    That I should do what I abhor to name,
    Or else thou diest tomorrow.

Claudio.   Thou shalt not do't.

Isabella. O, were it but my life,
    I'd throw it down for your deliverance   *105*
    As frankly as a pin.

Claudio.   Thanks, dear Isabel.

Isabella. Be ready, Claudio, for your death tomorrow.

Claudio. Yes. Has he affections° in him,
    That thus can make him bite the law by th' nose,
    When he would force° it? Sure, it is no sin,   *110*
    Or of the deadly seven° it is the least.

Isabella. Which is the least?

Claudio. If it were damnable, he being so wise,
    Why would he for the momentary trick
    Be perdurably fined?° O Isabel!   *115*

Isabella. What says my brother?

Claudio.   Death is a fearful thing.

Isabella. And shamèd life a hateful.

Claudio. Ay, but to die, and go we know not where,
    To lie in cold obstruction° and to rot,
    This sensible° warm motion° to become   *120*
    A kneaded clod; and the delighted° spirit
    To bathe in fiery floods, or to reside

108 *affections* sensual appetites   110 *force* enforce   111 *deadly
seven* (pride, envy, wrath, sloth, avarice, gluttony, lechery)   114–15
Why . . . fined i.e., why for the momentary trifle (of sexual intercourse) would he be eternally damned   119 *obstruction* motionless-
ness   120 *sensible* feeling   120 *motion* organism   121 *delighted*
capable of delight

In thrilling region of thick-ribbèd ice;
To be imprisoned in the viewless winds,
125 And blown with restless violence round about
The pendent° world; or to be worse than worst
Of those that lawless and incertain thought
Imagine howling—'tis too horrible!
The weariest and most loathèd worldly life
130 That age, ache, penury, and imprisonment
Can lay on nature is a paradise
To what we fear of death.

Isabella. Alas, alas.

Claudio.   Sweet sister, let me live:
What sin you do to save a brother's life,
135 Nature dispenses with° the deed so far
That it becomes a virtue.

Isabella.   O you beast,
O faithless coward, O dishonest wretch!
Wilt thou be made a man out of my vice?
Is't not a kind of incest, to take life
From thine own sister's shame? What should I
140   think?
Heaven shield my mother played my father fair,
For such a warpèd slip of wilderness°
Ne'er issued from his blood. Take my defiance,
Die, perish! Might but my bending down
145 Reprieve thee from thy fate, it should proceed.
I'll pray a thousand prayers for thy death,
No word to save thee.

Claudio. Nay, hear me, Isabel.

Isabella.   O, fie, fie, fie!
Thy sin's not accidental, but a trade.
150 Mercy to thee would prove itself a bawd,
'Tis best that thou diest quickly.

Claudio.   O, hear me, Isabella!

---

126 *pendent* hanging in space   135 *dispenses with* grants a dispensa-
tion for   142 *wilderness* wild nature without nurture

[*The Duke comes forward.*]

Duke. Vouchsafe a word, young sister, but one word.

Isabella. What is your will?

Duke. Might you dispense with your leisure, I would
   by and by have some speech with you: the satis-   155
   faction I would require is likewise your own benefit.

Isabella. I have no superfluous leisure; my stay must
   be stolen out of other affairs, but I will attend you
   awhile.

Duke. [*Aside to Claudio*] Son, I have overheard what   160
   hath passed between you and your sister. Angelo
   had never the purpose to corrupt her; only he hath
   made an assay° of her virtue to practice his judgment with the disposition of natures. She, having
   the truth of honor in her, hath made him that   165
   gracious denial which he is most glad to receive. I
   am confessor to Angelo, and I know this to be true;
   therefore prepare yourself to death. Do not satisfy
   your resolution with hopes that are fallible. Tomorrow you must die; go to your knees, and make   170
   ready.

Claudio. Let me ask my sister pardon. I am so out
   of love with life, that I will sue to be rid of it.

Duke. Hold you there; farewell. [*Exit Claudio.*] Provost, a word with you.   175

[*Enter Provost.*]

Provost. What's your will, father?

Duke. That now you are come, you will be gone.
   Leave me awhile with the maid. My mind promises
   with my habit° no loss shall touch her by my company.   180

Provost. In good time.°   *Exit.*

Duke. The hand that hath made you fair hath made

163 *assay* test   179 *habit* religious dress   181 *In good time* very
well

you good. The goodness that is cheap in beauty
makes beauty brief in goodness; but grace, being
185 the soul of your complexion,° shall keep the body
of it ever fair. The assault that Angelo hath made
to you, fortune hath conveyed to my understanding, and, but that frailty hath examples for his falling, I should wonder at Angelo. How will you do
190 to content this substitute, and to save your brother?

Isabella. I am now going to resolve° him. I had rather
my brother die by the law than my son should be
unlawfully born. But O, how much is the good
Duke deceived in Angelo! If ever he return and I
195 can speak to him, I will open my lips in vain, or
discover his government.°

Duke. That shall not be much amiss. Yet, as the matter now stands, he will avoid your accusation: he
made trial of you only. Therefore fasten your ear
200 on my advisings; to the love I have in doing good
a remedy presents itself. I do make myself believe
that you may most uprighteously do a poor
wronged lady a merited benefit; redeem your
brother from the angry law; do no stain to your
205 own gracious person; and much please the absent
Duke, if peradventure he shall ever return to have
hearing of this business.

Isabella. Let me hear you speak farther. I have spirit
to do anything that appears not foul in the truth
210 of my spirit.

Duke. Virtue is bold, and goodness never fearful.
Have you not heard speak of Mariana, the sister
of Frederick, the great soldier who miscarried at
sea?

215 *Isabella.* I have heard of the lady, and good words
went with her name.

185 *complexion* character   191 *resolve* answer   196 *discover his
government* expose his rule

Duke. She should this Angelo have married; was affianced to her by oath, and the nuptial appointed:
between which time of the contract and limit of the
solemnity,° her brother Frederick was wracked at   *220*
sea, having in that perished vessel the dowry of his
sister. But mark how heavily this befell to the poor
gentlewoman: there she lost a noble and renowned
brother, in his love toward her ever most kind and
natural; with him, the portion and sinew of her for-   *225*
tune, her marriage dowry; with both, her com-
binate° husband, this well-seeming Angelo.

Isabella. Can this be so? Did Angelo so leave her?

Duke. Left her in her tears, and dried not one of them
with his comfort; swallowed his vows whole, pre-   *230*
tending in her discoveries of dishonor: in few, bestowed her on her own lamentation, which she yet
wears for his sake; and he, a marble to her tears,
is washed with them, but relents not.

Isabella. What a merit were it in death to take this
poor maid from the world! What corruption in this
life, that it will let this man live! But how out of
this can she avail?°

Duke. It is a rupture that you may easily heal, and
the cure of it not only saves your brother, but   *240*
keeps you from dishonor in doing it.

Isabella. Show me how, good father.

Duke. This forenamed maid hath yet in her the continuance of her first affection; his unjust unkindness, that in all reason should have quenched her   *245*
love, hath, like an impediment in the current, made
it more violent and unruly. Go you to Angelo;
answer his requiring with a plausible obedience;
agree with his demands to the point; only refer
yourself to this advantage: first, that your stay with   *250*
him may not be long; that the time may have all

219–20 *limit of the solemnity* date set for the marriage ceremony
226–27 *combinate* betrothed   238 *avail* benefit

shadow and silence in it; and the place answer to
convenience. This being granted in course—and
now follows all—we shall advise this wronged maid
255 to stead up° your appointment, go in your place.
If the encounter° acknowledge itself hereafter, it
may compel him to her recompense: and here, by
this, is your brother saved, your honor untainted,
the poor Mariana advantaged, and the corrupt dep-
260 uty scaled.° The maid will I frame° and make fit
for his attempt. If you think well to carry this, as
you may, the doubleness of the benefit defends the
deceit from reproof. What think you of it?

Isabella. The image of it gives me content already,
265 and I trust it will grow to a most prosperous per-
fection.

Duke. It lies much in your holding up. Haste you
speedily to Angelo: if for this night he entreat you
to his bed, give him promise of satisfaction. I will
270 presently to Saint Luke's; there at the moated
grange° resides this dejected Mariana. At that
place call upon me, and dispatch with Angelo, that
it may be quickly.

Isabella. I thank you for this comfort. Fare you well,
275 good father.   *Exit.*

[Scene II. *Before the prison.*]

*Enter, [to the Duke,] Elbow, Clown
[Pompey, and] Officers.*

Elbow. Nay, if there be no remedy for it, but that
you will needs buy and sell men and women like

255 *stead up* keep   256 *encounter* i.e., sexual union   260 *scaled*
weighed   260 *frame* prepare   271 *grange* farm

beasts, we shall have all the world drink brown and
white bastard.°

Duke. O heavens! What stuff is here?   5

Pompey. 'Twas never merry world since, of two
usuries, the merriest was put down, and the worser
allowed by order of law a furred gown to keep him
warm; and furred with fox and lamb skins too, to
signify that craft, being richer than innocency,   10
stands for the facing.°

Elbow. Come your way, sir. 'Bless you, good father
friar.

Duke. And you, good brother father. What offense
hath this man made you, sir?   15

Elbow. Marry, sir, he hath offended the law; and, sir,
we take him to be a thief too, sir; for we have
found upon him, sir, a strange picklock, which we
have sent to the deputy.

Duke. Fie, sirrah, a bawd, a wicked bawd!   20
The evil that thou causest to be done,
That is thy means to live. Do thou but think
What 'tis to cram a maw° or clothe a back
From such a filthy vice; say to thyself,
From their abominable and beastly touches   25
I drink, I eat, array myself, and live.
Canst thou believe thy living is a life,
So stinkingly depending? Go mend, go mend.

Pompey. Indeed, it does stink in some sort, sir; but
yet, sir, I would prove—   30

Duke. Nay, if the devil have given thee proofs for sin,
Thou wilt prove his. Take him to prison, officer.
Correction and instruction must both work
Ere this rude beast will profit.

Elbow. He must before the deputy, sir; he has given   35
him warning. The deputy cannot abide a whore-

III.ii.4 *bastard* sweet Spanish wine   11 *stands for the facing* represents the trimming   23 *maw* belly

master; if he be a whoremonger, and comes before
him, he were as good go a mile on his errand.°

Duke. That we were all, as some would seem to be,
40   From our faults, as faults from seeing, free!

Enter Lucio.

Elbow. His neck will come to your waist—a cord, sir.

Pompey. I spy comfort; I cry bail. Here's a gentleman
and a friend of mine.

Lucio. How now, noble Pompey! What, at the wheels
45   of Caesar? Art thou led in triumph? What, is there
none of Pygmalion's images,° newly made woman,
to be had now, for putting the hand in the pocket
and extracting it clutched? What reply, ha? What
say'st thou to this tune, matter and method? Is't not
50   drowned i' th' last rain, ha? What say'st thou, Trot?
Is the world as it was, man? Which is the way? Is
it sad, and few words? Or how? The trick of it?

Duke. Still thus, and thus; still worse.

Lucio. How doth my dear morsel, thy mistress? Pro-
55   cures she still, ha?

Pompey. Troth, sir, she hath eaten up all her beef,°
and she is herself in the tub.°

Lucio. Why, 'tis good. It is the right of it; it must be
so: ever your fresh whore and your powdered bawd,
60   an unshunned consequence; it must be so. Art going
to prison, Pompey?

Pompey. Yes, faith, sir.

Lucio. Why, 'tis not amiss, Pompey. Farewell; go, say

---

38 *he were . . . errand* i.e., he has a hard (or fruitless?) journey
ahead   46 *Pygmalion's images* i.e., prostitutes (Pompey is compared
to Pygmalion, sculptor of a female statue that came to life)
56 *beef* prostitutes (who serve as flesh-food)   57 *in the tub* taking
the cure for venereal disease (a tub was also used for corning
beef, hence the reference to powdering—pickling—in Lucio's next
speech)

I sent thee thither. For debt, Pompey? Or how?

Elbow. For being a bawd, for being a bawd.   65

Lucio. Well, then, imprison him. If imprisonment be
the due of a bawd, why, 'tis his right. Bawd is he
doubtless, and of antiquity too, bawd-born. Farewell, good Pompey. Commend me to the prison,
Pompey, you will turn good husband° now, Pom-   70
pey, you will keep the house.

Pompey. I hope, sir, your good worship will be my
bail.

Lucio. No, indeed, will I not, Pompey, it is not the
wear.° I will pray, Pompey, to increase your bond-   75
age. If you take it not patiently, why, your mettle°
is the more. Adieu, trusty Pompey. 'Bless you, friar.

Duke. And you.

Lucio. Does Bridget paint still, Pompey, ha?

Elbow. Come your ways, sir, come.   80

Pompey. You will not bail me then, sir?

Lucio. Then, Pompey, nor now. What news abroad,
friar, what news?

Elbow. Come your ways, sir, come.

Lucio. Go to kennel, Pompey, go. [*Exeunt Elbow,*   85
Pompey, and Officers.] What news, friar, of the
Duke?

Duke. I know none. Can you tell me of any?

Lucio. Some say he is with the Emperor of Russia;
other some, he is in Rome: but where is he, think   90
you?

Duke. I know not where; but wheresoever, I wish him
well.

Lucio. It was a mad fantastical trick of him to steal

70 *husband* housekeeper, manager   75 *wear* fashion   76 *mettle*
spirit (pun on metal of chains)

95 from the state, and usurp the beggary he was never
born to. Lord Angelo dukes it well in his absence;
he puts transgression to't.

Duke. He does well in't.

Lucio. A little more lenity to lechery would do no
100 harm in him; something too crabbed that way, friar.

Duke. It is too general a vice, and severity must
cure it.

Lucio. Yes, in good sooth, the vice is of a great
kindred, it is well allied; but it is impossible to
105 extirp it quite, friar, till eating and drinking be
put down. They say this Angelo was not made by
man and woman after this downright way of creation. Is it true, think you?

Duke. How should he be made, then?

110 *Lucio.* Some report a sea maid° spawned him; some,
that he was begot between two stockfishes.° But it
is certain that when he makes water his urine is
congealed ice; that I know to be true. And he is a
motion generative;° that's infallible.

115 *Duke.* You are pleasant, sir, and speak apace.

Lucio. Why, what a ruthless thing is this in him, for
the rebellion of a codpiece to take away the life of
a man! Would the Duke that is absent have done
this? Ere he would have hanged a man for the get-
120 ting a hundred bastards, he would have paid for
the nursing a thousand. He had some feeling of the
sport; he knew the service, and that instructed him
to mercy.

Duke. I never heard the absent Duke much detected
125 for° women; he was not inclined that way.

Lucio. O, sir, you are deceived.

---

110 *sea maid* (to explain his piscatory coldness)   111 *stockfishes*
dried cod   114 *motion generative* masculine puppet   124–25 *detected for* accused of

Duke. 'Tis not possible.

Lucio. Who, not the Duke? Yes, your beggar of fifty, and his use was to put a ducat in her clack-dish;° the Duke had crotchets° in him. He would be drunk 130 too; that let me inform you.

Duke. You do him wrong, surely.

Lucio. Sir, I was an inward° of his. A shy fellow was the Duke, and I believe I know the cause of his withdrawing. 135

Duke. What, I prithee, might be the cause?

Lucio. No, pardon; 'tis a secret must be locked within the teeth and the lips; but this I can let you understand, the greater file° of the subject held the Duke to be wise. 140

Duke. Wise! Why, no question but he was.

Lucio. A very superficial, ignorant, unweighing fellow.

Duke. Either this is envy in you, folly, or mistaking. The very stream of his life and the business he hath helmed must, upon a warranted need,° give him a 145 better proclamation. Let him be but testimonied in his own bringings-forth,° and he shall appear to the envious a scholar, a statesman, and a soldier. Therefore you speak unskillfully; or if your knowledge be more, it is much dark'ned in your malice. 150

Lucio. Sir, I know him, and I love him.

Duke. Love talks with better knowledge, and knowledge with dearer love.

Lucio. Come, sir, I know what I know.

Duke. I can hardly believe that, since you know not 155 what you speak. But, if ever the Duke return, as our prayers are he may, let me desire you to make

---

129 *clack-dish* beggar's bowl (metaphorical here)   130 *crotchets* whims   133 *inward* intimate companion   139 *greater file* majority 145 *upon a warranted need* if proof be demanded   147 *bringings-forth* actions

your answer before him. If it be honest you have
spoke, you have courage to maintain it. I am bound
160   to call upon you, and I pray you, your name?

Lucio. Sir, my name is Lucio, well known to the Duke.

Duke. He shall know you better, sir, if I may live to
report you.

Lucio. I fear you not.

165   *Duke.* O, you hope the Duke will return no more, or
you imagine me too unhurtful an opposite. But,
indeed, I can do you little harm; you'll forswear
this again.

Lucio. I'll be hanged first; thou art deceived in me,
170   friar. But no more of this. Canst thou tell if Claudio
die tomorrow or no?

Duke. Why should he die, sir?

Lucio. Why? For filling a bottle with a tundish.° I
would the Duke we talk of were returned again;
175   this ungenitured° agent will unpeople the province
with continency; sparrows must not build in his
house-eaves, because they are lecherous. The Duke
yet would have dark deeds darkly answered; he
would never bring them to light. Would he were
180   returned! Marry, this Claudio is condemned for untrussing.° Farewell, good friar; I prithee, pray for
me. The Duke, I say to thee again, would eat mutton on Fridays.° He's now past it, yet, and I say
to thee, he would mouth with a beggar, though she
185   smelled brown bread and garlic. Say that I said so.
Farewell.   *Exit.*

Duke. No might nor greatness in mortality
Can censure 'scape; back-wounding calumny
The whitest virtue strikes. What king so strong

173 *tundish* funnel   175 *ungenitured* sexless   180–81 *untrussing*
undressing   182–83 *eat mutton on Fridays* (the Duke allegedly
ate mutton on a Friday, which was a fast day, and also practiced
venery; "mutton" also means "harlot," and Friday is the day of the
planet Venus)

Can tie the gall up in the slanderous tongue?   190
But who comes here?

Enter Escalus, Provost, and [Officers with]
Bawd [Mistress Overdone].

Escalus. Go, away with her to prison!

Mistress Overdone. Good my lord, be good to me.
Your honor is accounted a merciful man, good my
lord.   195

Escalus. Double and treble admonition, and still forfeit in the same kind! This would make mercy
swear, and play the tyrant.

Provost. A bawd of eleven years' continuance, may
it please your honor.   200

Mistress Overdone. My lord, this is one Lucio's information against me. Mistress Kate Keepdown was
with child by him in the Duke's time; he promised
her marriage; his child is a year and a quarter old,
come Philip and Jacob;° I have kept it myself, and   205
see how he goes about to abuse me.

Escalus. That fellow is a fellow of much license; let
him be called before us. Away with her to prison.
Go to, no more words. [*Exeunt Officers with Mis-*
tress Overdone.] Provost, my brother Angelo will   210
not be altered; Claudio must die tomorrow. Let him
be furnished with divines, and have all charitable
preparation. If my brother wrought by my pity,
it should not be so with him.

Provost. So please you, this friar hath been with him,   215
and advised him for th' entertainment of death.

Escalus. Good even, good father.

Duke. Bliss and goodness on you!

Escalus. Of whence are you?

205 *Philip and Jacob* May 1st

220 *Duke.* Not of this country, though my chance is now
          To use it for my time; I am a brother
          Of gracious order, late come from the See
          In special business from his Holiness.

Escalus. What news abroad i' th' world?

225 *Duke.* None, but that there is so great a fever on good-
          ness, that the dissolution of it must cure it,° novelty
          is only in request,° and it is as dangerous to be
          aged° in any kind of course as it is virtuous to be
          constant in any undertaking. There is scarce truth
230   enough alive to make societies secure, but security°
          enough to make fellowships° accursed. Much upon
          this riddle runs the wisdom of the world. This news
          is old enough, yet it is every day's news. I pray
          you, sir, of what disposition was the Duke?

235 *Escalus.* One that, above all other strifes, contended
          especially to know himself.

Duke. What pleasure was he given to?

Escalus. Rather rejoicing to see another merry, than
          merry at anything which professed to make him
240   rejoice: a gentleman of all temperance. But leave
          we him to his events, with a prayer they may prove
          prosperous, and let me desire to know how you
          find Claudio prepared. I am made to understand
          that you have lent him visitation.

245 *Duke.* He professes to have received no sinister meas-
          ure from his judge, but most willingly humbles him-
          self to the determination of justice; yet had he
          framed to himself, by the instruction of his frailty,
          many deceiving promises of life; which I, by my
250   good leisure, have discredited to him, and now is
          he resolved to die.

Escalus. You have paid the heavens your function,

___

225–26 *fever . . . cure it* i.e., the dissolution of the fever alone can
now restore goodness to its pristine health   226–27 *novelty is only
in request* change is urgently needed   228 *aged* old and worn out
230 *security* heedlessness   231 *fellowships* human societies

and the prisoner the very debt of your calling. I
have labored for the poor gentleman to the extremest shore of my modesty,° but my brother   255
justice have I found so severe, that he hath forced
me to tell him he is indeed Justice.

Duke. If his own life answer the straitness of his proceeding, it shall become him well; wherein if he
chance to fail, he hath sentenced himself.   260

Escalus. I am going to visit the prisoner. Fare you
well.

Duke. Peace be with you!
                    [*Exeunt Escalus and Provost.*]
He who the sword of heaven will bear
Should be as holy as severe;   265
Pattern in himself to know,
Grace to stand, and virtue go;°
More nor less to others paying
Than by self-offenses weighing.
Shame to him whose cruel striking   270
Kills for faults of his own liking.
Twice treble shame on Angelo,
To weed my° vice and let his grow.
O, what may man within him hide,
Though angel on the outward side!   275
How may likeness made in crimes,
Making practice on the times,
To draw with idle spiders' strings
Most ponderous and substantial things?
Craft against vice I must apply: 280
With Angelo tonight shall lie
His old betrothèd but despisèd;
So disguise shall, by th' disguisèd,
Pay with falsehood false exacting,
And perform an old contracting.   285
                              Exit.

254–55 *extremest shore of my modesty* i.e., as far as is proper
266–67 *Pattern . . . go* i.e., he should have a model in himself of
grace which will stand if virtue elsewhere ebbs   273 *my* (used
impersonally)

ACT IV

Scene I. [*The moated grange.*]

Enter Mariana and Boy singing.

SONG

Take, O, take those lips away,
  That so sweetly were forsworn;
And those eyes, the break of day,
  Lights that do mislead the morn;
But my kisses bring again, bring again;
Seals of love, but sealed in vain, sealed in vain.

Enter Duke [disguised as before].

Mariana. Break off thy song, and haste thee quick
    away.
Here comes a man of comfort, whose advice
Hath often stilled my brawling discontent.

                             [*Exit Boy.*]

I cry you mercy, sir; and well could wish
You had not found me here so musical.
Let me excuse me, and believe me so,
My mirth it much displeased, but pleased my woe.

Duke. 'Tis good; though music oft hath such a charm

To make bad good, and good provoke to harm. 15
I pray you, tell me, hath anybody inquired for me
here today? Much upon this time have I promised
here to meet.

Mariana. You have not been inquired after; I have
sat here all day. 20

Enter Isabella.

Duke. I do constantly believe you. The time is come
even now. I shall crave your forbearance a little;
may be I will call upon you anon, for some advantage to yourself.

Mariana. I am always bound to you. *Exit.* 25

Duke. Very well met, and well come.
What is the news from this good deputy?

Isabella. He hath a garden circummured° with brick,
Whose western side is with a vineyard backed;
And to that vineyard is a planchèd° gate, 30
That makes his opening with this bigger key.
This other doth command a little door
Which from the vineyard to the garden leads.
There have I made my promise
Upon the heavy middle of the night 35
To call upon him.

Duke. But shall you on your knowledge find this way?

Isabella. I have ta'en a due and wary note upon't.
With whispering and most guilty diligence,
In action all of precept,° he did show me 40
The way twice o'er.

Duke.   Are there no other tokens
Between you 'greed concerning her observance?°

Isabella. No, none, but only a repair i' th' dark,
And that I have possessed° him my most stay

IV.i.28 *circummured* walled around 30 *planchèd* planked 40 *In
. . . precept* teaching by gestures 42 *her observance* what she must
do 44 *possessed* informed

45 Can be but brief; for I have made him know
    I have a servant comes with me along,
    That stays upon° me, whose persuasion° is
    I come about my brother.

Duke.   'Tis well borne up.
    I have not yet made known to Mariana
50 A word of this. What, ho, within! Come forth.

Enter Mariana.

    I pray you, be acquainted with this maid;
    She comes to do you good.

Isabella.   I do desire the like.

Duke. Do you persuade yourself that I respect you?

Mariana. Good friar, I know you do, and have found
    it.

55 *Duke.* Take, then, this your companion by the hand,
    Who hath a story ready for your ear.
    I shall attend your leisure, but make haste;
    The vaporous night approaches.

Mariana. Will't please you walk aside?
                    Exit [*with Isabella*].

60 *Duke.* O place and greatness, millions of false eyes
    Are stuck upon thee; volumes of report
    Run with these false and most contrarious quests°
    Upon thy doings; thousand escapes° of wit
    Make thee the father of their idle dreams,
    And rack thee in their fancies.

Enter Mariana and Isabella.

65   Welcome, how agreed?

Isabella. She'll take the enterprise upon her, father,
    If you advise it.

Duke.   It is not my consent

47 *stays upon* waits for   47 *persuasion* conviction   62 *quests* cry
of the hound on the scent   63 *escapes* sallies

But my entreaty too.

Isabella.   Little have you to say
When you depart from him, but, soft and low,
"Remember now my brother."

Mariana.   Fear me not.   70

Duke. Nor, gentle daughter, fear you not at all.
He is your husband on a precontract;°
To bring you thus together, 'tis no sin,
Sith that the justice of your title to him
Doth flourish the deceit. Come, let us go: 75
Our corn's to reap, for yet our tithe's° to sow.
                                        Exeunt.

Scene II. [*The prison.*]

Enter Provost and Clown [Pompey].

Provost. Come hither, sirrah. Can you cut off a man's
head?

Pompey. If the man be a bachelor, sir, I can; but if he
be a married man, he's his wife's head,° and I can
never cut off a woman's head.   5

Provost. Come, sir, leave me your snatches,° and yield
me a direct answer. Tomorrow morning are to die
Claudio and Barnardine. Here is in our prison a
common executioner, who in his office lacks a
helper. If you will take it on you to assist him, it   10
shall redeem you from your gyves;° if not, you
shall have your full time of imprisonment, and your

72 *precontract* legally binding betrothal agreement   76 *tithe* tithe
corn   IV.ii.4 *he's his wife's head* (see Ephesians 5:23: "For the
husband is the head of the wife")   6 *snatches* quibbles   11 *gyves*
shackles

deliverance with an unpitied whipping, for you
have been a notorious bawd.

15 *Pompey.* Sir, I have been an unlawful bawd time out
of mind, but yet I will be content to be a lawful
hangman. I would be glad to receive some instruction from my fellow partner.

Provost. What, ho, Abhorson!° Where's Abhorson,
20 there?

Enter Abhorson.

Abhorson. Do you call, sir?

Provost. Sirrah, here's a fellow will help you tomorrow in your execution. If you think it meet, com-
pound° with him by the year, and let him abide
25 here with you; if not, use him for the present, and
dismiss him. He cannot plead his estimation° with
you; he hath been a bawd.

Abhorson. A bawd, sir? Fie upon him! He will discredit our mystery.°

30 *Provost.* Go to, sir; you weigh equally; a feather will
turn the scale.   *Exit.*

Pompey. Pray, sir, by your good favor—for surely,
sir, a good favor° you have, but that you have a
hanging look—do you call, sir, your occupation
35 a mystery?

Abhorson. Ay, sir; a mystery.

Pompey. Painting, sir, I have heard say, is a mystery;
and your whores, sir, being members of my occupation, using painting, do prove my occupation a
40 mystery; but what mystery there should be in hanging, if I should be hanged, I cannot imagine.

Abhorson. Sir, it is a mystery.

---

19 *Abhorson* (pun on "ab, whore, son," son from a whore)   23–
24 *compound* settle   26 *estimation* reputation   29 *mystery* craft
33 *favor* countenance

Pompey. Proof?

Abhorson. Every true man's apparel fits your thief: if
it be too little for your thief, your true man thinks it
big enough; if it be too big for your thief, your thief   45
thinks it little enough: so every true man's apparel
fits your thief.°

Enter Provost.

Provost. Are you agreed?

Pompey. Sir, I will serve him; for I do find your hang-   50
man is a more penitent trade than your bawd; he
doth oft'ner ask forgiveness.°

Provost. You, sirrah, provide your block and your ax
tomorrow four o'clock.

Abhorson. Come on, bawd. I will instruct thee in my   55
trade; follow.

Pompey. I do desire to learn, sir; and I hope, if you
have occasion to use me for your own turn,°
you shall find me yare;° for, truly, sir, for your
kindness I owe you a good turn.   60

Provost. Call hither Barnardine and Claudio.

Exit [Pompey with Abhorson].

Th' one has my pity; not a jot the other,
Being a murderer, though he were my brother.

Enter Claudio.

Look, here's the warrant, Claudio, for thy death.
'Tis now dead midnight, and by eight tomorrow   65
Thou must be made immortal. Where's Barnardine?

Claudio. As fast locked up in sleep as guiltless labor
When it lies starkly° in the traveler's bones;
He will not wake.

44–48 *every . . . thief* (interpretation uncertain)   52 *ask forgiveness*
(the executioner always asked the condemned man to forgive him)
58 *turn* execution (pun)   59 *yare* ready   68 *starkly* stiffly

Provost.   Who can do good on him?
 Well, go, prepare yourself. [*Knocking within.*] But,
70 hark, what noise?—
 Heaven give your spirits comfort. [*Exit Claudio.*]
  By and by.
 I hope it is some pardon or reprieve
 For the most gentle Claudio. Welcome, father.

Enter Duke [disguised as before].

Duke. The best and wholesom'st spirits of the night
 Envelop you, good provost! Who called here of
75 late?

Provost. None since the curfew rung.

Duke. Not Isabel?

Provost.   No.

Duke.   They will, then, ere't be long.

Provost. What comfort is for Claudio?

Duke. There's some in hope.

80 *Provost.* It is a bitter deputy.

Duke. Not so, not so; his life is paralleled
 Even with the stroke and line of his great justice.
 He doth with holy abstinence subdue
 That in himself which he spurs on his pow'r
85 To qualify° in others; were he mealed° with that
 Which he corrects, then were he tyrannous;
 But this being so, he's just.   [*Knocking within.*]
       Now are they come.
        [*Exit Provost.*]
 This is a gentle provost—seldom when
 The steelèd jailer is the friend of men.
        [*Knocking within.*]
 How now, what noise? That spirit's possessed with
90 haste

85 *qualify* moderate   85 *mealed* stained

That wounds th' unsisting° postern° with these
  strokes.

[Enter Provost.]

Provost. There he must stay until the officer
  Arise to let him in; he is called up.

Duke. Have you no countermand for Claudio yet,
  But he must die tomorrow?

Provost.   None, sir, none.   *95*

Duke. As near the dawning, provost, as it is,
  You shall hear more ere morning.

Provost.   Happily
  You something know; yet I believe there comes
  No countermand; no such example have we.
  Besides, upon the very siege° of justice   *100*
  Lord Angelo hath to the public ear
  Professed the contrary.

Enter a Messenger.

                  This is his lord's man.

Duke. And here comes Claudio's pardon.

Messenger. My lord hath sent you this note, and by
  me this further charge, that you swerve not from   *105*
  the smallest article of it, neither in time, matter,
  or other circumstance. Good morrow; for, as I
  take it, it is almost day.

Provost. I shall obey him.

                  [Exit Messenger.]

Duke. *[Aside]* This is his pardon, purchased by such
  sin   *110*
  For which the pardoner himself is in.
  Hence hath offense his quick celerity,

---

91 *unsisting* (perhaps "unassisting," perhaps a printer's slip for
"resisting")   91 *postern* small door   100 *siege* seat

When it is borne in high authority.
When vice makes mercy, mercy's so extended,
115 That for the fault's love is th' offender friended.
Now, sir, what news?

Provost. I told you. Lord Angelo, belike° thinking
me remiss in mine office, awakens me with this un-
wonted putting-on;° methinks strangely, for he hath
120 not used it before.

Duke. Pray you, let's hear.

Provost. [*Reads*] *the letter.* "Whatsoever you may hear
to the contrary, let Claudio be executed by four
of the clock; and in the afternoon Barnardine. For
125 my better satisfaction, let me have Claudio's head
sent me by five. Let this be duly performed with a
thought that more depends on it than we must yet
deliver. Thus fail not to do your office, as you will
answer it at your peril."
130 What say you to this, sir?

Duke. What is that Barnardine who is to be executed
in th' afternoon?

Provost. A Bohemian born, but here nursed up and
bred; one that is a prisoner nine years old.

135 *Duke.* How came it that the absent Duke had not
either delivered him to his liberty or executed him?
I have heard it was ever his manner to do so.

Provost. His friends still wrought reprieves for him;
and, indeed, his fact,° till now in the government
140 of Lord Angelo, came not to an undoubtful proof.

Duke. It is now apparent?

Provost. Most manifest, and not denied by himself.

Duke. Hath he borne himself penitently in prison?
How seems he to be touched?

145 *Provost.* A man that apprehends death no more dreadfully but as a drunken sleep; careless, reckless, and

117 *belike* perhaps   119 *putting-on* urging   139 *fact* evil deed

fearless of what's past, present, or to come; in-
sensible of mortality, and desperately mortal.°

Duke. He wants° advice.

Provost. He will hear none. He hath evermore had the 150
liberty of the prison; give him leave to escape hence,
he would not: drunk many times a day, if not many
days entirely drunk. We have very oft awaked him,
as if to carry him to execution, and showed him a
seeming warrant for it; it hath not moved him at all. 155

Duke. More of him anon. There is written in your
brow, provost, honesty and constancy: if I read it
not truly, my ancient skill beguiles me; but, in the
boldness of my cunning,° I will lay myself in hazard.° Claudio, whom here you have warrant to exe- 160
cute, is no greater forfeit to the law than Angelo who
hath sentenced him. To make you understand this
in a manifested effect,° I crave but four days' res-
pite, for the which you are to do me both a
present° and a dangerous courtesy. 165

Provost. Pray, sir, in what?

Duke. In the delaying death.

Provost. Alack, how may I do it, having the hour limited,° and an express command, under penalty, to
deliver his head in the view of Angelo? I may make 170
my case as Claudio's, to cross this in the smallest.

Duke. By the vow of mine Order I warrant you, if my
instructions may be your guide. Let this Barnardine
be this morning executed, and his head borne to
Angelo. 175

Provost. Angelo hath seen them both, and will discover the favor.°

Duke. O, death's a great disguiser; and you may add

148 *desperately mortal* about to die without hope of the future
149 *wants* needs   159 *cunning* knowledge   159–60 *lay myself in
hazard* take a risk   163 *in a manifested effect* by open proof
165 *present* immediate   168–69 *limited* determined   176–77 *discover the favor* recognize the face

to it. Shave the head, and tie the beard; and say it
180　was the desire of the penitent to be so bared° before his death; you know the course is common.
If anything fall to you upon this, more than thanks
and good fortune, by the saint whom I profess, I
will plead against it with my life.

185 *Provost.* Pardon me, good father; it is against my oath.

Duke. Were you sworn to the Duke, or to the deputy?

Provost. To him, and to his substitutes.

Duke. You will think you have made no offense, if the
Duke avouch the justice of your dealing?

190 *Provost.* But what likelihood is in that?

Duke. Not a resemblance, but a certainty. Yet since
I see you fearful,° that neither my coat, integrity,
nor persuasion can with ease attempt° you, I will
go further than I meant, to pluck all fears out of
195　you. Look you, sir, here is the hand and seal of the
Duke. You know the character,° I doubt not, and
the signet is not strange to you.

Provost. I know them both.

Duke. The contents of this is the return of the Duke.
200　You shall anon overread it at your pleasure, where
you shall find, within these two days he will be
here. This is a thing that Angelo knows not; for he
this very day receives letters of strange tenor, perchance of the Duke's death, perchance entering into
205　some monastery, but by chance nothing of what is
writ. Look, th' unfolding star° calls up the shepherd. Put not yourself into amazement how these
things should be: all difficulties are but easy when
they are known. Call your executioner, and off with
210　Barnardine's head; I will give him a present shrift,°

180 *bared* shaved   192 *fearful* full of fear   193 *attempt* move
196 *character* handwriting   206 *unfolding star* morning star (signal-
ing the shepherd to lead the sheep from the fold)   210 *shrift*
absolution

and advise him for a better place. Yet you are
amazed; but this shall absolutely resolve° you.
Come away; it is almost clear dawn.

Exit [*with Provost*].

Scene III. [*The prison.*]

Enter Clown [*Pompey*].

Pompey. I am as well acquainted here as I was in our
   house of profession: one would think it were Mistress Overdone's own house, for here be many of
   her old customers. First, here's young Master Rash;
   he's in for a commodity° of brown paper and old   5
   ginger, ninescore and seventeen pounds, of which
   he made five marks,° ready money; marry, then
   ginger was not much in request, for the old women
   were all dead. Then is there here one Master Caper,
   at the suit of Master Three-pile the mercer, for   10
   some four suits of peach-colored satin, which now
   peaches° him a beggar. Then have we here young
   Dizzy, and young Master Deep-vow, and Master
   Copper-spur,° and Master Starve-lackey, the rapier
   and dagger man, and young Drop-heir that killed   15
   lusty Pudding, and Master Forthright the tilter,°
   and brave Master Shoe-tie° the great traveler, and
   wild Half-can° that stabbed Pots, and, I think,
   forty more; all great doers in our trade, and are
   now "for the Lord's sake."°   20

212 *resolve* convince IV.iii.5 *commodity* (worthless goods whose
purchase at a heavy price was forced on a debtor in dire need by
a usurious creditor, who thus circumvented the contemporary laws
against usury) 7 *marks* (a mark was about two-thirds of a pound)
12 *peaches* betrays 14 *Copper-spur* i.e., Master Pretentious (cop-
per was a bogus substitute for gold) 16 *tilter* fighter 17 *Shoe-tie*
rosette (worn by gallants) 18 *Half-can* (a larger vessel than a
pot) 20 *"for the Lord's sake"* (the cry of prisoners begging alms
from passers-by)

Enter Abhorson.

Abhorson. Sirrah, bring Barnardine hither.

Pompey. Master Barnardine! You must rise and be hanged, Master Barnardine!

Abhorson. What, ho, Barnardine!

25 *Barnardine.* (*Within*) A pox o' your throats! Who makes that noise there? What are you?

Pompey. Your friends, sir; the hangman. You must be so good, sir, to rise and be put to death.

Barnardine. [*Within*] Away, you rogue, away! I am 30 sleepy.

Abhorson. Tell him he must awake, and that quickly too.

Pompey. Pray, Master Barnardine, awake till you are executed, and sleep afterwards.

35 *Abhorson.* Go into him, and fetch him out.

Pompey. He is coming, sir, he is coming; I hear his straw rustle.

Enter Barnardine.

Abhorson. Is the ax upon the block, sirrah?

Pompey. Very ready, sir.

40 *Barnardine.* How now, Abhorson? What's the news with you?

Abhorson. Truly, sir, I would desire you to clap into your prayers; for, look you, the warrant's come.

Barnardine. You rogue, I have been drinking all night; 45 I am not fitted for't.

Pompey. O, the better, sir: for he that drinks all night, and is hanged betimes° in the morning, may sleep the sounder all the next day.

47 *betimes* early

Enter Duke [disguised as before].

Abhorson. Look you, sir; here comes your ghostly°
 father. Do we jest now, think you?   50

Duke. Sir, induced by my charity, and hearing how
 hastily you are to depart, I am come to advise you,
 comfort you, and pray with you.

Barnardine. Friar, not I: I have been drinking hard
 all night, and I will have more time to prepare me,   55
 or they shall beat out my brains with billets.° I will
 not consent to die this day, that's certain.

Duke. O, sir, you must; and therefore I beseech you
 Look forward on the journey you shall go.

Barnardine. I swear I will not die today for any man's   60
 persuasion.

Duke. But hear you—

Barnardine. Not a word. If you have anything to say
 to me, come to my ward, for thence will not I today.
                                                    Exit.

Enter Provost.

Duke. Unfit to live or die. O gravel heart!   65
 After him, fellows; bring him to the block.
                  [Exeunt Abhorson and Pompey.]

Provost. Now, sir, how do you find the prisoner?

Duke. A creature unprepared, unmeet for death;
 And to transport him in the mind he is
 Were damnable.

Provost.   Here in the prison, father,   70
 There died this morning of a cruel fever
 One Ragozine, a most notorious pirate,
 A man of Claudio's years, his beard and head
 Just of his color. What if we do omit
 This reprobate till he were well inclined,   75
 And satisfy the deputy with the visage

49 *ghostly* spiritual   56 *billets* cudgels

Of Ragozine, more like to Claudio?

Duke. O, 'tis an accident that heaven provides.
Dispatch it presently;° the hour draws on
80 Prefixed° by Angelo. See this be done,
And sent according to command, whiles I
Persuade this rude wretch willingly to die.

Provost. This shall be done, good father, presently;
But Barnardine must die this afternoon,
85 And how shall we continue Claudio,
To save me from the danger that might come
If he were known alive?

Duke.   Let this be done:
Put them in secret holds,° both Barnardine and
Claudio.
Ere twice the sun hath made his journal° greeting
90 To yonder generation, you shall find
Your safety manifested.

Provost. I am your free dependant.°

Duke. Quick, dispatch, and send the head to Angelo.
Exit [*Provost*].
Now will I write letters to Angelo—
95 The provost, he shall bear them—whose contents
Shall witness to him I am near at home,
And that by great injunctions I am bound
To enter publicly. Him I'll desire
To meet me at the consecrated fount,
100 A league below the city; and from thence,
By cold gradation° and well-balanced form,
We shall proceed with Angelo.

Enter Provost.

Provost. Here is the head; I'll carry it myself.

Duke. Convenient is it. Make a swift return,

79 *presently* at once   80 *Prefixed* predetermined   88 *holds* cells
89 *journal* daily   92 *your free dependant* freely at your service
101 *cold gradation* deliberate steps

For I would commune with you of such things   105
That want° no ear but yours.

Provost.   I'll make all speed.
                                              Exit.

Isabella. (*Within*) Peace, ho, be here!

Duke. The tongue of Isabel. She's come to know
If yet her brother's pardon be come hither.
But I will keep her ignorant of her good,   110
To make her heavenly comforts of despair
When it is least expected.

                    Enter Isabella.

Isabella.   Ho, by your leave!

Duke. Good morning to you, fair and gracious daugh-
    ter.

Isabella. The better, given me by so holy a man.
    Hath yet the deputy sent my brother's pardon?   115

Duke. He hath released him, Isabel, from the world;
    His head is off, and sent to Angelo.

Isabella. Nay, but it is not so.

Duke. It is no other. Show your wisdom, daughter,
    In your close° patience.   120

Isabella. O, I will to him and pluck out his eyes!

Duke. You shall not be admitted to his sight.

Isabella. Unhappy Claudio, wretched Isabel,
    Injurious world, most damnèd Angelo!

Duke. This nor hurts him nor profits you a jot;   125
    Forbear it therefore, give your cause to heaven.
    Mark what I say, which you shall find
    By every syllable a faithful verity.
    The Duke comes home tomorrow—nay, dry your
        eyes—
    One of our covent,° and his confessor,   130

106 *want* need   120 *close* deep, secret   130 *covent* convent

Gives me this instance:° already he hath carried
Notice to Escalus and Angelo,
Who do prepare to meet him at the gates,
There to give up their pow'r. If you can, pace°
   your wisdom
135 In that good path that I would wish it go,
And you shall have your bosom° on this wretch,
Grace of the Duke, revenges to your heart,
And general honor.

Isabella.   I am directed by you.

Duke. This letter, then, to Friar Peter give;
140 'Tis that he sent me of the Duke's return.
Say, by this token, I desire his company
At Mariana's house tonight. Her cause and yours
I'll perfect him withal, and he shall bring you
Before the Duke; and to the head of Angelo
145 Accuse him home and home. For my poor self,
I am combinèd° by a sacred vow,
And shall be absent. Wend you with this letter;
Command these fretting waters from your eyes
With a light heart; trust not my holy Order,
150 If I pervert your course. Who's here?

Enter Lucio.

Lucio. Good even. Friar, where's the provost?

Duke. Not within, sir.

Lucio. O pretty Isabella, I am pale at mine heart to
see thine eyes so red; thou must be patient. I am
155 fain to dine and sup with water and bran; I dare
not for my head fill my belly; one fruitful meal
would set me to't. But they say the Duke will be
here tomorrow. By my troth, Isabel, I loved thy
brother. If the old fantastical Duke of dark cor-
160 ners had been at home, he had lived.
                    [Exit Isabella.]

131 *instance* proof 134 *pace* conduct 136 *bosom* desire 146
combinèd bound

Duke. Sir, the Duke is marvelous little beholding to
  your reports; but the best is, he lives not in them.

Lucio. Friar, thou knowest not the Duke so well as I
  do; he's a better woodman° than thou tak'st him
  for.   *165*

Duke. Well, you'll answer this one day. Fare ye well.

Lucio. Nay, tarry, I'll go along with thee: I can tell
  thee pretty tales of the Duke.

Duke. You have told me too many of him already,   *170*
  sir, if they be true; if not true, none were enough.

Lucio. I was once before him for getting a wench
  with child.

Duke. Did you such a thing?

Lucio. Yes, marry, did I; but I was fain to forswear
  it: they would else have married me to the rotten   *175*
  medlar.°

Duke. Sir, your company is fairer than honest. Rest
  you well.

Lucio. By my troth, I'll go with thee to the lane's end.
  If bawdy talk offend you, we'll have very little of   *180*
  it. Nay, friar, I am a kind of burr; I shall stick.
                                                    Exeunt.

Scene IV. [*A room.*]

Enter Angelo and Escalus.

Escalus. Every letter he hath writ hath disvouched
  other.

---

164 *woodman* hunter (here, of women)   176 *medlar* applelike fruit
edible only when partly decayed (here, a prostitute)

Angelo. In most uneven and distracted manner. His
actions show much like to madness; pray heaven
5 his wisdom be not tainted. And why meet him at
the gates, and redeliver our authorities there?

Escalus. I guess not.

Angelo. And why should we proclaim it in an hour
before his ent'ring, that if any crave redress of in-
10 justice, they should exhibit their petitions in the
street?

Escalus. He shows his reason for that: to have a dispatch of complaints, and to deliver us from devices°
hereafter which shall then have no power to stand
15 against us.

Angelo. Well, I beseech you, let it be proclaimed.
Betimes i' th' morn I'll call you at your house. Give
notice to such men of sort and suit° as are to meet
him.

20 *Escalus.* I shall, sir. Fare you well. *Exit.*

Angelo. Good night.
 This deed unshapes me quite, makes me unpreg-
  nant,°
 And dull to all proceedings. A deflow'red maid,
 And by an eminent body that enforced
25 The law against it! But that her tender shame
 Will not proclaim against her maiden loss,°
 How might she tongue me! Yet reason dares her no;
 For my authority bears of a credent bulk,°
 That no particular scandal once can touch
 But it confounds the breather. He should have
30 lived,
 Save that his riotous youth, with dangerous sense,°
 Might in the times to come have ta'en revenge,
 By so receiving a dishonored life

IV.iv.13 *devices* false complaints   18 *men of sort and suit* noble-
men   22 *unpregnant* unreceptive   26 *maiden loss* loss of maiden-
hood   28 *bears of a credent bulk* is derived from trusted material
31 *sense* feeling

With ransom of such shame. Would yet he had
  lived!
Alack, when once our grace we have forgot,   35
Nothing goes right; we would, and we would not.

Exit.

Scene V. [*Outside the town.*]

Enter Duke [*in his own habit*] *and Friar Peter.*

Duke. These letters at fit time deliver me.°
  The provost knows our purpose and our plot.
  The matter being afoot, keep your instruction,
  And hold you ever to our special drift,
  Though sometimes you do blench° from this to that,   5
  As cause doth minister. Go call at Flavius' house,
  And tell him where I stay; give the like notice
  To Valencius, Rowland, and to Crassus,
  And bid them bring the trumpets to the gate;
  But send me Flavius first.

Friar Peter.   It shall be speeded well.   10

                                      [*Exit.*]

              Enter Varrius.

Duke. I thank thee, Varrius; thou hast made good
  haste.
  Come, we will walk. There's other of our friends
  Will greet us here anon, my gentle Varrius.   *Exeunt.*

IV.v.1 *me* for me   5 *blench* deviate

Scene VI. [*Near the city gate.*]

Enter Isabella and Mariana.

Isabella. To speak so indirectly I am loath:
I would say the truth; but to accuse him so,
That is your part. Yet I am advised to do it,
He says, to veil full purpose.

Mariana.   Be ruled by him.

5 *Isabella.* Besides, he tells me that, if peradventure
He speak against me on the adverse side,
I should not think it strange; for 'tis a physic
That's bitter to sweet end.

Mariana. I would Friar Peter—

Enter Friar Peter.

Isabella.   O peace! The friar is come.

Friar Peter. Come, I have found you out a stand most
10   fit
Where you may have such vantage° on the Duke,
He shall not pass you. Twice have the trumpets
    sounded.
The generous° and gravest citizens
Have hent° the gates, and very near upon
15 The Duke is ent'ring: therefore, hence, away!

                              Exeunt.

IV.vi.11 *vantage* advantageous position   13 *generous* highborn   14
hent gathered at

ACT V

Scene I. [*The city gate.*]

Enter Duke, Varrius, Lords, Angelo, Escalus,
Lucio, [Provost, Officers, and] Citizens, at
several doors.

Duke. My very worthy cousin,° fairly met.
  Our old and faithful friend, we are glad to see you.

Angelo, Escalus. Happy return be to your royal
  Grace.

Duke. Many and hearty thankings to you both.
  We have made inquiry of you, and we hear   *5*
  Such goodness of your justice, that our soul
  Cannot but yield you forth to public thanks,
  Forerunning more requital.°

Angelo.   You make my bonds still greater.

Duke. O, your desert speaks loud, and I should wrong
  it
  To lock it in the wards of covert bosom,°   *10*

V.i.1 *cousin* (a sovereign's address to a nobleman) 8 *Forerunning*
more requital preceding additional reward 10 *To . . . bosom* i.e.,
to keep it locked hidden in my heart

When it deserves, with characters of brass,
A forted residence 'gainst the tooth of time
And razure° of oblivion. Give me your hand,
And let the subject see, to make them know
15   That outward courtesies would fain proclaim
Favors that keep° within. Come, Escalus,
You must walk by us on our other hand—
And good supporters are you.

Enter [Friar] Peter and Isabella.

Friar Peter. Now is your time: speak loud, and kneel
before him.

20 *Isabella.* Justice, O royal Duke! Vail your regard°
Upon a wronged—I would fain have said, a maid.
O worthy prince, dishonor not your eye
By throwing it on any other object
Till you have heard me in my true complaint,
25   And given me justice, justice, justice, justice!

Duke. Relate your wrongs. In what? By whom? Be
brief.
Here is Lord Angelo shall give you justice;
Reveal yourself to him.

Isabella.   O worthy Duke,
You bid me seek redemption of the devil.
30   Hear me yourself, for that which I must speak
Must either punish me, not being believed,
Or wring redress from you. Hear me, O hear me,
here!

Angelo. My lord, her wits, I fear me, are not firm.
She hath been a suitor to me for her brother
Cut off by course of justice—

35 *Isabella.*   By course of justice!

Angelo. And she will speak most bitterly and strange.

Isabella. Most strange, but yet most truly, will I speak.

13 *razure* erasure   16 *keep* dwell   20 *Vail your regard* cast your
attention

That Angelo's forsworn, is it not strange?
That Angelo's a murderer, is't not strange?
That Angelo is an adulterous thief,   40
An hypocrite, a virgin-violator;
Is it not strange, and strange?

Duke.   Nay, it is ten times strange.

Isabella. It is not truer he is Angelo
Than this is all as true as it is strange.
Nay, it is ten times true, for truth is truth   45
To th' end of reck'ning.

Duke.   Away with her! Poor soul,
She speaks this in th' infirmity of sense.

Isabella. O prince, I conjure thee, as thou believ'st
There is another comfort than this world,
That thou neglect me not, with that opinion   50
That I am touched with madness. Make not impos-
   sible
That which but seems unlike. 'Tis not impossible
But one, the wicked'st caitiff on the ground,
May seem as shy, as grave, as just, as absolute°
As Angelo; even so may Angelo,   55
In all his dressings, caracts,° titles, forms,
Be an arch-villain. Believe it, royal prince;
If he be less, he's nothing; but he's more,
Had I more name for badness.

Duke.   By mine honesty,
If she be mad, as I believe no other,   60
Her madness hath the oddest frame of sense,
Such a dependency of thing on thing,
As e'er I heard in madness.

Isabella.   O gracious Duke,
Harp not on that; nor do not banish reason
For inequality,° but let your reason serve   65
To make the truth appear where it seems hid,
And hide the false seems° true.

54 *absolute* perfect   56 *caracts* symbols of office   65 *inequality* injustice   67 *seems* which seems

Duke.   Many that are not mad
  Have, sure, more lack of reason. What would you
    say?

Isabella. I am the sister of one Claudio,
70 Condemned upon the act of fornication
  To lose his head, condemned by Angelo.
  I, in probation° of a sisterhood,
  Was sent to by my brother, one Lucio
  As then the messenger—

Lucio.   That's I, and't like° your Grace.
75 I came to her from Claudio, and desired her
  To try her gracious fortune with Lord Angelo
  For her poor brother's pardon.

Isabella.   That's he indeed.

Duke. You were not bid to speak.

Lucio.   No, my good lord,
  Nor wished to hold my peace.

Duke.   I wish you now, then;
80 Pray you, take note of it, and when you have
  A business for yourself, pray heaven you then
  Be perfect.°

Lucio.   I warrant your honor.

Duke. The warrant's° for yourself; take heed to't.

Isabella. This gentleman told somewhat of my tale—

85 *Lucio.* Right.

Duke. It may be right; but you are i' the wrong
  To speak before your time. Proceed.

Isabella.   I went
  To this pernicious caitiff deputy—

Duke. That's somewhat madly spoken.

72 *probation* novitiate   74 *and't like* if it please   82 *perfect* thoroughly prepared   83 *warrant* warning

Isabella.   Pardon it;
  The phrase is to the matter.°   *90*

Duke. Mended again. The matter: proceed.

Isabella. In brief, to set the needless process by,
  How I persuaded, how I prayed, and kneeled,
  How he refelled° me, and how I replied—
  For this was of much length—the vild° conclusion   *95*
  I now begin with brief and shame to utter.
  He would not, but by gift of my chaste body
  To his concupiscible intemperate lust,
  Release my brother; and after much debatement,
  My sisterly remorse° confutes mine honor,   *100*
  And I did yield to him; but the next morn betimes,
  His purpose surfeiting,° he sends a warrant
  For my poor brother's head.

Duke.   This is most likely!

Isabella. O, that it were as like as it is true!

Duke. By heaven, fond wretch, thou know'st not what
    thou speak'st,   *105*
  Or else thou art suborned against his honor
  In hateful practice.° First, his integrity
  Stands without blemish. Next, it imports° no reason
  That with such vehemency he should pursue
  Faults proper° to himself: if he had so offended,   *110*
  He would have weighed thy brother by himself,
  And not have cut him off. Someone hath set you on;
  Confess the truth, and say by whose advice
  Thou cam'st here to complain.

Isabella.   And is this all?
  Then, O you blessèd ministers above,   *115*
  Keep me in patience, and with ripened time
  Unfold the evil which is here wrapped up
  In countenance. Heaven shield your Grace from
    woe,

---

90 *to the matter* appropriate   94 *refelled* refuted   95 *vild* vile
100 *remorse* pity   102 *surfeiting* satiating   107 *practice* plot   108
imports signifies   110 *proper* belonging

As I, thus wronged, hence unbelievèd go!

120 *Duke.* I know you'd fain be gone. An officer,
To prison with her! Shall we thus permit
A blasting and a scandalous breath to fall
On him so near us? This needs must be a practice.
Who knew of your intent and coming hither?

125 *Isabella.* One that I would were here, Friar Lodowick.

Duke. A ghostly father, belike. Who knows that
Lodowick?

Lucio. My lord, I know him; 'tis a meddling friar,
I do not like the man. Had he been lay,° my lord,
For certain words he spake against your Grace
130 In your retirement, I had swinged° him soundly.

Duke. Words against me! This's a good friar, belike!
And to set on this wretched woman here
Against our substitute! Let this friar be found.

Lucio. But yesternight, my lord, she and that friar,
135 I saw them at the prison; a saucy friar,
A very scurvy° fellow.

Friar Peter. Blessed be your royal Grace!
I have stood by, my lord, and I have heard
Your royal ear abused. First, hath this woman
140 Most wrongfully accused your substitute,
Who is as free from touch or soil with her
As she from one ungot.

Duke.   We did believe no less.
Know you that Friar Lodowick that she speaks of?

Friar Peter. I know him for a man divine and holy;
145 Not scurvy, nor a temporary meddler,°
As he's reported by this gentleman;
And, on my trust, a man that never yet
Did, as he vouches, misreport your Grace.

Lucio. My lord, most villainously; believe it.

128 *lay* layman   130 *swinged* thrashed   136 *scurvy* worthless   145 *temporary meddler* meddler in temporal affairs

Friar Peter. Well, he in time may come to clear him-
　　self,   150
　But at this instant he is sick, my lord,
　Of a strange fever. Upon his mere request,
　Being come to knowledge that there was complaint
　Intended 'gainst Lord Angelo, came I hither,
　To speak, as from his mouth, what he doth know   155
　Is true and false; and what he with his oath
　And all probation° will make up full clear,
　Whensoever he's convented.° First, for this woman,
　To justify this worthy nobleman,
　So vulgarly and personally accused,   160
　Her shall you hear disprovèd to her eyes,
　Till she herself confess it.

Duke.   Good friar, let's hear it.
　　　　　[Isabella is carried off guarded.]

Enter Mariana.

　Do you not smile at this, Lord Angelo?
　O heaven, the vanity of wretched fools!
　Give us some seats. Come, cousin Angelo,   165
　In this I'll be impartial; be you judge
　Of your own cause. Is this the witness, friar?
　First, let her show her face, and after speak.

Mariana. Pardon, my lord; I will not show my face
　Until my husband bid me.   170

Duke. What, are your married?

Mariana. No, my lord.

Duke. Are you a maid?

Mariana. No, my lord.

Duke. A widow, then?   175

Mariana. Neither, my lord.

Duke. Why, you are nothing, then: neither maid,
　widow, nor wife?

157 *probation* proof   158 *convented* sent for

Lucio. My lord, she may be a punk;° for many of
180   them are neither maid, widow, nor wife.

Duke. Silence that fellow. I would he had some cause
To prattle for himself.

Lucio. Well, my lord.

Mariana. My lord, I do confess I ne'er was married,
185   And I confess, besides, I am no maid.
I have known° my husband; yet my husband
Knows not that ever he knew me.

Lucio. He was drunk, then, my lord; it can be no
better.

190   *Duke.* For the benefit of silence, would thou wert so
too!

Lucio. Well, my lord.

Duke. This is no witness for Lord Angelo.

Mariana. Now I come to't, my lord:
195   She that accuses him of fornication,
In selfsame manner doth accuse my husband,
And charges him, my lord, with such a time
When I'll depose I had him in mine arms
With all th' effect of love.

Angelo. Charges she moe than me?

200   *Mariana.*   Not that I know.

Duke. No? You say your husband?

Mariana. Why, just, my lord, and that is Angelo,
Who thinks he knows that he ne'er knew my body,
But knows he thinks that he knows Isabel's.

205   *Angelo.* This is a strange abuse. Let's see thy face.

Mariana. My husband bids me; now I will unmask.
                                            [*Unveiling.*]
This is that face, thou cruel Angelo,

179 *punk* harlot   186 *known* had intercourse with

Which once thou swor'st was worth the looking on;
This is the hand which, with a vowed contract,
Was fast belocked in thine; this is the body   210
That took away the match° from Isabel,
And did supply thee at thy garden house
In her imagined person.

Duke.   Know you this woman?

Lucio. Carnally, she says.

Duke.   Sirrah, no more!

Lucio. Enough, my lord.   215

Angelo. My lord, I must confess I know this woman:
  And five years since there was some speech of mar-
      riage
  Betwixt myself and her, which was broke off,
  Partly for that her promisèd proportions°
  Came short of composition,° but in chief,   220
  For that her reputation was disvalued
  In levity;° since which time of five years
  I never spake with her, saw her, nor heard from her,
  Upon my faith and honor.

Mariana.   Noble prince,
  As there comes light from heaven and words from
      breath,   225
  As there is sense in truth and truth in virtue,
  I am affianced this man's wife as strongly
  As words could make up vows; and, my good lord,
  But Tuesday night last gone in's garden house
  He knew me as a wife. As this is true,   230
  Let me in safety raise me from my knees,
  Or else forever be confixèd° here,
  A marble monument.

Angelo.   I did but smile till now;
  Now, good my lord, give me the scope of justice;
  My patience here is touched. I do perceive   235

211 *match* meeting   219 *proportions* dowry   220 *composition* previous agreement   221–22 *disvalued/In levity* discredited for lightness   232 *confixèd* fixed firmly

These poor informal° women are no more
But instruments of some more mightier member
That sets them on. Let me have way, my lord,
To find this practice out.

Duke.   Ay, with my heart,
240 And punish them to your height of pleasure.
Thou foolish friar and thou pernicious woman,
Compact° with her that's gone, think'st thou thy oaths,
Though they would swear down each particular saint,
Were testimonies against his worth and credit,
245 That's sealed in approbation?° You, Lord Escalus,
Sit with my cousin; lend him your kind pains
To find out this abuse, whence 'tis derived.
There is another friar that set them on;
Let him be sent for.

Friar Peter. Would he were here, my lord, for he, in-
250 deed,
Hath set the women on to this complaint:
Your provost knows the place where he abides,
And he may fetch him.

Duke.   Go, do it instantly. [*Exit Provost.*]
And you, my noble and well-warranted cousin,
255 Whom it concerns to hear this matter forth,
Do with your injuries as seems you best,
In any chastisement. I for a while
Will leave you, but stir not you till you have
Well determined upon these slanderers.

260 *Escalus.* My lord, we'll do it throughly.   *Exit* [*Duke*].
Signior Lucio, did not you say you knew that Friar
Lodowick to be a dishonest person?

Lucio. Cucullus non facit monachum;° honest in
nothing but in his clothes, and one that hath spoke
265 most villainous speeches of the Duke.

236 *informal* (1) rash (2) informing   242 *Compact* in collusion
245 *approbation* attested integrity   263 *Cucullus non facit mona-chum* the cowl does not make the monk (Latin)

Escalus. We shall entreat you to abide here till he
come, and enforce them against him; we shall find
this friar a notable° fellow.

Lucio. As any in Vienna, on my word.

Escalus. Call that same Isabel here once again; I   *270*
would speak with her. [*Exit an Attendant.*] Pray
you, my lord, give me leave to question; you shall
see how I'll handle her.

Lucio. Not better than he, by her own report.

Escalus. Say you?   *275*

Lucio. Marry, sir, I think, if you handled her pri-
vately, she would sooner confess; perchance, publicly, she'll be ashamed.

   Enter Duke [as friar], Provost, Isabella,
     [and Officers].

Escalus. I will go darkly° to work with her.

Lucio. That's the way; for women are light at mid- *280*
night.

Escalus. Come on, mistress, here's a gentlewoman
denies all that you have said.

Lucio. My lord, here comes the rascal I spoke of—
here with the provost.   *285*

Escalus. In very good time. Speak not you to him till
we call upon you.

Lucio. Mum.

Escalus. Come, sir, did you set these women on to
slander Lord Angelo? They have confessed you did. *290*

Duke. 'Tis false.

Escalus. How! Know you where you are?

Duke. Respect to your great place; and let the devil

268 *notable* notorious 279 *darkly* slyly, subtly

Be sometime honored for his burning throne.
295 Where is the Duke? 'Tis he should hear me speak.

Escalus. The Duke's in us, and we will hear you speak.
Look you speak justly.

Duke. Boldly, at least. But, O poor souls,
Come you to seek the lamb here of the fox?
300 Good night to your redress. Is the Duke gone?
Then is your cause gone too. The Duke's unjust,
Thus to retort° your manifest° appeal,
And put your trial in the villain's mouth
Which here you come to accuse.

305 *Lucio.* This is the rascal; this is he I spoke of.

Escalus. Why, thou unreverend and unhallowed friar,
Is't not enough thou hast suborned these women
To accuse this worthy man, but in foul mouth,
And in the witness of his proper° ear,
310 To call him villain? And then to glance from him
To th' Duke himself, to tax him with injustice?
Take him hence; to th' rack with him. We'll touse°
    you
Joint by joint, but we will know his purpose.
What, "unjust"!

Duke.   Be not so hot. The Duke
315 Dare no more stretch this finger of mine than he
Dare rack his own: his subject am I not,
Nor here provincial.° My business in this state
Made me a looker-on here in Vienna,
Where I have seen corruption boil and bubble
320 Till it o'errun the stew. Laws for all faults,
But faults so countenanced, that the strong statutes
Stand like the forfeits° in a barber's shop,
As much in mock as mark.°

Escalus. Slander to th' state! Away with him to prison!

---

302 *retort* refer back   302 *manifest* clear   309 *proper* very   312
touse pull   317 *provincial* belonging to the province or state
322 *forfeits* extracted teeth (barbers acted as dentists)   323 *As
much . . . mark* to be mocked at as much as to be seen

Angelo. What can you vouch against him, Signior 325
Lucio? Is this the man that you did tell us of?

Lucio. 'Tis he, my lord. Come hither, goodman bald-
pate; do you know me?

Duke. I remember you, sir, by the sound of your
voice. I met you at the prison, in the absence of 330
the Duke.

Lucio. O, did you so? And do you remember what
you said of the Duke?

Duke. Most notedly, sir.

Lucio. Do you so, sir? And was the Duke a flesh- 335
monger, a fool, and a coward, as you then reported
him to be?

Duke. You must, sir, change persons with me, ere you
make that my report. You, indeed, spoke so of
him; and much more, much worse. 340

Lucio. O thou damnable fellow! Did not I pluck thee
by the nose for thy speeches?

Duke. I protest I love the Duke as I love myself.

Angelo. Hark, how the villain would close° now, after
his treasonable abuses. 345

Escalus. Such a fellow is not to be talked withal.
Away with him to prison! Where is the provost?
Away with him to prison, lay bolts enough upon
him, let him speak no more. Away with those gig-
lets° too, and with the other confederate compan- 350
ion.

Duke. [*To the Provost*] Stay, sir; stay awhile.

Angelo. What, resists he? Help him, Lucio.

Lucio. Come, sir; come, sir; come, sir; foh, sir! Why,
you bald-pated, lying rascal, you must be hooded, 355
must you? Show your knave's visage, with a pox

344 *close* come to agreement   349–50 *giglets* wanton women

to you. Show your sheep-biting° face, and be
hanged an hour. Will't not off?
[*Pulls off the friar's hood, and discovers the Duke.*]

Duke. Thou art the first knave that e'er mad'st a
Duke.
360 First, provost, let me bail these gentle three.
[*To Lucio*] Sneak not away, sir; for the friar and
you
Must have a word anon. Lay hold on him.

Lucio. This may prove worse than hanging.

Duke [*To Escalus*] What you have spoke I pardon.
Sit you down.
We'll borrow place of him. [*To Angelo*] Sir, by
365 your leave.
Hast thou or word, or wit, or impudence,
That yet can do thee office?° If thou hast,
Rely upon it till my tale be heard,
And hold no longer out.

Angelo.   O my dread lord,
370 I should be guiltier than my guiltiness,
To think I can be undiscernible,
When I perceive your Grace, like pow'r divine,
Hath looked upon my passes.° Then, good prince,
No longer session° hold upon my shame,
375 But let my trial be mine own confession.
Immediate sentence then, and sequent death,
Is all the grace I beg.

Duke.   Come hither, Mariana.
Say, wast thou e'er contracted to this woman?

Angelo. I was, my lord.

380 *Duke.* Go take her hence, and marry her instantly.
Do you the office, friar, which consummate,
Return him here again. Go with him, provost.

Exit [*Angelo with Mariana, Friar Peter, and Provost*].

357 *sheep-biting* currish   367 *office* service   373 *passes* trespasses   374
session trial

Escalus. My lord, I am more amazed at his dishonor
    Than at the strangeness of it.

Duke.   Come hither, Isabel.
    Your friar is now your prince. As I was then   385
    Advertising and holy° to your business,
    Not changing heart with habit, I am still
    Attorneyed at your service.

Isabella.   O, give me pardon,
    That I, your vassal, have employed and pained
    Your unknown sovereignty!

Duke.   You are pardoned, Isabel: 390
    And now, dear maid, be you as free to us.
    Your brother's death, I know, sits at your heart,
    And you may marvel why I obscured myself,
    Laboring to save his life, and would not rather
    Make rash remonstrance of my hidden pow'r   395
    Than let him so be lost. O most kind maid,
    It was the swift celerity of his death,
    Which I did think with slower foot came on,
    That brained my purpose. But, peace be with him.
    That life is better life, past fearing death,   400
    Than that which lives to fear. Make it your comfort,
    So happy is your brother.

    Enter Angelo, Mariana, [Friar] Peter, Provost.

Isabella.   I do, my lord.

Duke. For this new-married man, approaching here,
    Whose salt° imagination yet hath wronged
    Your well-defended honor, you must pardon   405
    For Mariana's sake. But as he adjudged your
        brother,
    Being criminal, in double violation,
    Of sacred chastity, and of promise-breach,
    Thereon dependent, for your brother's life,
    The very mercy of the law cries out   410

---

386 *Advertising and holy* attentive and devoted   404 *salt* lecherous

Most audible, even from his proper tongue,
"An Angelo for Claudio, death for death!"
Haste still pays haste, and leisure answers leisure;
Like doth quit like, and Measure still for Measure.°

415 Then, Angelo, thy fault's thus manifested;
Which, though thou wouldst deny, denies thee vantage.
We do condemn thee to the very block
Where Claudio stooped to death, and with like haste.
Away with him.

Mariana.   O my most gracious lord,
420 I hope you will not mock me with a husband.

Duke. It is your husband mocked you with a husband.
Consenting to the safeguard of your honor,
I thought your marriage fit; else imputation,°
For that he knew you, might reproach your life,
425 And choke your good to come. For his possessions,
Although by confiscation they are ours,
We do instate and widow you withal,
To buy you a better husband.

Mariana.   O my dear lord,
I crave no other, nor no better man.

430 *Duke.* Never crave him; we are definitive.°

Mariana. Gentle my liege—   [*Kneeling.*]

Duke.   You do but lose your labor.
Away with him to death! [*To Lucio*] Now, sir, to you.

Mariana. O my good lord! Sweet Isabel, take my part,
Lend me your knees, and all my life to come
435 I'll lend you all my life to do you service.

Duke. Against all sense you do importune her;

414 *Measure still for Measure* (see Matthew 7:1–2: "Judge not, that ye be not judged. For with what judgment ye judge, ye shall be judged: and with what measure ye mete, it shall be measured to you again")   423 *imputation* accusation   430 *definitive* determined

Should she kneel down in mercy of this fact,°
Her brother's ghost his pavèd° bed would break,
And take her hence in horror.

Mariana.   Isabel,
Sweet Isabel, do yet but kneel by me,   440
Hold up your hands, say nothing, I'll speak all.
They say, best men are molded out of faults;
And, for the most, become much more the better
For being a little bad; so may my husband.
O Isabel, will you not lend a knee?   445

Duke. He dies for Claudio's death.

Isabella. [*Kneeling*]   Most bounteous sir,
Look, if it please you, on this man condemned,
As if my brother lived. I partly think
A due sincerity governèd his deeds,
Till he did look on me. Since it is so,   450
Let him not die. My brother had but justice,
In that he did the thing for which he died.
For Angelo,
His act did not o'ertake his bad intent,
And must be buried but as an intent   455
That perished by the way. Thoughts are no sub·
    jects,°
Intents but merely thoughts.

Mariana.   Merely, my lord.

Duke. Your suit's unprofitable; stand up, I say.
I have bethought me of another fault.
Provost, how came it Claudio was beheaded   460
At an unusual hour?

Provost.   It was commanded so.

Duke. Had you a special warrant for the deed?

Provost. No, my good lord; it was by private message.

Duke. For which I do discharge you of your office;
    Give up your keys.

---

437 *fact* crime   438 *pavèd* slab-covered   456 *no subjects* i.e., not
subject to law

465 *Provost.*   Pardon me, noble lord.
    I thought it was a fault, but knew it not;°
    Yet did repent me, after more advice;°
    For testimony whereof, one in the prison,
    That should by private order else have died,
    I have reserved alive.

    Duke.   What's he?

470 *Provost.*   His name is Barnardine.

    Duke. I would thou hadst done so by Claudio.
    Go fetch him hither; let me look upon him.
                                [*Exit Provost.*]

    Escalus. I am sorry, one so learnèd and so wise
    As you, Lord Angelo, have still° appeared,
475 Should slip so grossly, both in the heat of blood,
    And lack of tempered judgment afterward.

    Angelo. I am sorry that such sorrow I procure,
    And so deep sticks it in my penitent heart,
    That I crave death more willingly than mercy;
480 'Tis my deserving, and I do entreat it.

        Enter Barnardine and Provost,
          Claudio [*muffled*], *Juliet.*

    Duke. Which is that Barnardine?

    Provost.   This, my lord.

    Duke. There was a friar told me of this man.
    Sirrah, thou art said to have a stubborn soul,
    That apprehends no further than this world,
    And squar°st thy life according. Thou'rt con-
485   demned;
    But, for those earthly faults, I quit° them all,
    And pray thee take this mercy to provide
    For better times to come. Friar, advise him;
    I leave him to your hand. What muffled fellow's
        that?

    _____

    466 *knew it not* was not sure   467 *advice* thought   474 *still*
    ever   485 *squar'st* regulate   486 *quit* pardon

Provost. This is another prisoner that I saved,   490
    Who should have died when Claudio lost his head;
    As like almost to Claudio as himself.
                                    [*Unmuffles Claudio.*]

Duke. [*To Isabella*] If he be like your brother, for his
        sake
    Is he pardoned; and, for your lovely sake,
    Give me your hand, and say you will be mine,
    He is my brother too; but fitter time for that.   495
    By this Lord Angelo perceives he's safe;
    Methinks I see a quick'ning° in his eye.
    Well, Angelo, your evil quits you well;
    Look that you love your wife; her worth, worth
        yours.
    I find an apt remission° in myself,   500
    And yet here's one in place I cannot pardon.
    [*To Lucio*] You, sirrah, that knew me for a fool, a
        coward,
    One all of luxury,° an ass, a madman;
    Wherein have I so deserved of you,
    That you extol me thus?   505

Lucio. 'Faith, my lord, I spoke it but according to the
    trick.° If you will hang me for it, you may; but I
    had rather it would please you I might be whipped.

Duke. Whipped first, sir, and hanged after.   510
    Proclaim it, provost, round about the city,
    If any woman wronged by this lewd fellow—
    As I have heard him swear himself there's one
    Whom he begot with child—let her appear,
    And he shall marry her. The nuptial finished,   515
    Let him be whipped and hanged.

Lucio. I beseech your highness, do not marry me to a
    whore. Your highness said even now, I made you a
    duke: good my lord, do not recompense me in
    making me a cuckold.   520

---

498 *quick'ning* animation   501 *remission* wish to forgive   504 *lux-
ury* lust   508 *trick* fashion

Duke. Upon mine honor, thou shalt marry her.
Thy slanders I forgive; and therewithal
Remit thy other forfeits. Take him to prison,
And see our pleasure herein executed.

525 *Lucio.* Marrying a punk, my lord, is pressing to death,
whipping, and hanging.

Duke. Slandering a prince deserves it.
                    [*Exeunt Officers with Lucio.*]
She, Claudio, that you wronged, look you restore.°
Joy to you, Mariana. Love her, Angelo;
530 I have confessed her, and I know her virtue.
Thanks, good friend Escalus, for thy much good-
      ness;
There's more behind° that is more gratulate.°
Thanks, provost, for thy care and secrecy;
We shall employ thee in a worthier place.
535 Forgive him, Angelo, that brought you home
The head of Ragozine for Claudio's;
Th' offense pardons itself. Dear Isabel,
I have a motion° much imports your good,
Whereto if you'll a willing ear incline,
540 What's mine is yours, and what is yours is mine.
So, bring us to our palace, where we'll show
What's yet behind, that's meet° you all should
      know.   [*Exeunt.*]

FINIS.

Textual Note

Our only authority for the text of *Measure for Measure* is the First Folio, whose text is on the whole a good one, probably based on a transcript of Shakespeare's manuscripts made by Ralph Crane, the scrivener of the King's Players. It seems a little disturbed in Act IV; the Duke's speech on "place and greatness" in this act would be more appropriate preceding his lines in III.ii, after the exit of Lucio. In the present text the act and scene divisions are translated from Latin and in two places depart from the Folio in order to correspond to the Globe text (the Globe's divisions are used in most books on Shakespeare): Globe I.ii is split in the Folio into a new scene after the exit of Pompey, and Globe III.ii is not marked in the Folio. The present edition corrects obvious typographical errors, modernizes spelling and punctuation, expands and regularizes speech prefixes, adjusts the lineation of a few passages, transfers the indication of locale ("The Scene: Vienna") and the *dramatis personae* ("The names of all the actors.") from the end to the beginning, and slightly alters the position of a few stage directions. Other substantial departures from the Folio are listed below, the present reading in italics and then the Folio reading in roman.

I.iii.27 *Becomes more* More   43 *it* in

I.iv.54 *givings-out* giuing-out

II.i.12 *your* our   39 *breaks* brakes

II.ii.96 *new* now   111 *ne'er* neuer

II.iv.9 *seared* feard   53 *or, to* and to   76 *Let me be* Let be   94 *all-binding* all-building

III.i.31 *serpigo* Sapego   52 *Bring me to hear them* Bring them to heare me   69 *Though* Through   130 *penury* periury   218 *by oath* oath

III.ii.26 *eat, array* eate away   48 *extracting it* extracting   153 *dearer* deare   227 *and it* and as it   278 *strings* stings

IV.i.62 *quests* Quest   64 *dreams* dreame

IV.ii.44–48 *If it be too little . . . fits your thief* [F gives to Pompey]

IV.iii.16 *Forthright* Forthlight   90 *yonder* yond

IV.iv.6 *redeliver* reliuer

V.i.13 *me* we   168 *her face* your face   426 *confiscation* confutation   542 *that's* that

A Note on
the Sources of *Measure for Measure*

The principal sources of *Measure for Measure* are George Whetstone's play of *Promos and Cassandra* (1578) and its prose redaction in the same author's *Heptameron of Civil Discourses* (1582). Whetstone's own source was Giraldi Cinthio's *Hecatommithi* (1565); and Shakespeare almost certainly knew this work, which contains the story of Othello. He may, in addition, have also known Cinthio's posthumously published play of *Epitia* (1583). Brief summaries of these sources are given here for comparison with Shakespeare's treatment of the story.

CINTHIO's *Hecatommithi*, DECADE 8, NOVELLA 5

The Emperor Maximian appoints one of his trusted men, Juriste, to rule over the city of Innsbruck. He charges him particularly to observe justice scrupulously. Juriste, who lacks all self-knowledge, accepts the grave responsibility with alacrity and for a while he is a model ruler.

A young man called Vico is brought before Juriste for violating a virgin, and is condemned to death according to the laws of the city. Vico's sister, Epitia, who is a student of philosophy and has a sweet way of speaking, pleads for her brother. Her brother is very young; he was moved by the impulse of love; the ravished maiden is unmarried and Vico is willing to marry her. The law was made so severe only to deter would-be offenders, not really to be enforced. Captivated by Epitia's beauty and eloquence, Juriste promises to reconsider the case. When she meets him again, he proposes that she should lie with him if she wants her brother's sentence to be mitigated. Epitia refuses unless Juriste is willing to marry her afterward. Juriste does not promise to do this, though he hints at the possibility. When Epitia goes to the prison to prepare her brother for his fate, Vico pleads passionately with her and appeals to her sisterly affection to save him. So Epitia reluctantly consents to Juriste's proposal. Juriste, however, orders the execution of Vico before lying with her.

In the morning Epitia goes home to find that Juriste has indeed kept his promise to release her brother—dead. She thinks of revenge, but instead appeals to the Emperor. The Emperor sends for Juriste and finds that the complaint is true. He first forces Juriste to marry Epitia, who is quite unwilling, and then he orders that Juriste be put to death. Now that Juriste is her husband, Epitia is in a cruel dilemma. She discourses to the Emperor on the superiority of clemency to justice. The Emperor is impressed with her forgiving nature and pardons Juriste. Epitia and her husband live happily ever after.

CINTHIO's *Epitia*

The story is much the same as that in the *Hecatommithi,* but there are some new characters and the brother is secretly saved by the captain of the prison. The latter announces this fact at the end of the play, to the astonishment of the other characters and also the reader, who is not given a hint of it in the prefatory "argument."

Principal among the new characters are Angela, Juriste's sister, who conveys an offer of marriage from him to Epitia and testifies against him before the Emperor when

THE SOURCES OF MEASURE FOR MEASURE 141

Juriste breaks his word; a secretary and a podesta who argue respectively for and against forgiving Vico; a messenger who reports how Vico was put to death on special commission from the podesta, who had Juriste's authority to do so; and the captain of the prison, who brings the supposed head of Vico to Epitia.

Epitia refuses to plead for Juriste until she learns that her brother is alive. Believing that Juriste should be punished for evil intent, the Emperor is at first unwilling to pardon him even after Vico reappears, but he finally grants Epitia's suit in order that she may have "complete contentment."

WHETSTONE'S *Promos and Cassandra* AND *Heptameron*

In the play, Promos is appointed to rule over the city of Julio, and declares his resolve to render justice impartially. Reviving a defunct law, he sentences Andrugio to death for incontinence. The law will not accept marriage as sufficient recompense for the wrong. Andrugio's sister, Cassandra, weeps over the hard fate of her young brother, who appeals to her to plead with Promos. She therefore meets Promos and obtains a postponement of the execution. After she has left, Promos reveals in a soliloquy that he has fallen in love with her but is determined to overcome the temptation. However, having been encouraged by his corrupt servant, Phallax, to believe that Cassandra might be overcome, he is unable to subdue his desire for her. When she meets him again to know his final decision, he first defends the law and then, when she pleads for mercy, makes his infamous proposal.

Amazed and horrified, Cassandra refuses. Promos promises to make her his wife and gives her two days in which to think it over. She goes to her brother's cell to inform him of Promos' vile condition and to prepare him for death. Andrugio, taken aback that a judge of Promos' supposed integrity has been corrupted by the same lust for which he would condemn another, appeals to his sister to accept the proposed terms and thereby save his life.

Brother and sister argue, but finally Cassandra is won over.

After satisfying his desire, Promos decides to break his word, since no one knows of his promise and Cassandra cannot reveal her own shame. He orders that Andrugio should be executed secretly and his head sent to Cassandra. While the girl is eagerly looking forward to welcoming her brother, the jailer brings her the severed head. She conceals her grief, pretending to be quite satisfied. She thinks of suicide, but later decides to appeal to the King. The jailer has in fact brought her the head of an executed criminal and released Andrugio, who goes into hiding. Promos is secretly troubled at what he has done.

In the second part of the play, the King comes to Julio. He hears Cassandra's story and promises to see that justice is done. Upon examination, Promos at once confesses, and the King orders that he first be married to Cassandra and then put to death. Promos pleads for mercy, but in vain. In the meantime, Andrugio, hiding in the woods, comes to know what is happening. Cassandra bewails her hard fate. Duty commands that she should love the husband for whose sentence she has been responsible. She appeals to the King to pardon him, but the ruler is adamant. Andrugio, now in the city under a disguise, sees his sister's unhappiness and resolves to surrender himself to the King at the risk of being put to death. Promos makes a sincere confession of his misdeeds and is led out to execution. Andrugio's boy enters with the news that his master is alive. The King pardons Andrugio, and then pardons Promos for the sake of Cassandra, exhorting Promos always to measure grace with justice. He restores him to the governorship of the city. "The lost sheep found, for joy the feast was made."

Whetstone's play has also a comic underplot, involving a courtesan, unscrupulous officers, informers, and bawds. With the corruption of the magistrates, all the city becomes corrupt.

The version in the *Heptameron* is substantially the same as that of the play. Andrugio is disguised as a hermit, and reveals himself after hearing the King say that Promos might be pardoned if Andrugio were alive. The entire story is narrated by one Isabella.

Summary

Measure for Measure is generally closer to Whetstone's versions than to *Epitia;* but it does show significant correspondences with Cinthio's play at certain points where Whetstone differs markedly. "The relation of *Measure for Measure* to Giraldi's *novella* is ambiguous, since some of the correspondences to that might have come through Whetstone, some through *Epitia.*"[1] Among the similarities between *Measure for Measure* and *Epitia* may be mentioned the following: the secretary in *Epitia* protests to the podesta of the harshness of the law and the severity of its enforcement; in a soliloquy he comments on the rigor of those in power (compare Escalus' protests to Angelo in II.i); the criminal whose head is substituted for that of Vico is hopelessly evil (compare Ragozine, described as a notorious pirate); like Isabella, Epitia also distinguishes between act and intention. Some close verbal parallels have been noted by Kenneth Muir.[2]

1 Madeleine Doran, *Endeavors of Art: A Study of Form in Elizabethan Drama.* Madison, Wisconsin: University of Wisconsin Press, 1954, pp. 386–387.

2 *Shakespeare's Sources.* London: Methuen & Co., Ltd., 1957, I, 104–05.

Commentaries

WILLIAM HAZLITT

from *Characters of Shakespear's Plays*

This is a play as full of genius as it is of wisdom. Yet there is an original sin in the nature of the subject, which prevents us from taking a cordial interest in it. "The height of moral argument" which the author has maintained in the intervals of passion or blended with the more powerful impulses of nature, is hardly surpassed in any of his plays. But there is in general a want of passion; the affections are at a stand; our sympathies are repulsed and defeated in all directions. The only passion which influences the story is that of Angelo; and yet he seems to have a much greater passion for hypocrisy than for his mistress. Neither are we greatly enamored of Isabella's rigid chastity, though she could not act otherwise than she did. We do not feel the same confidence in the virtue that is "sublimely good" at another's expense, as if it had been put to some less disinterested trial. As to

From *Characters of Shakespear's Plays* by William Hazlitt. 2nd ed. London: Taylor & Hessey, 1818.

the Duke, who makes a very imposing and mysterious stage character, he is more absorbed in his own plots and gravity than anxious for the welfare of the state; more tenacious of his own character than attentive to the feelings and apprehensions of others. Claudio is the only person who feels naturally; and yet he is placed in circumstances of distress which almost preclude the wish for his deliverance. Mariana is also in love with Angelo, whom we hate. In this respect, there may be said to be a general system of cross purposes between the feelings of the different characters and the sympathy of the reader or the audience. This principle of repugnance seems to have reached its height in the character of Master Barnardine, who not only sets at defiance the opinions of others, but has even thrown off all self-regard—"one that apprehends death no more dreadfully but as a drunken sleep; careless, reckless, and fearless of what's past, present, and to come." He is a fine antithesis to the morality and the hypocrisy of the other characters of the play. Barnardine is Caliban transported from Prospero's wizard island to the forests of Bohemia or the prisons of Vienna. He is the creature of bad habits as Caliban is of gross instincts. He has however a strong notion of the natural fitness of things, according to his own sensations—"He has been drinking hard all night, and he will not be hanged that day"—and Shakespear has let him off at last. We do not understand why the philosophical German critic, Schlegel, should be so severe on those pleasant persons, Lucio, Pompey, and Master Froth, as to call them "wretches." They appear all mighty comfortable in their occupations, and determined to pursue them, "as the flesh and fortune should serve." A very good exposure of the want of self-knowledge and contempt for others, which is so common in the world, is put into the mouth of Abhorson, the jailor, when the Provost proposes to associate Pompey with him in his office—"A bawd, sir? Fie upon him, he will discredit our mystery." And the same answer will serve in nine instances out of ten to the same kind of remark, "Go to, sir, you weigh equally; a feather will turn the scale." Shakespear was in one sense the least moral of all writers; for morality (commonly so called) is made up of antipathies; and his talent consisted in sympathy with human nature, in all its shapes, degrees, depressions, and elevations. The object of the pedantic moralist is to find out the bad in everything: his was to show that "there is some soul of goodness in things evil." Even Master Barnardine is not left to the mercy of what others think of him; but when he comes in, speaks for himself, and pleads his own cause, as well as if counsel had been assigned him. In one sense, Shakespear was no moralist at all: in another, he was the greatest of all moralists. He was a moralist in the same sense in which nature is one. He taught what he had learnt from her. He showed the greatest knowledge of humanity with the greatest fellow-feeling for it.

WALTER PATER

"Measure for Measure"

In *Measure for Measure,* as in some other of his plays,
Shakespeare has remodeled an earlier and somewhat
rough composition to "finer issues," suffering much to
remain as it had come from the less skillful hand, and not
raising the whole of his work to an equal degree of intensity. Hence perhaps some of that depth and weighti-
ness which make this play so impressive, as with the true
seal of experience, like a fragment of life itself, rough and
disjointed indeed, but forced to yield in places its profounder meaning. In *Measure for Measure,* in contrast
with the flawless execution of *Romeo and Juliet,* Shakespeare has spent his art in just enough modification of the
scheme of the older play to make it exponent of this
purpose, adapting its terrible essential incidents, so that
Coleridge found it the only painful work among Shakespeare's dramas, and leaving for the reader of today more
than the usual number of difficult expressions; but infus-
ing a lavish color and a profound significance into it, so
that under his touch certain select portions of it rise far
above the level of all but his own best poetry, and working
out of it a morality so characteristic that the play might
well pass for the central expression of his moral judgments. It remains a comedy, as indeed is congruous with
the bland, half-humorous equity which informs the whole

From *Appreciations* (1889).

composition, sinking from the heights of sorrow and terror into the rough scheme of the earlier piece; yet it is hardly less full of what is really tragic in man's existence than if Claudio had indeed "stooped to death." Even the humorous concluding scenes have traits of special grace, retaining in less emphatic passages a stray line or word of power, as it seems, so that we watch to the end for the traces where the nobler hand has glanced along, leaving its vestiges, as if accidentally or wastefully, in the rising of the style.

The interest of *Measure for Measure,* therefore, is partly that of an old story told over again. We measure with curiosity that variety of resources which has enabled Shakespeare to refashion the original material with a higher motive; adding to the intricacy of the piece, yet so modifying its structure as to give the whole almost the unity of a single scene; lending, by the light of a philosophy which dwells much on what is complex and subtle in our nature, a true human propriety to its strange and unexpected turns of feeling and character, to incidents so difficult as the fall of Angelo, and the subsequent reconciliation of Isabella, so that she pleads successfully for his life. It was from Whetstone, a contemporary English writer, that Shakespeare derived the outline of Cinthio's "rare history" of *Promos and Cassandra,* one of that numerous class of Italian stories, like Boccaccio's *Tancred of Salerno,* in which the mere energy of southern passion has everything its own way, and which, though they may repel many a northern reader by a certain crudity in their coloring, seem to have been full of fascination for the Elizabethan age. This story, as it appears in Whetstone's endless comedy, is almost as rough as the roughest episode of actual criminal life. But the play seems never to have been acted, and some time after its publication Whetstone himself turned the thing into a tale, included in his *Heptameron of Civil Discourses,* where it still figures as a genuine piece, with touches of undesigned poetry, a quaint field-flower here and there of diction or sentiment, the whole strung up to an effective brevity, and with the fragrance of that admirable age of literature all about it. Here, then, there is something of the original Italian color: in this narrative Shakespeare may well have caught the first glimpse of a composition with nobler proportions; and some artless sketch from his own hand, perhaps, putting together his first impressions, insinuated itself between Whetstone's work and the play as we actually read it. Out of these insignificant sources Shakespeare's play rises, full of solemn expression, and with a profoundly designed beauty, the new body of a higher, though sometimes remote and difficult poetry, escaping from the imperfect relics of the old story, yet not wholly transformed, and even as it stands but the preparation only, we might think, of a still more imposing design. For once we have in it a real example of that sort of writing which is sometimes described as *suggestive,* and which by the help of certain subtly calculated hints only, brings into distinct shape the reader's own half-developed imaginings. Often the quality is attributed to writing merely vague and unrealized, but in *Measure for Measure,* quite certainly, Shakespeare has directed the attention of sympathetic readers along certain channels of meditation beyond the immediate scope of his work.

Measure for Measure, therefore, by the quality of these higher designs, woven by his strange magic on a texture of poorer quality, is hardly less indicative than *Hamlet* even, of Shakespeare's reason, of his power of moral interpretation. It deals, not like *Hamlet* with the problems which beset one of exceptional temperament, but with mere human nature. It brings before us a group of persons, attractive, full of desire, vessels of the genial, seed-bearing powers of nature, a gaudy existence flowering out over the old court and city of Vienna, a spectacle of the fullness and pride of life which to some may seem to touch the verge of wantonness. Behind this group of people, behind their various actions, Shakespeare inspires in us the sense of a strong tyranny of nature and circumstance. Then what shall there be on this side of it—on our side, the spectators' side, of this painted screen, with its puppets who are really glad or sorry all the time? what philosophy of life, what sort of equity?

Stimulated to read more carefully by Shakespeare's own profounder touches, the reader will note the vivid reality, the subtle interchange of light and shade, the strongly contrasted characters of this group of persons, passing across the stage so quickly. The slightest of them is at least not ill-natured: the meanest of them can put forth a plea for existence—*Truly, sir, I am a poor fellow that would live!*—they are never sure of themselves, even in the strong tower of a cold unimpressible nature: they are capable of many friendships and of a true dignity in danger, giving each other a sympathetic, if transitory, regret—one sorry that another "should be foolishly lost at a game of tick-tack." Words which seem to exhaust man's deepest sentiment concerning death and life are put on the lips of a gilded, witless youth; and the saintly Isabella feels fire creep along her, kindling her tongue to eloquence at the suggestion of shame. In places the shadow deepens: death intrudes itself on the scene, as among other things "a great disguiser," blanching the features of youth and spoiling its goodly hair, touching the fine Claudio even with its disgraceful associations. As in Orcagna's fresco at Pisa, it comes capriciously, giving many and long reprieves to Barnardine, who has been waiting for it nine years in prison, taking another thence by fever, another by mistake of judgment, embracing others in the midst of their music and song. The little mirror of existence, which reflects to each for a moment the stage on which he plays, is broken at last by a capricious accident; while all alike, in their yearning for untasted enjoyment, are really discounting their days, grasping so hastily and accepting so inexactly the precious pieces. The Duke's quaint but excellent moralizing at the beginning of the third act does but express, like the chorus of a Greek play, the spirit of the passing incidents. To him in Shakespeare's play, to a few here and there in the actual world, this strange practical paradox of our life, so unwise in its eager haste, reveals itself in all its clearness.

The Duke disguised as a friar, with his curious moralizing on life and death, and Isabella in her first mood of

renunciation, a thing "ensky'd and sainted," come with
the quiet of the cloister as a relief to this lust and pride
of life: like some gray monastic picture hung on the wall
of a gaudy room, their presence cools the heated air of
the piece. For a moment we are within the placid conventual walls, whither they fancy at first that the Duke
has come as a man crossed in love, with Friar Thomas
and Friar Peter, calling each other by their homely, English names, or at the nunnery among the novices, with
their little limited privileges, where

> If you speak you must not show your face,
> Or if you show your face you must not speak.
>
> (I.iv.12–13)

Not less precious for this relief in the general structure
of the piece, than for its own peculiar graces is the episode
of Mariana, a creature wholly of Shakespeare's invention,
told, by way of interlude, in subdued prose. The moated
grange, with its dejected mistress, its long, listless, discon-
tented days, where we hear only the voice of a boy broken
off suddenly in the midst of one of the loveliest songs
of Shakespeare, or of Shakespeare's school,[1] is the pleas-
antest of many glimpses we get here of pleasant places—
the fields without the town, Angelo's gardenhouse, the
consecrated fountain. Indirectly it has suggested two of
the most perfect compositions among the poetry of our
own generation. Again it is a picture within a picture,
but with fainter lines and a grayer atmosphere: we have
here the same passions, the same wrongs, the same continuance of affection, the same crying out upon death,
as in the nearer and larger piece, though softened, and
reduced to the mood of a more dreamy scene.

Of Angelo we may feel at first sight inclined to say
only *guarda e passa!* or to ask whether he is indeed psychologically possible. In the old story, he figures as an
embodiment of pure and unmodified evil, like "Hyliogaba-
lus of Rome or Denis of Sicyll." But the embodiment of
pure evil is no proper subject of art, and Shakespeare,
in the spirit of a philosophy which dwells much on the

---

[1] Fletcher, in the *Bloody Brother*, gives the rest of it.

complications of outward circumstance with men's incli-
nations, turns into a subtle study in casuistry this incident
of the austere judge fallen suddenly into utmost corruption by a momentary contact with supreme purity. But the
main interest in *Measure for Measure* is not, as in *Promos
and Cassandra,* in the relation of Isabella and Angelo,
but rather in the relation of Claudio and Isabella.

Greek tragedy in some of its noblest products has taken
for its theme the love of a sister, a sentiment unimpas-
sioned indeed, purifying by the very spectacle of its pas-
sionlessness, but capable of a fierce and almost animal
strength if informed for a moment by pity and regret. At
first Isabella comes upon the scene as a tranquilizing influence in it. But Shakespeare, in the development of the
action, brings quite different and unexpected qualities out
of her. It is his characteristic poetry to expose this cold,
chastened personality, respected even by the worldly
Lucio as "something ensky'd and sainted, and almost
an immortal spirit," to two sharp, shameful trials, and
wring out of her a fiery, revealing eloquence. Thrown
into the terrible dilemma of the piece, called upon to
sacrifice that cloistral whiteness to sisterly affection, become in a moment the ground of strong, contending passions, she develops a new character and shows herself
suddenly of kindred with those strangely conceived women,
like Webster's Vittoria, who unite to a seductive sweetness something of a dangerous and tigerlike changefulness
of feeling. The swift, vindictive anger leaps, like a white
flame, into this white spirit, and, stripped in a moment
of all convention, she stands before us clear, detached,
columnar, among the tender frailties of the piece. Cassandra, the original of Isabella in Whetstone's tale, with
the purpose of the Roman Lucretia in her mind, yields
gracefully enough to the conditions of her brother's safety;
and to the lighter reader of Shakespeare there may seem
something harshly conceived, or psychologically impossible even, in the suddenness of the change wrought in
her, as Claudio welcomes for a moment the chance of
life through her compliance with Angelo's will, and he
may have a sense here of flagging skill, as in words less

finely handled than in the preceding scene. The play, though still not without traces of nobler handiwork, sinks down, as we know, at last into almost homely comedy, and it might be supposed that just here the grander manner deserted it. But the skill with which Isabella plays upon Claudio's well-recognized sense of honor, and endeavors by means of that to insure him beforehand from the acceptance of life on baser terms, indicates no coming laxity of hand just in this place. It was rather that there rose in Shakespeare's conception, as there may for the reader, as there certainly would in any good acting of the part, something of that terror, the seeking for which is one of the notes of romanticism in Shakespeare and his circle. The stream of ardent natural affection, poured as sudden hatred upon the youth condemned to die, adds an additional note of expression to the horror of the prison where so much of the scene takes place. It is not here only that Shakespeare has conceived of such extreme anger and pity as putting a sort of genius into simple women, so that their "lips drop eloquence," and their intuitions interpret that which is often too hard or fine for manlier reason; and it is Isabella with her grand imaginative diction, and that poetry laid upon the "prone and speechless dialect" there is in mere youth itself, who gives utterance to the equity, the finer judgments of the piece on men and things.

From behind this group with its subtle lights and shades, its poetry, its impressive contrasts, Shakespeare, as I said, conveys to us a strong sense of the tyranny of nature and circumstance over human action. The most powerful expressions of this side of experience might be found here. The bloodless, impassible temperament does but wait for its opportunity, for the almost accidental coherence of time with place, and place with wishing, to annul its long and patient discipline, and become in a moment the very opposite of that which under ordinary conditions it seemed to be, even to itself. The mere resolute self-assertion of the blood brings to others special temptations, temptations which, as defects or overgrowths, lie in the very qualities which make them otherwise imposing or attractive; the

very advantage of men's gifts of intellect or sentiment
being dependent on a balance in their use so delicate
that men hardly maintain it always. Something also must
be conceded to influences merely physical, to the complexion of the heavens, the skyey influences, shifting as
the stars shift; as something also to the mere caprice of
men exercised over each other in the dispensations of
social or political order, to the chance which makes the
life or death of Claudio dependent on Angelo's will.

The many veins of thought which render the poetry of
this play so weighty and impressive unite in the image
of Claudio, a flowerlike young man, whom, prompted by
a few hints from Shakespeare, the imagination easily
clothes with all the bravery of youth, as he crosses the
stage before us on his way to death, coming so hastily to
the end of his pilgrimage. Set in the horrible blackness
of the prison, with its various forms of unsightly death,
this flower seems the braver. Fallen by "prompture of the
blood," the victim of a suddenly revived law against the
common fault of youth like his, he finds his life forfeited
as if by the chance of a lottery. With that instinctive
clinging to life, which breaks through the subtlest casuistries of monk or sage apologizing for an early death, he
welcomes for a moment the chance of life through his
sister's shame, though he revolts hardly less from the
notion of perpetual imprisonment so repulsive to the
buoyant energy of youth. Familiarized, by the words alike
of friends and the indifferent, to the thought of death,
he becomes gentle and subdued indeed, yet more perhaps
through pride than real resignation, and would go down
to darkness at last hard and unblinded. Called upon suddenly to encounter his fate, looking with keen and resolute
profile straight before him, he gives utterance to some of
the central truths of human feeling, the sincere, concen-
trated expression of the recoiling flesh. Thoughts as profound and poetical as Hamlet's arise in him; and but
for the accidental arrest of sentence he would descend
into the dust, a mere gilded, idle flower of youth indeed,
but with what are perhaps the most eloquent of all Shakespeare's words upon his lips.

As Shakespeare in *Measure for Measure* has refashioned, after a nobler pattern, materials already at hand, so that the relics of other men's poetry are incorporated into his perfect work, so traces of the old "morality," that early form of dramatic composition which had for its function the inculcating of some moral theme, survive in it also, and give it a peculiar ethical interest. This ethical interest, though it can escape no attentive reader, yet, in accordance with that artistic law which demands the predominance of form everywhere over the mere matter or subject handled, is not to be wholly separated from the special circumstances, necessities, embarrassments, of these particular dramatic persons. The old "moralities" exemplified most often some rough-and-ready lesson. Here the very intricacy and subtlety of the moral world itself, the difficulty of seizing the true relations of so complex a material, the difficulty of just judgment, of judgment that shall not be unjust, are the lessons conveyed. Even in Whetstone's old story this peculiar vein of moralizing comes to the surface: even there, we notice the tendency to dwell on mixed motives, the contending issues of action, the presence of virtues and vices alike in unexpected places, on "the hard choice of two evils," on the "imprisoning" of men's "real intents." *Measure for Measure* is full of expressions drawn from a profound experience of these casuistries, and that ethical interest becomes predominant in it: it is no longer *Promos and Cassandra,* but *Measure for Measure,* its new name expressly suggesting the subject of *poetical justice.* The action of the play, like the action of life itself for the keener observer, develops in us the conception of this poetical justice, and the yearning to realize it, the true justice of which Angelo knows nothing, because it lies for the most part beyond the limits of any acknowledged law. The idea of justice involves the idea of rights. But at bottom rights are equivalent to that which really is, to facts; and the recognition of his rights therefore, the justice he requires of our hands, or our thoughts, is the recognition of that which the person, in his inmost nature, really is; and as sympathy alone can discover that which really is in matters of feeling and

thought, true justice is in its essence a finer knowledge
through love.

> 'Tis very pregnant:
> The jewel that we find we stoop and take it,
> Because we see it; but what we do not see
> We tread upon, and never think of it.
>
> (II.i.23–26)

It is for this finer justice, a justice based on a more delicate appreciation of the true conditions of men and things,
a true respect of persons in our estimate of actions, that
the people in *Measure for Measure* cry out as they pass
before us; and as the poetry of this play is full of the
peculiarities of Shakespeare's poetry, so in its ethics it is
an epitome of Shakespeare's moral judgments. They are
the moral judgments of an observer, of one who sits as a
spectator, and knows how the threads in the design before
him hold together under the surface: they are the judgments of the humorist also, who follows with a half-
amused but always pitiful sympathy, the various ways of
human disposition, and sees less distance than ordinary
men between what are called respectively great and little
things. It is not always that poetry can be the exponent
of morality; but it is this aspect of morals which it represents most naturally, for this true justice is dependent on
just those finer appreciations which poetry cultivates in
us the power of making, those peculiar valuations of
action and its effect which poetry actually requires.
[1874]

G. WILSON KNIGHT

"Measure for Measure" and the Gospels

In *Measure for Measure* we have a careful dramatic pattern, a studied explication of a central theme: the moral nature of man in relation to the crudity of man's justice, especially in the matter of sexual vice. There is, too, a clear relation existing between the play and the Gospels, for the play's theme is this:

> Judge not, that ye be not judged. For with what judgment ye judge, ye shall be judged: and with what measure ye mete, it shall be measured to you again.
> (Matthew 7:1–2)

The ethical standards of the Gospels are rooted in the thought of *Measure for Measure*. Therefore, in this analysis we shall, while fixing attention primarily on the play, yet inevitably find a reference to the New Testament continually helpful, and sometimes essential.

Measure for Measure is a carefully constructed work. Not until we view it as a deliberate artistic pattern of certain pivot ideas determining the play's action throughout shall we understand its peculiar nature. Though there is consummate psychological insight here and at least one

From *The Wheel of Fire* by G. Wilson Knight. 4th ed. rev. London: Methuen & Co., Ltd.; New York: British Book Centre, 1949. Reprinted by permission of Methuen & Co., Ltd.

person of most vivid and poignant human interest, we
must first have regard to the central theme, and only
second look for exact verisimilitude to ordinary processes
of behavior. We must be careful not to let our human
interest in any one person distort our single vision of the
whole pattern. The play tends towards allegory or symbolism. The poet elects to risk a certain stiffness, or arbi-
trariness, in the directing of his plot rather than fail to
express dramatically, with variety and precision, the full
content of his basic thought. Any stiffness in the matter
of human probability is, however, more than balanced
by its extreme fecundity and compacted significance of
dramatic symbolism. The persons of the play tend to illustrate certain human qualities chosen with careful reference
to the main theme. Thus Isabella stands for sainted purity,
Angelo for Pharisaical righteousness, the Duke for a psychologically sound and enlightened ethic. Lucio represents
indecent wit, Pompey and Mistress Overdone professional
immorality. Barnardine is hardheaded, criminal insensi-
tiveness. Each person illumines some facet of the central
theme: man's moral nature. The play's attention is con-
fined chiefly to sexual ethics: which in isolation is naturally the most pregnant of analysis and the most universal
of all themes. No other subject provides so clear a contrast between human consciousness and human instinct;
so rigid a distinction between the civilized and the natural
qualities of man; so amazing, yet so slight, a boundary set
in the public mind between the foully bestial and the
ideally divine in humanity. The atmosphere, purpose, and
meaning of the play are throughout ethical. The Duke,
lord of this play in the exact sense that Prospero is lord of
The Tempest, is the prophet of an enlightened ethic. He
controls the action from start to finish, he allots, as it were,
praise and blame, he is lit at moments with divine suggestion comparable with his almost divine power of fore-
knowledge, and control, and wisdom. There is an enigmatic, otherworldly mystery suffusing his figure and the
meaning of his acts: their results, however, in each case
justify their initiation; wherein we see the allegorical nature
of the play, since the plot is so arranged that each person

receives his deserts in the light of the Duke's—which is really the Gospel—ethic.

The poetic atmosphere is one of religion and critical morality. The religious coloring is orthodox, as in *Hamlet*. Isabella is a novice among "the votarists of St. Clare" (I.iv.5); the Duke disguises himself as a Friar, exercising the divine privileges of his office towards Juliet, Barnardine, Claudio, Pompey. We hear of "the consecrated fount a league below the city" (IV.iii.99). The thought of death's eternal damnation, which is prominent in *Hamlet,* recurs in Claudio's speech:

> Ay, but to die and go we know not where;
> To lie in cold obstruction and to rot;
> This sensible warm motion to become
> A kneaded clod; and the delighted spirit
> To bathe in fiery floods, or to reside
> In thrilling region of thick-ribbed ice;
> To be imprison'd in the viewless winds,
> And blown with restless violence round about
> The pendant world; or to be worse than worst
> Of those that lawless and incertain thoughts
> Imagine howling: 'tis too horrible!
> The weariest and most loathed worldly life
> That age, ache, penury, and imprisonment
> Can lay on nature is a paradise
> To what we fear in death.
>
> (III.i.118–32)

So powerful can orthodox eschatology be in *Measure for Measure*: it is not, as I shall show, all-powerful. Nor is the play primarily a play of death philosophy: its theme is rather that of the Gospel ethic. And there is no more beautiful passage in all Shakespeare on the Christian redemption than Isabella's lines to Angelo:

> Alas! Alas!
> Why, all the souls that were, were forfeit once;
> And He, that might the vantage best have took,
> Found out the remedy. How would you be,
> If He which is the top of judgment, should

But judge you as you are? O, think on that;
And mercy then will breathe within your lips,
Like man new made.

                                    (II.ii.72–79)

This is the natural sequence to Isabella's earlier lines:

                        Well, believe this,
No ceremony that to great ones 'longs,
Not the king's crown, nor the deputed sword,
The marshal's truncheon, nor the judge's robe,
Become them with one half so good a grace
As mercy does.   (II.ii.58–63)

These thoughts are a repetition of those in Portia's famous
"mercy" speech. There they come as a sudden, gleaming,
almost irrelevant beam of the ethical imagination. But
here they are not irrelevant: they are intrinsic with the
thought of the whole play, the pivot of its movement.
In *The Merchant of Venice* the Gospel reference is explicit:

                . . . we do pray for mercy;
And that same prayer doth teach us all to render
The deeds of mercy.   (IV.i)

And the central idea of *Measure for Measure* is this:

And forgive us our debts as we forgive our debtors.
                              (Matthew 6:12)

Thus "justice" is a mockery: man, himself a sinner, cannot
presume to judge. That is the lesson driven home in
Measure for Measure.

The atmosphere of Christianity pervading the play
merges into the purely ethical suggestion implicit in the
inter-criticism of all the persons. Though the Christian
ethic be the central theme, there is a wider setting of
varied ethical thought, voiced by each person in turn,
high or low. The Duke, Angelo, and Isabella are clearly
obsessed with such ideas and criticize freely in their dif-

ferent fashions. So also Elbow and the officers bring in
Froth and Pompey, accusing them. Abhorson is severely
critical of Pompey:

> A bawd? Fie upon him! He will discredit our mystery.
> (IV.ii.28–29)

Lucio traduces the Duke's character, Mistress Overdone
informs against Lucio. Barnadine is universally despised.
All, that is, react to each other in an essentially ethical
mode: which mode is the peculiar and particular vision
of this play. Even music is brought to the bar of the
ethical judgment:

> . . . music oft hath such a charm
> To make bad good, and good provoke to harm.
> (IV.i.14–15)

Such is the dominating atmosphere of this play. Out of it
grow the main themes, the problem and the lesson of
Measure for Measure. There is thus a pervading atmosphere of orthodoxy and ethical criticism, in which is cen-
tered the mysterious holiness, the profound death-philoso-
phy, the enlightened human insight and Christian ethic
of the protagonist, the Duke of Vienna.

The satire of the play is directed primarily against self-
conscious, self-protected righteousness. The Duke starts
the action by resigning his power to Angelo. He addresses
Angelo, outspoken in praise of his virtues, thus:

> Angelo,
> There is a kind of character in thy life,
> That to the observer doth thy history
> Fully unfold. Thyself and thy belongings
> Are not thine own so proper, as to waste
> Thyself upon thy virtue, they on thee.
> Heaven doth with us as we with torches do;
> Not light them for themselves; for if our virtues
> Did not go forth of us, 'twere all alike
> As if we had them not. Spirits are not finely touch'd,
> But to fine issues, nor Nature never lends

The smallest scruple of her excellence,
But, like a thrifty goddess, she determines
Herself the glory of a creditor,
Both thanks and use.   (I.i.26–40)

The thought is similar to that of the Sermon on the Mount:

Ye are the light of the world. A city that is set on an
hill cannot be hid. Neither do men light a candle, and
put it under a bushel, but on a candlestick; and it giveth
light unto all that are in the house.

(Matthew 5:14–15)

Not only does the Duke's "torch" metaphor clearly recall
this passage, but his development of it is vividly paralleled
by other of Jesus' words. The Duke compares "Nature"
to "a creditor," lending qualities and demanding both
"thanks and use." Compare:

For the Kingdom of Heaven is as a man traveling
into a far country, who called his own servants, and
delivered unto them his goods.
And unto one he gave five talents, to another two,
and to another one; to every man according to his several ability; and straightway took his journey.

(Matthew 25:14–15)

The sequel needs no quotation. Now, though Angelo
modestly refuses the honor, the Duke insists, forcing it on
him. Later, in conversation with Friar Thomas, himself
disguised as a Friar now, he gives us reason for his strange
act:

We have strict statutes and most biting laws,
The needful bits and curbs to headstrong steeds,
Which for this nineteen years we have let slip;
Even like an o'ergrown lion in a cave,
That goes not out to prey. Now, as fond fathers,
Having bound up the threatening twigs of birch,
Only to stick it in their children's sight
For terror, not to use, in time the rod
Becomes more mock'd than fear'd; so our decrees,

Dead to infliction, to themselves are dead;
And liberty plucks justice by the nose;
The baby beats the nurse, and quite athwart
Goes all decorum.   (I.iii.19–31)

Therefore he has given Angelo power and command to
"strike home." Himself he will not exact justice, since he
has already, by his laxity, as good as bade the people sin
by his "permissive pass": the people could not readily
understand such a change in himself—with a new governor it would be different. But these are not his only reasons. He ends:

> Moe reasons for this action
> At our more leisure shall I render you;
> Only, this one: Lord Angelo is precise;
> Stands at a guard with envy; scarce confesses
> That his blood flows, or that his appetite
> Is more to bread than stone: hence shall we see
> If power change purpose, what our seemers be.
>   (I.iii.48–54)

The rest of the play slowly unfolds the rich content of the
Duke's plan, and the secret, too, of his lax rule.
   Escalus tells us that the Duke was

> One that, above all other strifes, contended especially to
> know himself.   (III.ii.235–36)

But he has studied others, besides himself. He prides himself on his knowledge:

> There is written in your brow, provost, honesty and
> constancy: if I read it not truly, my ancient skill be-
> guiles me . . .   (IV.ii.156–58)

Herein are the causes of his leniency. His government
has been inefficient, not through an inherent weakness or
laxity in him, but rather because meditation and self-
analysis, together with profound study of human nature,
have shown him that all passions and sins from other men

have reflected images in his own soul. He is no weakling:
he has been "a scholar, a statesman, and a soldier"
(III.ii.148). But to such a philosopher government and
justice may begin to appear a mockery, and become ab-
horrent. His judicial method has been original: all crimi-
nals were either executed promptly or else freely released
(IV.ii.135–37). Nowhere is the peculiar modernity of the
Duke in point of advanced psychology more vividly apparent. It seems, too, if we are to judge by his treatment
of Barnadine (IV.iii.65–82), that he could not tolerate
an execution without the criminal's own approval! The
case of Barnadine troubles him intensely:

> A creature unprepared, unmeet for death;
> And to transport him in the mind he is
> Were damnable.   (IV.iii.68–70)

The Duke's sense of human responsibility is delightful
throughout: he is like a kindly father, and all the rest are
his children. Thus he now performs the experiment of
handing the reins of government to a man of ascetic purity
who has an hitherto invulnerable faith in the rightness and
justice of his own ideals—a man of spotless reputation
and self-conscious integrity, who will have no fears as to
the "justice" of enforcing precise obedience. The scheme
is a plot, or trap: a scientific experiment to see if extreme
ascetic righteousness can stand the test of power.

The Duke, disguised as the Friar, moves through the
play, a dark figure, directing, watching, moralizing on the
actions of the other persons. As the play progresses and
his plot on Angelo works he assumes an ever-increasing
mysterious dignity, his original purpose seems to become
more and more profound in human insight, the action
marches with measured pace to its appointed and logical
end. We have ceased altogether to think of the Duke as
merely a studious and unpractical governor, incapable
of office. Rather he holds, within the dramatic universe,
the dignity and power of a Prospero, to whom he is
strangely similar. With both, their plot and plan is the
plot and plan of the play: they make and forge the play,

and thus are automatically to be equated in a unique sense with the poet himself—since both are symbols of the poet's controlling, purposeful, combined, movement of the chessmen of the drama. Like Prospero, the Duke tends to assume proportions evidently divine. Once he is actually compared to the Supreme Power:

> O my dread lord,
> I should be guiltier than my guiltiness,
> To think I can be undiscernible,
> When I perceive your grace, like power divine,
> Hath look'd upon my passes.   (V.i.369–73)

So speaks Angelo at the end. We are prepared for it long before. In the rhymed octosyllabic couplets of the Duke's soliloquy in III.ii there is a distinct note of supernatural authority, forecasting the rhymed mystic utterances of divine beings in the Final Plays. He has been talking with Escalus and the Provost, and dismisses them with the words:

> Peace be with you!

They leave him and he soliloquizes:

> He who the sword of Heaven will bear
> Should be as holy as severe;
> Pattern in himself to know
> Grace to stand and virtue go;
> More nor less to other paying
> Than by self-offenses weighing.
> Shame to him whose cruel striking
> Kills for faults of his own liking!
> Twice treble shame on Angelo,
> To weed my vice and let his grow!
> O what may man within him hide,
> Though angel on the outward side!
> How may likeness made in crimes,
> Making practice on the times,
> To draw with idle spiders' strings
> Most ponderous and substantial things!

> Craft against vice I must apply:
> With Angelo tonight shall lie
> His old betrothed but despised;
> So disguise shall, by the disguised,
> Pay with falsehood false exacting,
> And perform an old contracting.

>   (III.ii.264–85)

This fine soliloquy gives us the Duke's philosophy: the philosophy that prompted his original plan. And it is important to notice the mystical, prophetic tone of the speech.

The Duke, like Jesus, is the prophet of a new order of ethics. This aspect of the Duke as teacher and prophet is also illustrated by his cryptic utterance to Escalus just before this soliloquy:

> *Escalus.* Good even, good father.
>
> *Duke.* Bliss and goodness on you.
>
> *Escalus.* Of whence are you?
>
> *Duke.* Not of this country, though my chance is now
> To use it for my time: I am a brother
> Of gracious order, late come from the See
> In special business from his Holiness.
>
> *Escalus.* What news abroad i' the world?
>
> *Duke.* None, but that there is so great a fever on good-
> ness, that the dissolution of it must cure it: novelty is
> only in request; and it is as dangerous to be aged in
> any kind of course, as it is virtuous to be constant in
> any undertaking. There is scarce truth enough alive to
> make societies secure; but security enough to make
> fellowships accursed: much upon this riddle runs the
> wisdom of the world. This news is old enough, yet it
> is every day's news. I pray you, sir, of what disposition
> was the Duke?
>
> *Escalus.* One that, above all other strifes, contended es-
> pecially to know himself.   (III.ii.217–36)

This remarkable speech, with its deliberate, incisive, cryptic sentences, has a profound quality and purpose which reaches the very heart of the play. It deserves exact attention. Its expanded paraphrase runs thus:

> No news, but that goodness is suffering such a disease that a complete dissolution of it (goodness) is needed to cure it. That is, our whole system of conventional ethics should be destroyed and rebuilt. A change (novelty) never gets beyond request, that is, is never actually put in practice. And it is as dangerous to continue indefinitely a worn-out system or order of government, as it is praiseworthy to be constant in any individual undertaking. There is scarcely enough knowledge of human nature current in the world to make societies safe; but ignorant self-confidence (i.e., in matters of justice) enough to make human intercourse within a society a miserable thing. This riddle holds the key to the wisdom of the world (probably, both the false wisdom of the unenlightened, and the true wisdom of great teachers). This news is old enough, and yet the need for its understanding sees daily proof.

I paraphrase freely, admittedly interpreting difficulties in the light of the recurring philosophy of this play on the blindness of men's moral judgments, and especially in the light of the Duke's personal moral attitude as read from his other words and actions. This speech holds the poetry of ethics. Its content, too, is very close to the Gospel teaching, the insistence on the blindness of the world, its habitual disregard of the truth exposed by prophet and teacher:

> And this is the condemnation, that light is come into the world, and men loved darkness rather than light, because their deeds were evil.   (John 3:19)

The same almost divine suggestion rings in many of the Duke's measured prose utterances. There are his supremely beautiful words to Escalus (IV.ii.206–09):

> Look, the unfolding star calls up the shepherd. Put

not yourself into amazement how these things should
be: all difficulties are but easy when they are known.

The first lovely sentence—a unique beauty of Shakespearean prose, in a style peculiar to this play—derives
part of its appeal from New Testament associations, and
the second sentence holds the mystic assurance of Matthew 10:26:

. . . for there is nothing covered, that shall not be revealed; and hid, that shall not be known.

The Duke exercises the authority of a teacher throughout
his disguise as a friar. He speaks authoritatively on repentance to Juliet:

> *Duke.*   . . . but lest you do repent,
> As that the sin hath brought you to this shame,
> Which sorrow is always towards ourselves, not Heaven,
> Showing we would not spare Heaven as we love it,
> But as we stand in fear——
>
> *Juliet.* I do repent me as it is an evil,
> And take the shame with joy.
>
> *Duke.* There rest . . .   (II.iii.30–36)

After rebuking Pompey the bawd very sternly but not
unkindly, he concludes:

> Go mend, go mend.   (III.ii.28)

His attitude is that of Jesus to the woman taken in adultery:

> Neither do I condemn thee: go, and sin no more.
>   (John 8:11)

Both are more kindly disposed towards honest impurity
than light and frivolous scandalmongers, such as Lucio,
or Pharisaic self-righteousness such as Angelo's.

The Duke's ethical attitude is exactly correspondent

with Jesus': the play must be read in the light of the
Gospel teaching, if its full significance is to be apparent.
So he, like Jesus, moves among men suffering grief at
their sins and deriving joy from an unexpected flower of
simple goodness in the deserts of impurity and hardness.
He finds softness of heart where he least expects it—in
the Provost of the prison:

> *Duke.* This is a gentle provost: seldom when
>   The steeled jailer is the friend of men.   (IV.ii.88–89)

So, too, Jesus finds in the centurion,

> a man under authority, having soldiers under me . . .
>   (Matthew 8:9)

a simple faith where he least expects it:

> . . . I say unto you, I have not found so great faith,
> no, not in Israel.

The two incidents are very similar in quality. Now, in that
he represents a perfected ethical philosophy joined to
supreme authority, the Duke is, within the dramatic universe, automatically comparable with Divinity; or we may
suggest that he progresses by successive modes, from
worldly power through the prophecy and moralizing of
the middle scenes, to the supreme judgment at the end,
where he exactly reflects the universal judgment as suggested by many Gospel passages. There is the same apparent injustice, the same tolerance and mercy. The Duke
is, in fact, a symbol of the same kind as the Father in the
Parable of the Prodigal Son (Luke 15) or the Lord in that
of the Unmerciful Servant (Matthew 18). The simplest
way to focus correctly the quality and unity of *Measure
for Measure* is to read it on the analogy of Jesus' parables.
  Though his ethical philosophy is so closely related to
the Gospel teaching, yet the Duke's thoughts on death
are devoid of any explicit belief in immortality. He addresses Claudio, who is to die, and his words at first appear
vague, agnostic: but a deeper acquaintance renders their

profundity and truth. Claudio fears death. The Duke comforts him by concentrating not on death, but on life. In
a series of pregnant sentences he asserts the negative
nature of any single life-joy. First, life is slave to death
and may fail at any chance moment; however much you
run from death, yet you cannot but run still towards it;
nobility in man is inextricably twined with "baseness"
(this is, indeed, the moral of *Measure for Measure*), and
courage is ever subject to fear; sleep is man's "best rest,"
yet he fears death which is but sleep; man is not a single
independent unit, he has no solitary self to lose, but rather
is compounded of universal "dust"; he is always discontent, striving for what he has not, forgetful of that which
he succeeds in winning; man is a changing, wavering substance; his riches he wearily carries till death unloads
him; he is tortured by disease and old age. The catalogue
is strong in unremittent condemnation of life:

> Thou hast nor youth nor age,
> But, as it were, an after-dinner's sleep,
> Dreaming on both; for all thy blessed youth
> Becomes as aged, and doth beg the alms
> Of palsied eld; and when thou art old and rich,
> Thou hast neither heat, affection, limb, nor beauty,
> To make thy riches pleasant. What's yet in this
> That bears the name of life? Yet in this life
> Lie hid moe thousand deaths: yet death we fear,
> That makes these odds all even.   (III.i.32–41)

Life is therefore a sequence of unrealities, strung together
in a time succession. Everything it can give is in turn
killed. Regarded thus, it is unreal, a delusion, a living
death. The thought is profound. True, the Duke has con-
centrated especially on the temporal aspect of life's appearances, regarding only the shell of life and neglecting
the inner vital principle of joy and hope; he has left deeper
things untouched. He neglects love and all immediate
transcendent intuitions. But since it is only this temporal
aspect of decayed appearances which death is known to
end, since it is only the closing of this very time-succession
which Claudio fears, it is enough to prove this succession

valueless. Claudio is thus comforted. The death of such
a life is indeed not death, but rather itself a kind of life:

> I humbly thank you.
> To sue to live, I find I seek to die;
> And seeking death, find life: let it come on.
>   (III.i.41–43)

Now he "will encounter darkness as a bride," like Antony
(III.i.84). The Duke's death philosophy is thus the philosophy of the great tragedies to follow—of *Timon of
Athens,* of *Antony and Cleopatra.* So, too, his ethic is the
ethic of *King Lear.* In this problem play we find the profound thought of the supreme tragedies already emergent
and given careful and exact form, the Duke in this respect
being analogous to Agamemnon in *Troilus and Cressida.*
Both his ethical and his death thinking are profoundly
modern. But Claudio soon reverts to the crude time-
thinking (and fine poetry) of his famous death speech,
in which he regards the afterlife in terms of orthodox
eschatology, thinking of it as a temporal process, like
Hamlet:

> Ay, but to die, and go we know not where . . .
>   (III.i.118)

In the Shakespearean mode of progressive thought it is
essential first to feel death's reality strongly as the ender
of what we call "life": only then do we begin to feel the
tremendous pressure of an immortality not known in
terms of time. We then begin to attach a different meaning to the words "life" and "death." The thought of this
scene thus wavers between the old and the new death
philosophies.

The Duke's plot pivots on the testing of Angelo. Angelo
is a man of spotless reputation, generally respected. Escalus says

> If any in Vienna be of worth
> To undergo such ample grace and honor,
> It is Lord Angelo.   (I.i.22–24)

Angelo, hearing the Duke's praise, and his proposed trust, modestly declines, as though he recognizes that his virtue is too purely idealistic for the rough practice of state affairs:

> Now, good my lord,
> Let there be some more test made of my metal,
> Before so noble and so great a figure
> Be stamp'd upon it.   (I.i.47–50)

Angelo is not a conscious hypocrite: rather a man whose chief faults are self-deception and pride in his own righteousness—an unused and delicate instrument quite useless under the test of active trial. This he half-recognizes, and would first refuse the proffered honor. The Duke insists: Angelo's fall is thus entirely the Duke's responsibility. So this man of ascetic life is forced into authority. He is

> A man whose blood
> Is very snow-broth; one who never feels
> The wanton stings and motions of the sense,
> But doth rebate and blunt his natural edge
> With profits of the mind, study and fast.
>   (I.iv.57–61)

Angelo, indeed, does not know himself: no one receives so great a shock as he himself when temptation overthrows his virtue. He is no hypocrite. He cannot, however, be acquitted of Pharisaical pride: his reputation means much to him, he "stands at a guard with envy" (I.iii.51). He "takes pride" in his "gravity" (II.iv.10). Now, when he is first faced with the problem of Claudio's guilt of adultery—and commanded, we must presume, by the Duke's sealed orders to execute stern punishment wholesale, for this is the Duke's ostensible purpose—Angelo pursues his course without any sense of wrongdoing. Escalus hints that surely all men must know sexual desire—how then is Angelo's procedure just? Escalus thus adopts the Duke's ethical point of view, exactly:

> Let but your honor know

(Whom I believe to be most strait in virtue),
That, in the working of your own affections,
Had time cohered with place, or place with wishing,
Or that the resolute acting of your blood
Could have attain'd the effect of your own purpose,
Whether you had not, some time in your life,
Err'd in this point, which now you censure him,
And pull'd the law upon you.   (II.i.8–16)

Which reflects the Gospel message:

Ye have heard that it was said by them of old time,
Thou shalt not commit adultery:
But I say unto you, that whosoever looketh on a
woman to lust after her hath committed adultery with
her already in his heart.   (Matthew 5:27–28)

Angelo's reply, however, is sound sense:

'Tis one thing to be tempted, Escalus,
Another thing to fall.   (II.i.17–18)

Isabella later uses the same argument as Escalus:

. . . Go to your bosom;
Knock there, and ask your heart what it doth know
That's like my brother's fault: if it confess
A natural guiltiness, such as is his,
Let it not sound a thought upon your tongue
Against my brother's life.   (II.ii.136–41)

We are reminded of Jesus' words to the Scribes and Phari-
sees concerning the woman "taken in adultery":

He that is without sin among you, let him first cast a
stone at her.   (John 8:7)

Angelo is, however, sincere: terribly sincere. He feels no
personal responsibility, since he is certain that he does
right. We believe him when he tells Isabella:

It is the law, not I, condemn your brother:

>   Were he my kinsman, brother, or my son,
>   It should be thus with him.   (II.ii.80–82)

To execute justice, he says, is kindness, not cruelty, in the
long run.

Angelo's arguments are rationally conclusive. A thing
irrational breaks them, however: his passion for Isabella.
Her purity, her idealism, her sanctity enslave him—she
who speaks to him of

>   true prayers
>   That shall be up at heaven and enter there
>   Ere sunrise, prayers from preserved souls,
>   From fasting maids whose minds are dedicate
>   To nothing temporal.   (II.ii.151–55)

Angelo is swiftly enwrapped in desire. He is finely shown
as falling a prey to his own love of purity and asceticism:

>   What is't I dream on?
>   O cunning enemy, that, to catch a saint,
>   With saints dost bait thy hook!   (II.ii.178–80)

He "sins in loving virtue"; no strumpet could ever allure
him; Isabella subdues him utterly. Now he who built so
strongly on a rational righteousness, understands for the
first time the sweet unreason of love:

>   Ever till now,
>   When men were fond, I smiled and wonder'd how.
>   (II.ii.185–86)

Angelo struggles hard: he prays to Heaven, but his
thoughts "anchor" on Isabel (II.iv.4). His gravity and
learning—all are suddenly as nothing. He admits to himself that he has taken "pride" in his well-known austerity,
adding "let no man hear me"—a pathetic touch which
casts a revealing light both on his shallow ethic and his
honest desire at this moment to understand himself. The
violent struggle is short. He surrenders, his ideals all top-
pled over like ninepins:

Blood, thou art blood:
Let's write good angel on the Devil's horn,
'Tis not the Devil's crest.   (II.iv.15–17)

Angelo is now quite adrift: all his old contacts are irrevocably severed. Sexual desire has long been anathema to him, so his warped idealism forbids any healthy love. Good and evil change places in his mind, since this passion is immediately recognized as good, yet, by every one of his stock judgments, condemned as evil. The Devil becomes a "good angel." And this wholesale reversion leaves Angelo in sorry plight now: he has no moral values left. Since sex has been synonymous with foulness in his mind, this new love, reft from the start of moral sanction in a man who "scarce confesses that his blood flows," becomes swiftly a devouring and curbless lust:

I have begun,
And now I give my sensual race the rein.
(II.iv.159–60)

So he addresses Isabella. He imposes the vile condition of Claudio's life. All this is profoundly true: he is at a loss with this new reality—embarrassed as it were, incapable of pursuing a normal course of love. In proportion as his moral reason formerly denied his instincts, so now his instincts assert themselves in utter callousness of his moral reason. He swiftly becomes an utter scoundrel. He threatens to have Claudio tortured. Next, thinking to have had his way with Isabella, he is so conscience-stricken and tortured by fear that he madly resolves not to keep faith with her: he orders Claudio's instant execution. For, in proportion as he is nauseated at his own crimes, he is terror-struck at exposure. He is mad with fear, his story exactly pursues the Macbeth rhythm:

This deed unshapes me quite, makes me unpregnant
And dull to all proceedings. A deflower'd maid!
And by an eminent body that enforced
The law against it! But that her tender shame
Will not proclaim against her maiden loss,

> How might she tongue me! Yet reason dares her no;
> For my authority bears so credent bulk,
> That no particular scandal once can touch
> But it confounds the breather. He should have lived,
> Save that his riotous youth, with dangerous sense,
> Might in the times to come have ta'en revenge,
> By so receiving a dishonor'd life
> With ransom of such shame. Would yet he had lived!
> Alack, when once our grace we have forgot,
> Nothing goes right: we would, and we would not.
>   (IV.iv.22–36)

This is the reward of self-deception, of pharisaical pride, of an idealism not harmonized with instinct—of trying, to use the Duke's pregnant phrase:

> To draw with idle spiders' strings
> Most ponderous and substantial things. (III.ii.278–79)

Angelo has not been overcome with evil. He has been ensnared by good, by his own love of sanctity, exquisitely symbolized in his love of Isabella: the hook is baited with a saint, and the saint is caught. The cause of his fall is this and this only. The coin of his moral purity, which flashed so brilliantly, when tested does not ring true. Angelo is the symbol of a false intellectualized ethic divorced from the deeper springs of human instinct.

The varied close-inwoven themes of *Measure for Measure* are finally knit in the exquisite final act. To that point the action—reflected image always of the Ducal plot—marches

> By cold gradation and well-balanced form.
>   (IV.iii.101)

The last act of judgment is heralded by trumpet calls:

> Twice have the trumpets sounded;
> The generous and gravest citizens
> Have hent the gates, and very near upon
> The Duke is entering.   (IV.vi.12–15)

So all are, as it were, summoned to the final judgment. Now Angelo, Isabella, Lucio—all are understood most clearly in the light of this scene. The last act is the key to the play's meaning, and all difficulties are here resolved. I shall observe the judgment measured to each, noting retrospectively the especial significance in the play of Lucio and Isabella.

Lucio is a typical loose-minded, vulgar wit. He is the product of a society that has gone too far in condemnation of human sexual desires. He keeps up a running comment on sexual matters. His very existence is a condemnation of the society which makes him a possibility. Not that there is anything of premeditated villainy in him: he is merely superficial, enjoying the unnatural ban on sex which civilization imposes, because that very ban adds point and spice to sexual gratification. He is, however, sincerely concerned about Claudio, and urges Isabella to plead for him. He can be serious—for a while. He can speak sound sense, too, in the full flow of his vulgar wit:

> Yes, in good sooth, the vice is of a great kindred; it is well allied: but it is impossible to extirp it quite, friar, till eating and drinking be put down. They say this Angelo was not made by man and woman after this downright way of creation: is it true, think you?   (III.ii.103–08)

This goes to the root of our problem here. Pompey has voiced the same thought (II.i.238–54). This is, indeed, what the Duke has known too well: what Angelo and Isabella do not know. Thus Pompey and Lucio here at least tell downright facts—Angelo and Isabella pursue impossible and valueless ideals. Only the Duke holds the balance exact throughout. Lucio's running wit, however, pays no consistent regard to truth. To him the Duke's leniency was a sign of hidden immorality:

> Ere he would have hanged a man for getting a hundred bastards, he would have paid for the nursing of a thousand: he had some feeling of the sport; he knew the service, and that instructed him to mercy.   (III.ii.119–23)

He traduces the Duke's character wholesale. He does not pause to consider the truth of his words. Again, there is no intent to harm—merely a careless, shallow, truthless wit-philosophy which enjoys its own sex chatter. The type is common. Lucio is refined and vulgar, and the more vulgar because of his refinement; whereas Pompey, because of his natural coarseness, is less vulgar. Lucio can only exist in a society of smug propriety and self-deception: for his mind's life is entirely parasitical on those insincerities. His false—because fantastic and shallow— pursuit of sex, is the result of a false, fantastic denial of sex in his world. Like so much in *Measure for Measure* he is eminently modern. Now Lucio is the one person the Duke finds it all but impossible to forgive:

> I find an apt remission in myself;
> And yet here's one in place I cannot pardon.
>
> (V.i.501–02)

All the rest have been serious in their faults. Lucio's condemnation is his triviality, his insincerity, his profligate idleness, his thoughtless detraction of others' characters:

> You, sirrah, that knew me for a fool, a coward,
> One all of luxury, an ass, a madman;
> Wherein have I so deserved of you,
> That you extol me thus?   (V.i.503–06)

Lucio's treatment at the close is eminently, and fittingly, undignified. He is threatened thus: first he is to marry the mother of his child, about whose wrong he formerly boasted; then to be whipped and hanged. Lucio deserves some credit, however: he preserves his nature and answers with his characteristic wit. He cannot be serious. The Duke, his sense of humor touched, retracts the sentence:

> *Duke.* Upon mine honor, thou shalt marry her.
>   Thy slanders I forgive; and therewithal
>   Remit thy other forfeits. Take him to prison;
>   And see our pleasure herein executed.

> *Lucio.* Marrying a punk, my lord, is pressing to death, whipping, and hanging.
>
> *Duke.* Slandering a prince deserves it.   (V.i.521–27)

Idleness, triviality, thoughtlessness receive the Duke's strongest condemnation. The thought is this:

> But I say unto you, That every idle word that men shall speak, they shall give account thereof in the day of judgment.   (Matthew 12:36)

Exactly what happens to Lucio. His wit is often illuminating, often amusing, sometimes rather disgusting. He is never wicked, sometimes almost lovable, but terribly dangerous.[1]

Isabella is the opposite extreme. She is more saintly than Angelo, and her saintliness goes deeper, is more potent than his. When we first meet her, she is about to enter the secluded life of a nun. She welcomes such a life. She even wishes

> a more strict restraint
> Upon the sisterhood, the votarists of Saint Clare.
>   (I.iv.4–5)

Even Lucio respects her. She calls forth something deeper than his usual wit:

> I would not—though 'tis my familiar sin
> With maids to seem the lapwing and to jest,
> Tongue far from heart—play with all virgins so:
> I hold you as a thing ensky'd and sainted,
> By your renouncement an immortal spirit,
> And to be talk'd with in sincerity,
> As with a saint.   (I.iv.31–37)

Which contains a fine and exact statement of his shallow behavior, his habitual wit for wit's sake. Lucio is throughout a loyal friend to Claudio: truer to his cause, in fact, than Isabella. A pointed contrast. He urges her to help.

---

[1] For Lucio, see also *The Imperial Theme*, p. 20.

She shows a distressing lack of warmth. It is Lucio that talks of "your poor brother." She is cold:

> Lucio.   Assay the power you have.
>
> Isabella. My power; Alas, I doubt——
>
> Lucio.   Our doubts are traitors
> And make us lose the good we oft might win,
> By fearing to attempt.   (I.iv.76–79)

Isabella's self-centered saintliness is thrown here into strong contrast with Lucio's manly anxiety for his friend. So, contrasted with Isabella's ice-cold sanctity, there are the beautiful lines with which Lucio introduces the matter to her:

> Your brother and his lover have embraced:
> As those that feed grow full, as blossoming time
> That from the seedness the bare fallow brings
> To teeming foison, even so her plenteous womb
> Expresseth his full tilth and husbandry.   (I.iv.40–44)

Compare the pregnant beauty of this with the chastity of Isabella's recent lisping line:

> Upon the sisterhood, the votarists of Saint Clare.
>   (I.iv.5)

Isabella lacks human feeling. She starts her suit to Angelo poorly enough. She is lukewarm:

> There is a vice that most I do abhor,
> And most desire should meet the blow of justice;
> For which I would not plead but that I must;
> For which I must not plead, but that I am
> At war 'twixt will and will not.   (II.ii.29–33)

Lucio has to urge her on continually. We begin to feel that Isabella has no real affection for Claudio; has stifled all human love in the pursuit of sanctity. When Angelo at last proposes his dishonorable condition she quickly comes to her decision:

Then, Isabel, live chaste and, brother, die.
More than our brother is our chastity.

(II.iv.184–85)

When Shakespeare chooses to load his dice like this—
which is seldom indeed—he does it mercilessly. The
Shakespearean satire here strikes once, and deep: there
is no need to point it further. But now we know our
Isabel. We are not surprised that she behaves to Claudio,
who hints for her sacrifice, like a fiend:

Take my defiance!
Die, perish! Might but my bending down
Reprieve thee from thy fate, it should proceed:
I'll pray a thousand prayers for thy death,
No word to save thee.

(III.i.143–47)

Is her fall any less than Angelo's? Deeper, I think. With
whom is Isabel angry? Not only with her brother. She has
feared this choice—terribly: "O, I do fear thee, Claudio,"
she said (III.i.74). Even since Angelo's suggestion she
has been afraid. Now Claudio has forced the responsibility of choice on her. She cannot sacrifice herself. Her sex
inhibitions have been horribly shown her as they are,
naked. She has been stung—lanced on a sore spot of her
soul. She knows now that it is not all saintliness, she sees
her own soul and sees it as something small, frightened,
despicable, too frail to dream of such a sacrifice. Though
she does not admit it, she is infuriated not with Claudio,
but with herself. "Saints" should not speak like this.
Again, the comment of this play is terribly illuminating.
It is significant that she readily involves Mariana in illicit
love: it is only her own chastity which assumes, in her
heart, universal importance.[2]

Isabella, however, was no hypocrite, any more than
Angelo. She is a spirit of purity, grace, maiden charm:
but all these virtues the action of the play turns remorse-
lessly against herself. In a way, it is not her fault. Chastity
is hardly a sin—but neither, as the play emphasizes, is it

[2] I now doubt if Isabella's attitude to Mariana should be held against
her (1955).

the whole of virtue. And she, like the rest, has to find a
new wisdom. Mariana in the last act prays for Angelo's
life. Confronted by that warm, potent, forgiving, human
love, Isabella herself suddenly shows a softening, a sweet
humanity. Asked to intercede, she does so—she, who was
at the start slow to intercede for a brother's life, now implores the Duke to save Angelo, her wronger:

> I partly think
> A due sincerity govern'd his deeds,
> Till he did look on me.   (V.i.448–50)

There is a suggestion that Angelo's strong passion has
itself moved her, thawing her ice-cold pride. This is the
moment of her trial: the Duke is watching her keenly, to
see if she has learnt her lesson—nor does he give her any
help, but deliberately puts obstacles in her way. But she
stands the test: she bows to a love greater than her own
saintliness. Isabella, like Angelo, has progressed far during the play's action: from sanctity to humanity.

Angelo, at the beginning of this final scene, remains
firm in denial of the accusations leveled against him. Not
till the Duke's disguise as a friar is made known and he
understands that deception is no longer possible, does he
show outward repentance. We know, however, that his
inward thoughts must have been terrible enough. His earlier agonized soliloquies put this beyond doubt. Now, his
failings exposed, he seems to welcome punishment:

> Immediate sentence then and sequent death
> Is all the grace I beg.   (V.i.376–77)

Escalus expresses sorrow and surprise at his actions. He
answers:

> I am sorry that such sorrow I procure:
> And so deep sticks it in my penitent heart
> That I crave death more willingly than mercy;
> 'Tis my deserving and I do entreat it.   (V.i.477–80)

To Angelo, exposure seems to come as a relief: the horror of self-deception is at an end. For the first time in his life he is both quite honest with himself and with the world. So he takes Mariana as his wife. This is just: he threw her over because he thought she was not good enough for him,

> Partly for that her promised proportions
> Came short of composition, but in chief
> For that her reputation was disvalued
> In levity.   (V.i.219–22)

He aimed too high when he cast his eyes on the sainted Isabel: now, knowing himself, he will find his true level in the love of Mariana. He has become human. The union is symbolical. Just as his supposed love-contact with Isabel was a delusion, when Mariana, his true mate, was taking her place, so Angelo throughout has deluded himself. Now his acceptance of Mariana symbolizes his new self-knowledge. So, too, Lucio is to find his proper level in marrying Mistress Kate Keepdown, of whose child he is the father. Horrified as he is at the thought, he has to meet the responsibilities of his profligate behavior. The punishment of both is this only: to know, and to be, themselves. This is both their punishment and at the same time their highest reward for their sufferings: self-knowledge being the supreme, perhaps the only, good. We remember the parable of the Pharisee and the Publican (Luke 18).

So the Duke draws his plan to its appointed end. All, including Barnadine, are forgiven, and left, in the usual sense, unpunished. This is inevitable. The Duke's original leniency has been shown by his successful plot to have been right, not wrong. Though he sees "corruption boil and bubble" (V.i.319) in Vienna, he has found, too, that man's sainted virtue is a delusion: "judge not that ye be not judged." He has seen an Angelo to fall from grace at the first breath of power's temptation, he has seen Isabella's purity scarring, defacing her humanity. He has found more gentleness in "the steeled jailer" than in either of these. He has found more natural honesty in

Pompey the bawd than in Angelo the ascetic; more humanity in the charity of Mistress Overdone than in Isabella condemning her brother to death with venomed words in order to preserve her own chastity. Mistress Overdone has looked after Lucio's illegitimate child:

> ... Mistress Kate Keepdown was with child by him in the Duke's time; he promised her marriage; his child is a year and a quarter old, come Philip and Jacob: I have kept it myself ...

> (III.ii.202-05)

Human virtue does not flower only in high places: nor is it the monopoly of the pure in body. In reading *Measure for Measure* one feels that Pompey with his rough humor and honest professional indecency is the only one of the major persons, save the Duke, who can be called "pure in heart." Therefore, knowing all this, the Duke knows his tolerance to be now a moral imperative: he sees too far into the nature of man to pronounce judgment according to the appearances of human behavior. But we are not told what will become of Vienna. There is, however, a hint, for the Duke is to marry Isabel, and this marriage, like the others, may be understood symbolically. It is to be the marriage of understanding with purity; of tolerance with moral fervor. The Duke, who alone has no delusions as to the virtues of man, who is incapable of executing justice on vice since he finds forgiveness implicit in his wide and sympathetic understanding—he alone wins the "enskied and sainted" Isabel. More, we are not told. And we may expect her in future to learn from him wisdom, human tenderness, and love:

> What's mine is yours and what is yours is mine.

> (V.i.540)

If we still find this universal forgiveness strange—and many have done so—we might observe Mariana, who loves Angelo with a warm and realistically human love. She sees no fault in him, or none of any consequence:

> O my dear lord,
> I crave no other nor no better man.
>
> (V.i.428–29)

She knows that

> best men are molded out of faults,
> And, for the most, become much more the better
> For being a little bad.   (V.i.442–44)

The incident is profoundly true. Love asks no questions, sees no evil, transfiguring the just and unjust alike. This is one of the surest and finest ethical touches in this masterpiece of ethical drama. Its moral of love is, too, the ultimate splendor of Jesus' teaching.

Measure for Measure is indeed based firmly on that teaching. The lesson of the play is that of Matthew 5:20:

> For I say unto you, That except your righteousness shall exceed the righteousness of the scribes and Pharisees, ye shall in no case enter into the Kingdom of Heaven.

The play must be read, not as a picture of normal human affairs, but as a parable, like the parables of Jesus. The plot is, in fact, an inversion of one of those parables— that of the Unmerciful Servant (Matthew 18); and the universal and level forgiveness at the end, where all alike meet pardon, is one with the forgiveness of the Parable of the Two Debtors (Luke 7). Much has been said about the difficulties of *Measure for Measure*. But, in truth, no play of Shakespeare shows more thoughtful care, more deliberate purpose, more consummate skill in structural technique, and, finally, more penetrating ethical and psychological insight. None shows a more exquisitely inwoven pattern. And, if ever the thought at first sight seems strange, or the action unreasonable, it will be found to reflect the sublime strangeness and unreason of Jesus' teaching.

R. W. CHAMBERS

"Measure for Measure"

In *Measure for Measure* Shakespeare took as his source an old play, *Promos and Cassandra,* written by George Whetstone a quarter of a century before. Now, just as certainly as *Hamlet* was a story of revenge, so was *Promos and Cassandra* a story of forgiveness. In this play Cassandra (like Isabel) pleads for her brother, who (like Claudio) had been condemned to death for unchastity. The judge, Promos (like Angelo), will grant pardon only if Cassandra yield to his passion. Cassandra at last does so. That is the essential difference between the old plot, and Shakespeare's play. Nevertheless, Promos orders Cassandra's brother to be beheaded, and the head to be presented to her. Cassandra complains to the King; the King gives judgment that Promos first marry Cassandra, then lose *his* head. But, this marriage solemnized, Cassandra, now tied in the greatest bonds of affection to her husband, suddenly becomes an earnest suitor for his life. In the end it appears that the kindly jailer has in fact released the brother, and presented Cassandra with a felon's

From *Man's Unconquerable Mind* by R. W. Chambers. London: Jonathan Cape Limited, 1952; Philadelphia: Albert Saifer, Publisher, 1953. Reprinted by permission of Jonathan Cape Limited.

head instead. So, to renown the virtues of Cassandra, the King pardons both brother and judge, and all ends well.[1]

The story shows the violence of much Elizabethan drama. John Addington Symonds says, in *Shakespeare's Predecessors,* that the sympathies of a London audience were like "the chords of a warrior's harp, strung with twisted iron and bull's sinews, vibrating mightily, but needing a stout stroke to make them thrill." The playwrights "glutted their audience with horrors, cudgelled their horny fibres into sensitiveness."

Now mark how Shakespeare treats this barbarous story. According to Professor Dover Wilson, at the time when he wrote *Measure for Measure* Shakespeare "quite obviously believed in nothing; he was as cynical as Iago, as disillusioned as Macbeth, though he still retained, unlike the first, his sensitiveness, and, unlike the second, his hatred of cruelty, hypocrisy, and ingratitude."[2] According to Sir Edmund Chambers, in *Measure for Measure* his "remorseless analysis" "probes the inmost being of man, and strips him naked." "It is the temper of the inquisitor": "you can but shudder."[3]

Prepare then to shudder, as you observe William Iago Torquemada Shakespeare at work. Shakespeare, for all the "self-laceration," "disgust," and "general morbidity"[4] which is supposed to have obsessed him and his Jacobean contemporaries, removes from the play the really morbid scene of the heroine kissing the severed head of her supposed brother. Then, he divides the sorrows of the heroine between two characters, Isabel and Mariana. And the object of this duplication is, that, whatever their spiritual anguish, neither of them shall be placed in the "really intolerable situation"[5] of poor Cassandra. Mariana has been contracted to Angelo formally by oath. It is vital to re-

---

1. Whetstone retold the tale in prose (*Heptameron of Civil Discourses,* 1582). It is derived from the *Hecatommithi* of Cinthio (1565), who also wrote a play on the subject (*Epitia*). Shakespeare knew some of these, possibly all.

2. J. Dover Wilson, *The Essential Shakespeare,* p. 122.

3. *Ibid.,* p. 213.

4. *Ibid.,* pp. 117, 118.

5. G. L. Kittredge, ed., *Works of Shakespeare,* p. 97.

member that, according to Elizabethan ideas, Angelo and
Mariana are therefore man and wife. But Angelo has deserted Mariana. Now I grant that, according to our modern ideas, it is undignified for the deserted Mariana still
to desire union with the husband who has scorned her.
We may resent the elegiac and spaniel-like fidelity of
Mariana of the Moated Grange. *But is that the attitude of
the year 1604?* The tale of the deserted bride seeking her
husband in disguise is old, approved, beloved. It is a
mere anachronism to assume that Shakespeare, a practical dramatist, told this tale with some deep cynical and
self-lacerating intention unintelligible to his audience, but
now at last revealed to modern criticism. Shakespeare
made Mariana gentle and dignified. She, in all shadow
and silence, visits her husband in place of Isabel, to save
Claudio's life.

And our twentieth-century critics are scandalized over
the tale. This surprises me, a Late Victorian, brought up
on the Bible and Arthurian story. I did not know that our
modern age was so proper. A professor today cannot deliver a series of lectures on "The Application of Thought
to Textual Criticism" without its being reported as "The
Application of Thought to Sexual Criticism." Yet this
sex-obsessed age of ours is too modest to endure the old
story of the substituted bride. I learnt at my Early Victorian mother's knee how Jacob served seven years for
Rachel: "And it came to pass, that in the morning, behold, it was Leah,"[6] and Jacob had to serve another seven
years for his beloved. I did not exclaim: "Oh, my mother,
you are lacerating my feelings with this remorseless revelation of patriarchal polygamy." A child could grasp the
story of Jacob's service for Rachel, which "seemed unto
him but a few days, for the love he had to her."

Sir Edmund Chambers is entitled to say that the story
of the substituted bride "does not commend itself to the
modern conscience." Jaques was entitled to say that he
did not like the name of Rosalind. And Orlando was entitled to say, "There was no thought of pleasing you when
she was christened." In the sixteenth century the story

6. Genesis 29:25.

was a commonplace of romance, and Shakespeare used it in order to make more gentle one of the quite horrible situations of the pre-Shakespearean drama. There was a time when Shakespeare had not shrunk from staging the grossest horrors. It is to avoid them that he now introduces the substitution which offends "the modern conscience."

It may be objected that Shakespeare is "not for an age, but for all time," and that therefore he ought not to have condescended to use stories which, although current in his day, and although he made them less horrible, nevertheless would not appeal to future ages. But the great poets, Homer, Aeschylus, Sophocles, Dante, Shakespeare, speak to all time only through the language, conventions, and beliefs of their own age. How else?

A second fault of the old play is the crudity of the change from Cassandra's thirst for vengeance to her prayer for forgiveness. Shakespeare had permitted himself similar crudities in the past. Now he sets to work to make the plot consistent: he does this by making it turn, from first to last, on the problem of punishment and forgiveness. It is Shakespeare's addition to the story that the Duke is distressed by this problem. Fearing lest his rule has been too lax, he deputes his office to Angelo, whilst remaining, disguised as a friar, to "visit both prince and people." And here critics, among them Sir Walter Raleigh[7] and Sir Arthur Quiller-Couch,[8] object. It is not seemly for a Duke to "shirk his proper responsibility, and steal back incognito to play busybody and spy on his deputy."

I am reminded of one of the first essays ever shown up to me, by a Japanese student, some thirty-five years ago. He objected to *The Merchant of Venice*. "Sir, Bassanio," he said, "did not bring doctor in order that he tie up wound of friend. He did not recognize own spouse in masculine raiment."

There was every reason for a Japanese student to be puzzled when suddenly introduced to the world of west-

7. *Shakespeare*, p. 167.
8. New Cambridge Shakespeare, *Measure for Measure*, p. xxxiv.

ern romance, just as we in our turn are puzzled, when we first try to understand a translation of one of the *No* plays. But why do English critics today bring against *Measure for Measure* this kind of objection? They would be ashamed to bring it against Shakespeare's earlier comedies, or later romances.

Disguise and impersonation and misunderstanding are the very life of romantic comedy. The disguised monarch, who can learn the private affairs of his humblest subject, becomes a sort of earthly Providence, combining omniscience and omnipotence. That story has always had its appeal. "Thus hath the wise magistrate done in all ages";[9] although obviously to introduce into our daily life this ancient habit of the benevolent monarch would be to incur deserved satire.

When Professor Raleigh complains that the Duke "shirks his public duties," and when he likens him to a head of a college who "tries to keep the love of the rebels by putting his ugly duties upon the shoulders of a deputy," is he not falling into the mistake which he deplores in other critics, that of being so much more moral than Shakespeare himself? Is he not substituting for Shakespeare's Duke another, and a quite different one? Bernard Shaw has rewritten the last act of *Cymbeline,* as Shakespeare might have written it, if he had been post-Ibsen and post-Shaw. And that is a legitimate thing to do, compared with the modern habit of keeping Shakespeare's text, but putting upon it a construction which is post-Ibsen and post-Shaw; imposing an outlook and a morality not Shakespeare's.

Obviously, it is wrong for the master of a college deliberately to put his unpopular duties upon the vice-master; and it would be most improper for him to watch the result from the porter's lodge, disguised as a scout. It would be equally improper for a young lady to intervene in a lawsuit, by personating a K.C.; and in this way we might moralize amiss every one of Shakespeare's romantic plays. The question is not how Shaw might have satirized the Duke, had he rewritten *Measure for Measure.* The ques-

9. Jonson, *Bartholomew Fair*, II.i.

tion is how Shakespeare meant us to see the Duke; and since the Duke controls the whole action of the play, we must see him as Shakespeare meant us to do, or misunderstand the play.

Shakespeare makes the Duke describe himself as one who has ever loved the life removed; one who does not relish well the loud applause of the people. Under his friar's disguise, the Duke is stung by Lucio's slanders into defending himself as one who, by the business he has helmed, "shall appear to the envious a scholar, a statesman, and a soldier." To make it quite clear that we must take this seriously, Shakespeare makes Escalus, immediately after, confirm the Duke's words by describing him as

> One that, above all other strifes, contended especially to know himself. Rather rejoicing to see another merry, than merry at anything which professed to make him rejoice: a gentleman of all temperance.

Isabel, in her moment of direst distress, remembers him as "the good Duke." To Mariana he is, in his friar's disguise, "a man of comfort," who has often stilled her "brawling discontent." (This, of course, violates chronology, but Shakespeare never bothered about that.) Angelo, in his moment of deepest humiliation, addresses the Duke with profound reverence and awe. If our moderns prefer to follow the "fantastic" Lucio, and to regard the Duke cynically, they should remember that Lucio was but speaking according to the trick, and himself suggested a whipping as adequate punishment.

Shakespeare puts into the Duke's mouth a speech on Death which might have been uttered by Hamlet; and Shakespeare seems to have meant us to regard him as a man of Hamlet's thoughtful, scholarly type, but older, with much experience of government and of war: no longer "courtier, soldier, scholar," but "statesman, soldier, scholar"; yet still rather melancholy and distrustful of himself. Shakespeare, however, did not depict him with that intensity which makes his greatest characters come alive. The Duke remains somewhat impersonal, a controlling force; we never think of him by his name, Vincentio. But, though hardly a fully-realized character, he seems more than "a puppet, cleverly painted and adroitly manipulated."[10] Rather, he is the god in the machine: and we may concede that sometimes the machine creaks. But the Jacobeans did not mind if the machinery of their masques creaked a little, provided only it worked. And the Duke works: he is the source of the action of the play. Very truly he has been described as rather a power than a character.[11] So far from "shirking his proper responsibility," he controls the fate of all the characters in the play.

The Duke is deeply distressed because, after fourteen years of his rule, his subjects are still no better than they ought to be. To the moralists who say that he ought to have announced publicly and personally his intention of himself inflicting a little experimental decapitation, it is answer enough that thereby the plot, which needs the Duke as a power in reserve, would have been wrecked. In the world of romantic story, in which alone he moves, the Duke has the long-established right of adopting a disguise and appointing a deputy; who will, as he knows, elect to exercise his office with severity.

Perhaps there may be a touch of irony when Shakespeare makes the Duke, who is to end as the lover of Isabel, begin by declaring that the dribbling dart of love cannot pierce a complete bosom. But there is nothing unfriendly in such irony. Of course it is part of the fun of the story (and good fun too) that the Duke has to listen to slander upon himself; has to keep his end up by giving himself a handsome testimonial; is frustrated by Lucio's "Nay, friar, I am a kind of burr, I shall stick," when he tries to escape from his tormentor. But such are the inevitable misfortunes of the monarch in disguise; we do not honor King Alfred the less, because we enjoy his confusion when scolded for burning the cakes. Yet so great is the effect of persistent denigration, that even a wise critic, who is effectively defending the Duke, concedes to his detractors that he "punished Lucio merely for poking

---

10. W. W. Lawrence, *Shakespeare's Problem Comedies*, 1931, p. 112.
11. *The Times Literary Supplement*, 16 July 1931, p. 554.

fun at him behind his back."[12] But that is not what Shakespeare wrote. Lucio, in the old days, had escaped marrying the mother of his child, by denying his parentage. The Duke, when he learns the truth, merely carries out his original plan of making Lucio marry the woman to whom he had promised marriage.[13] The Duke markedly does *not* punish Lucio for his slanders: the suggestion that he does so is merely one more instance of the extraordinary prejudice which critics cherish against all the people in this play. They christen it "a dark comedy," and then darken the characters to justify their classification.

Not only does the Duke control the fate of all the characters; he profoundly alters the very nature of one: Angelo. The deputy, Angelo, is not so called for nothing. He *is* "angel on the outward side"—an ascetic saint in the judgment of his fellow citizens, and despite the meanness of his spirit, nay, because of it, a saint in his own esteem. His soliloquies prove this, and Isabel at the end gives him some credit for sincerity.

Now Claudio and Juliet have lived together as man and wife, although their contract has been secret: it has "lacked the denunciation of outward order." (The contract between Angelo and Mariana, on the other hand, had been public, and so had undoubtedly given them the rights of man and wife.) Angelo's puritanical revival of an ancient law, fourteen years out of date, renders Claudio's life forfeit. This Viennese law seems strange, but the Duke says the law is such. If we allow Portia to expound the even stranger law of Venice to the Duke and magnificoes, we may surely allow the Duke of Vienna to understand the law of his own state. It is a postulate of the story.

Critics speak as if Shakespeare had imagined Claudio a self-indulgent boy, a "poor weak soul."[14] Yet it is only Angelo's retrospective revival which makes Claudio's offense capital. "He hath but as offended in a dream," says the kindly Provost. He "was worth five thousand of you

12. Thaler, *Shakespeare's Silences*, p. 88.
13. III.ii.203, etc.; IV.iii.174, etc.
14. E. K. Chambers, *Shakespeare: A Survey*, p. 209.

all," says Mistress Overdone to Lucio and his friends. Claudio is first introduced, bearing himself with dignity under his sudden arrest. He sends his friend Lucio to his sister in her cloister, to beg her to intercede for him, because, he says,

> in her youth
> There is a prone and speechless dialect,
> Such as move men; beside, she hath prosperous art
> When she will play with reason and discourse,
> And well she can persuade.

Such descriptions of characters before they appear—perhaps before Shakespeare had written a word for them to speak—have surely a great weight. They show how Shakespeare wished the audience to see them. Isabel's characteristic when she does appear is exactly this mixture of winning silence with persuasive speech.

But before she can reach Angelo, his colleague Escalus has already interceded for Claudio, urging that, had time cohered with place, and place with wishing, Angelo might himself have fallen. Angelo replies:

> When I, that censure him, do so offend,
> Let mine own judgment pattern out my death,
> And nothing come in partial. Sir, he must die.

Isabel begins her pleading slowly and with characteristic silences: then she grows eloquent, and to Angelo's stern refusal she at last replies:

> I would to Heaven I had your potency,
> And you were Isabel! Should it then be thus?
> No; I would tell what 'twere to be a judge,
> And what a prisoner.

Isabel has no notion as yet of the depth of sin which may have to be pardoned in Angelo. But there is "dramatic irony" behind these two speeches, and we can forecast that in the end the places will be reversed: the fate of the convicted Angelo depending upon Isabel.

The phrase "dramatic irony" may be misunderstood. Shakespeare, like Sophocles, puts into the mouths of his characters words which they speak in all sincerity, but which, as the play proceeds, will be found to have a deeper meaning than the speaker knew. Dramatic irony does *not* mean that, at every turn, we are justified in suspecting that Shakespeare may have meant the reverse of what he makes his characters say. When he does that ("honest Iago") he leaves us in no doubt. As a great American critic has put it: "However much the *dramatis personae* mystify each other, the audience is never to be perplexed."[15]

It is a marked feature of the plays which Shakespeare was producing about the same time as *Measure for Measure,* that their early scenes contain "ironical," ominous lines, forecasting the conclusion:

Brabantio. She has deceived her father, and may thee.

Othello. My life upon her faith. Honest Iago . . .
(*Othello*, I.ii)

Lady Macbeth. A little water clears us of this deed.
(*Macbeth*, II.i)

This is meant to forecast her later:

What, will these hands ne'er be clean?
(*Macbeth*, V.i)

Edmund. Sir, I shall study deserving.

Gloster. He hath been out nine years, and away he shall again.
(*Lear*, I.i)

But before Gloster can send him out again, Edmund lies dying with the words "The wheel is come full circle."

To Angelo and to Isabel the wheel will come full circle. Will Isabel then remember the pleas which she now pours forth? "Well she can persuade." Her marvelous and impassioned pleadings, unsurpassed anywhere in Shake-

15. G. L. Kittredge, *op. cit.,* p. 20.

speare, are based on her Christian faith, and upon the Sermon on the Mount: all men are pardoned sinners, and *must* forgive:

> Why, all the souls that were, were forfeit once;
> And he that might the vantage best have took
> Found out the remedy.

"Judge not, that ye be not judged. For with what measure ye mete, it shall be measured to you again." *Measure for Measure*. But how is the Sermon on the Mount to be reconciled with the practical necessities of government? That is the problem which puzzles people—and particularly perhaps young people—so much today. In the Tudor Age men met it by exalting Government. The king is "the image of God's majesty": to him, and to his government, the divine office of rule and punishment is committed. The private man must submit and forgive. Accordingly, Angelo appeals to his "function": and there is real force in his answers to Isabel—if we remember, as we always must, that, for the purposes of the play, Claudio is supposed guilty of a capital offense.

Never does Shakespeare seem more passionately to identify himself with any of his characters than he does with Isabel, as she pleads for mercy against strict justice:

> O, it is excellent
> To have a giant's strength; but it is tyrannous
> To use it like a giant. . . .
>   man, proud man,
> Drest in a little brief authority . . .
>   like an angry ape
> Plays such fantastic tricks before high heaven
> As make the angels weep. . . .

"Man, proud man" is the man who, "drest in authority," condemns his fellow men. The "fantastic tricks" which such an unforgiving man plays "like an angry ape" make the angels weep; because it is the function of angels to rejoice over one sinner that repenteth. Yet portions of these lines are constantly quoted,[16] divorced from their context, as if they were Shakespeare's generalization about all actions of all mankind, when, in fact, they are the words he gives to a distressed sister pleading before a hardhearted, proud, self-righteous authoritarian. To Shakespeare, we are told, "man is now no more than 'an angry Ape.'" And so, Isabel's protest against the proud self-righteous man who condemns his fellow men, is turned by the critics into Shakespeare's proud, self-righteous condemnation of his fellow men.

But the unforgiving Angelo is himself about to fall, though not without a sincere struggle. More than one of Isabel's pleadings find a mark which she never meant:

> Go to your bosom;
> Knock there, and ask your heart what it doth know
> That's like my brother's fault . . .
> Hark how I'll bribe you . . .

Angelo has thought himself superior to human weakness, because he is free from the vulgar vices of a Lucio. And the "beauty of mind" of a distressed, noble woman throws him off his balance.[17] If we fail to see the nobility of Isabel, we cannot see the story as we should. The plot is rather like that of Calderon's *Magician,* where the scholarly, austere Cipriano is overthrown by speaking with the saintly Justina. Cipriano sells himself literally to the Devil to gain his end by magic. Angelo tempts Isabel in a second dialogue, as wonderful as the first. In her innocence Isabel is slow to see Angelo's drift, and it is only her confession of her own frailty that gives him a chance of making himself clear. "Nay," Isabel says,

> call us ten times frail;
> For we are soft as our complexions are,
> And credulous to false prints.

If Shakespeare is depicting in Isabel the self-righteous

16. E. K. Chambers, *op. cit.,* p. 213; J. Dover Wilson, *op. cit.,* p. 123; U. M. Ellis-Fermor, *The Jacobean Drama,* p. 261.
17. Cf. John Masefield, *William Shakespeare,* p. 179.

prude which some critics would make of her, he goes strangely to work.

But when she perceives Angelo's meaning, Isabel decides without hesitation. Now whatever we think of that instant decision, it is certainly not un-Christian. Christianity could never have lived through its first three hundred years of persecution, if its ranks had not been stiffened by men and women who never hesitated in the choice between righteousness and the ties to their kinsfolk. We may call this fanaticism: but it was well understood in Shakespeare's day. Foxe's *Martyrs* was read by all; old people could still remember seeing the Smithfield fires; year after year saw the martyrdoms of Catholic men (and sometimes of Catholic women like the Ven. Margaret Clitherow). It was a stern age—an age such as the founder of Christianity had foreseen when he uttered his stern warnings. "He that loveth father or mother more than me . . ." "If any man come to me, and hate not his father, and mother, . . . and brethren and sisters, . . . he cannot be my disciple."[18]

It is recorded of Linacre, the father of English medicine, that, albeit a priest, he opened his Greek New Testament for the first time late in life, and came on some of these hard sayings. "Either this is not the Gospel," he said, "or we are not Christians," and refusing to contemplate the second alternative, he flung the Book from him and returned to the study of medicine. Now it is open to us to say that we are not Christians: it is not open to us to say that Isabel is un-Christian. She goes to her brother, not because she hesitates, but that he may share with her the burden of her irrevocable decision. Claudio's first reply is, "O heavens! it cannot be"; "Thou shalt not do't." But the very bravest of men have quailed, within the four walls of a prison cell, waiting for the ax next day. I am amazed at the way critics condemn Claudio, when he breaks down, and utters his second thoughts, "Sweet sister, let me live." Isabel overwhelms him in the furious speech which we all know. And I am even more amazed at the dislike which the critics feel for the tor-

18. Matthew 10:37; Luke 14:26.

tured Isabel. But when they assure us that their feeling
towards both his creatures was shared by the gentle
Shakespeare, I am then most amazed of all.

It is admitted that no greater or more moving scenes
had appeared on any stage, since the masterpieces of
Attic drama ceased to be acted. Yet our critics tell us that
Shakespeare wrote them in a mood of "disillusionment
and cynicism," "self-laceration" and, strangest of all,
"weariness."[19] "A corroding atmosphere of moral suspicion"[20] hangs about this debate between "the sainted
Isabella, wrapt in her selfish chastity," and "the wretched
boy who in terror of death is ready to sacrifice his sister's
honor."[21] Isabel's chastity, they say, is "rancid," and she
is "not by any means such a saint as she looks";[22] her
inhumanity is pitiless, her virtue is self-indulgent, unimag-
inative, and self-absorbed.[23]

And yet, think of Rose Macaulay's war poem, "Many
sisters to many brothers," and let us believe that a sister
may suffer more in agony of mind than the brother can
suffer in physical wounds or death. Shakespeare has made
Isabel say to Claudio,

> O, were it but my life,
> I'ld throw it down for your deliverance
> As frankly as a pin.

It is standing the play on its head,[24] to say that Shakespeare wrote those words in irony and cynicism. How did
he convey that to his audience? If such assumptions are
allowed, we can prove anything we like, "eight years to-

19. J. Dover Wilson, *op. cit.,* pp. 116, 117.
20. E. K. Chambers, *op. cit.,* p. 214.
21. J. Dover Wilson, *op. cit.,* p. 116.
22. New Cambridge Shakespeare, *Measure for Measure,* p. xxx.
23. U. M. Ellis-Fermor, *op. cit.,* pp. 261, 262.
24. I borrow this very excellent phrase from W. W. Lawrence (p. 70).
The brevity of a lecture compels me to pass over many points that a critic
may think should have been more fully argued, but I do this the more
cheerfully, because they have been already so fully discussed by Lawrence
in his *Shakespeare's Problem Comedies,* 1931, and their moral emphasized
in an excellent leading article in *The Times Literary Supplement* of 16
July 1931.

gether, dinners and suppers and sleeping-hours excepted."

Isabel then, as Shakespeare sees her and asks us to see her, would frankly, joyously, give her life to save Claudio: and *"greater love hath no man than this."* And now Claudio is asking for what she cannot give, and she bursts out in agony. Have the critics never seen a human soul or a human body in the extremity of torment? Physical torture Isabel thinks she could have stood without flinching. She has said so to Angelo:

> The impression of keen whips I'ld wear as rubies,
> And strip myself to death, as to a bed
> That longing have been sick for, ere I'ld yield
> My body up to shame.

To suppose that Shakespeare gave these burning words to Isabel so that we should perceive her to be selfish and cold, is to suppose that he did not know his job. The honor of her family and her religion are more to her than mere life, her own or Claudio's.

There are those, like Sir George Greenwood, who prefer to the character of Isabel that of the heroine of the original story—Cassandra, who was willing to endure all shame to save her brother's life. The New Cambridge Shakespeare quotes this dictum of Sir George with more approval than it would give to his other dicta. And we may agree that from such a story a noble, if harrowing, tragedy might be made. There is no need to play the moralist, and to condemn either Cassandra or Isabel. "Wisdom is justified of all her children." Faced by a dire choice, different souls may make different decisions, which for each may be the right decision. Shakespeare has chosen to depict Isabel as one who cannot yield. And most of those who have criticized her, from Hazlitt downwards, agree that she cannot. And she has got to make that clear to Claudio. It is just here that her critics quarrel with her. Sir Arthur Quiller-Couch digs out Mrs. Charlotte Lennox from the obscurity of the mid-eighteenth century to tell us how the scene should have been written. Isabel, Charlotte says, should have made use of her superior understanding to reason down Claudio's fears, recall nobler ideas to his mind, teach him what was due to her honor and his own, and reconcile him to his approaching death by arguments drawn from that religion and virtue of which she made so high a profession.

"To reason down Claudio's fears!" "By arguments drawn from religion and virtue!" Why, the Duke had just preached to Claudio the most eloquent Sermon Against the Fear of Death that has ever been written since Lucretius completed his Third Book. Claudio had expressed himself convinced; and then the Duke's discourse had shriveled like a thread in the flame of Claudio's longing for life.

How will pi-jaw help Claudio? Shakespeare imagined Claudio as a good lad, but not, like his sister, devout; he doesn't keep devout company, exactly. Isabel "well can persuade." She is one of a few women in Shakespeare who can persuade. (Not Portia: "The quality of mercy is not strain'd" produces no persuasion in the soul of Shylock.) Volumnia is a special case. The other great persuaders are: Isabel, Beatrice, and Lady Macbeth. And they all use the same arguments—the arguments which, I expect, the first cave woman, when in dire straits, used to her cave man: You are a coward; You have no love or respect for me; I have no love for you.

Isabel is the most vehement of the three. Sisterly technique has its own rules; there is a peculiar freedom about the talk of those who have known each other from babyhood. And Isabel can appeal to the honor of the family. Escalus, when he first pleaded for Claudio, remembered his "most noble father." Isabel had exclaimed, when she first found Claudio firm,

> there my father's grave
> Did utter forth a voice.

And now she cries,

> Heaven shield my mother play'd my father fair.

Isabel appeals to the passion which, in an Elizabethan gentleman, may be presumed to be stronger than the fear of death—pride in his gentle birth and in the courage which should mark it. Don't people see that there are things about which we cannot argue calmly? The fierceness of Isabel's words is the measure of the agony of her soul. "The fortress which parleys, the woman who parleys, is lost." I grant that, at the end of a lifetime's training, a saint like Thomas More could smile on his daughter when she tempted him, "What, Mistress Eve?" But the young martyrs are apt to be more stern, whether it be Cordelia or Antigone, the spitfire St. Eulalia, or St. Juliana putting the fear of death upon the Devil. Who but a pedant would blame them? And it is our fault if we don't see that Isabel is suffering martyrdom none the less because her torment is mental, not physical.

One of the most significant of Shakespeare's alterations of his original is to make the heroine a "votarist of St. Clare." At the root of the movement of St. Francis and St. Clare was the intense remembrance of the sufferings of Christ, in atonement for the sins of the whole world—the "remedy" of which Isabel in vain reminds Angelo. Isabel, as a novice, is testing herself to see whether she is called to that utter renunciation which is the life of the "poor Clare." Whether she remains in the Convent or no, one who is contemplating such a life can no more be expected to sell herself into mortal sin, than a good soldier can be expected to sell a stronghold entrusted to him.

Imagine an officer and his subaltern commanded to hold to the uttermost a fortified post against rebels. In a sortie the rebels capture the subaltern, and threaten to shoot him unless the fort surrenders. The subaltern breaks down, and implores his commandant to save his life. I can imagine that the commandant would reply, firmly but gently, that surrender is impossible. But suppose the subaltern were his beloved younger brother, or his only son. I can imagine that then the commandant would reply to his son's appeal by passionate denunciation, telling him that he is a disgrace to his family. To discuss the matter calmly would lead to the surrender which he knows he

must not make: his instinct would tell him that. So, at
least, it seems to me in my ignorance. And when I find
Shakespeare in his wisdom depicting the matter so, I
don't see anything cynical about it.

Those who dislike the vehemence of Isabel would do
well, in Ben Jonson's phrase, to "call forth Sophocles to
us," and to ponder on the *Philoctetes.* In that play
Neoptolemus is asked to sell his honor and betray his
father's friend by a base lie, for the good of his country,
and for the ultimate good of the friend who is to be deceived. Neoptolemus refuses indignantly, but he lets himself be drawn into discussion, and so sells his honor and
his friend. But the anticipated good does not follow, and
Neoptolemus has to make amends to his friend, though
this means treason to the Greek army. The play is ending, with Neoptolemus deserting the army and even contemplating war against his own countrymen, when the
god appears from the machine to solve the knot. All this
follows because Neoptolemus listens and debates when
he hears the voice of the tempter: "Now give thyself to
me for one short, shameless day, and then, for the rest
of thy time, be called of all mortals the most righteous."
We cannot argue with the tempter, when our own desires
are already so much enlisted on his side. We can only
refuse, instinctively, vehemently.

It is precisely the alternation of vehemence with silence
which gives Isabel her individuality. When she first understands the drift of Angelo's temptation, the poor child
flies at him with a pathetic attempt at blackmail: "Sign
me a present pardon for my brother, or . . . I'll tell the
world . . ." When she is told that Angelo has slain Claudio, she exclaims:

O, I will to him and pluck out his eyes!

Shakespeare sometimes puts his heroines in pairs, cou-
pling the fierce, vehement girl with the gentle, swoon-
ing girl: Hermia with Helena, Beatrice with Hero, Isabel
with Mariana. For all her silence and modesty, Isabel has
the ferocity of the martyr. Yet I don't think Shakespeare

disliked his vixens. Hermia has nails which can reach her enemy's eyes. Benedick foresaw a predestinate scratched face for the husband of Beatrice. Yet would any of us take Hero in to dinner, if we could get Beatrice, or go hiking through the Athenian forest with Helena, if we could get Hermia?

Critics ask, as does Sir Edmund Chambers, whether Isabel too "has not had her ordeal, and in her turn failed," whether she was "wholly justified in the eyes of her creator." They are entitled to ask the question. But they ought to wait for the answer. The Duke enters, takes Claudio aside, and tells him there is no hope for him. And we find that Claudio, who before Isabel's outburst had been gripped by the mortal fear of death, is now again master of his soul:

> Let me ask my sister pardon. I am so out of love with life,
> that I will sue to be rid of it.

"Hold you there," says the Duke. Claudio does. Later, we see him quiet and self-possessed when the Provost shows him his death warrant. To the Provost he is "the most gentle Claudio": and to Shakespeare, the word "gentle" is a word of very high praise, not consistent with any want of spirit.[25] "Gentle" and "most gentle" is how his worthy friends and fellows—Ben Jonson, Heminges, Condell—described Shakespeare. Claudio, "most gentle" in his prison, has passed his ordeal well, showing quiet courage equally removed from the hilarity of a Posthumus and the insensibility of a Barnardine.

Mrs. Lennox says that Isabel ought to have taught Claudio what is due to her honor and his own. She has.

Now, if Isabel's speech had been intended to depict a "cold" and "remorseless" woman, "all for saving her own soul," acting cruelly to her brother in the "fiery ordeal" which (we are told) "his frail soul proves ill-fitted to endure," why does Shakespeare show Claudio, far from resenting his sister's reproaches, only wishing to ask her

25. "He's gentle, and not fearful," says Miranda to Prospero, warning him not to presume too much on Ferdinand's patience.

pardon, and henceforth courageous and resolute? Why, above all, does Shakespeare make the Duke, when he overhears Isabel's whole speech, comment on the beauty of her goodness? This is intelligible only if Shakespeare means Isabel's speech to be an agonized outcry, working on her brother as no calm reasoning could have done. If Shakespeare's critics think they could have written the scene better, they are welcome to try; but it does not follow that Shakespeare was a disillusioned cynic because he did not write Isabel's speech as Charlotte Lennox would have done.

When the Duke suggests that Isabel may yet be able to save her brother, she replies, "I have spirit to do any thing that appears not foul in the truth of my spirit." And now Isabel's critics disapprove of her because of the "businesslike" way in which she sets about saving her brother and assisting the Duke's plot. If Shakespeare's Jacobean audiences were as perverse as his modern critics, I can well understand how "gloom and dejection" may have driven the poor man "to the verge of madness," as critics assert that it did. That Shakespeare imagined Isabel as businesslike, should be clear to anyone who studies with care her words in the earlier scenes. She is a sensible Elizabethan girl, with no nonsense about her, and she knows that it is no sin to bring husband and wife together.

So Mariana takes Isabel's place, to save Claudio's life.

Again, if Shakespeare meant us to regard Isabel cynically, why did he picture her not only as touching by her goodness both Angelo and the Duke, though to different issues, but even as awing the frivolous Lucio into sobriety and sympathy? To Lucio she is "a thing ensky'd and sainted,"

> an immortal spirit;
> And to be talk'd with in sincerity,
> As with a saint.

Sir Arthur disqualifies Lucio's evidence because Lucio is a sensualist, and sensualists, he says, habitually divide women into angels and those who are "their animal prey."[26] Even if that be true, could Shakespeare seriously expect his audience to grasp such a subtlety? Critics see Isabel "hard as an icicle."[27] If Shakespeare meant that, why did he make Lucio see her differently: "O pretty Isabella, I am pale at mine heart to see thine eyes so red."[28] Even a sensualist can tell when people's eyes are red.

Angelo's own words make it clear that it is his conviction of the innocence and goodness of Isabel which overthrows him.

As for Claudio—the critics may despise him, but Angelo knows better. He knows that Claudio is a plucky lad who, "receiving a dishonor'd life with ransom of such shame," might take his revenge in time to come. So he commands Claudio's execution. The Duke, of course, prevents it, and continues to weave his toils round Angelo, till the moment when he will fall on him, and grind him to powder.

And, immediately, Angelo's remorse begins. He realizes what he really is: "This deed unshapes me quite." Yet his state is more gracious now, when he believes himself to be a perjured adulterer, than it was a few days before, when he believed himself to be a saint.

I pass over the agonies of Angelo's repentance. "Dull to all proceedings," he fights to maintain all that is left him, the "credent bulk" of a public esteem which has become a mockery to him. When Lucio brings the struggle to an end, by tearing the Friar's hood off the Duke, Angelo realizes that his master is one from whom no secrets are hid:

> *Duke.* Hast thou or word, or wit, or impudence,
> That yet can do thee office? . . .
>
> *Angelo.*   O my dread lord,
> I should be guiltier than my guiltiness,
> To think I can be undiscernible,

26. New Cambridge Shakespeare, p. xxvii.
27. U. M. Ellis-Fermor, *op. cit.*, p. 262.
28. IV.iii.153–54.

When I perceive your Grace, like power divine,
Hath looked upon my passes.

A cold-hearted, self-righteous prig is brought to a sense of what he is, in the sight of his master. A few hours before, Angelo had turned a deaf ear to the plea "Why, all the souls that were, were forfeit once." But now he can conceive no depth of guilt so deep as his own. "Guiltier than my guiltiness." It is like the repentance of Enobarbus, "I am alone the villain of the earth," or of Posthumus,

> it is I
> That all the abhorred things o' the earth amend
> By being worse than they.

For Angelo, as for Enobarbus and for Posthumus, nothing remains save a passionate prayer to be put out of his misery:

> Then, good prince,
> No longer session hold upon my shame,
> But let my trial be mine own confession:
> Immediate sentence then, and sequent death,
> Is all the grace I beg.

Surely it is concerning repentance like this that it is written, "There is joy in the presence of the angels of God." The ninety and nine just persons which need no repentance naturally think otherwise. Coleridge began the outcry against *Measure for Measure,* which he found "the most painful—say rather the only painful—part" of Shakespeare's genuine works. The pardon of Angelo, he says, "baffles the strong indignant claim of justice—(for cruelty, with lust and damnable baseness, cannot be forgiven, because we cannot conceive them as being morally repented of)."[29] Swinburne endorsed this judgment at great length. Justice, he said, "is buffeted, outraged, insulted, struck in the face." "We are tricked out of our dole, defeated of our due, lured and led on to look for

29. *Notes on Shakespeare.*

some equitable and satisfying upshot, defrauded and de-
rided and sent empty away."[30] Hazlitt could not allow
Mariana to love Angelo "whom we hate."[31] To enumerate
the ninety-six other just persons would be to write a bibliography of *Measure for Measure,* which is no part of
my intention. Rather I turn to Mariana as she implores
pardon for her husband. Coleridge thought the pardon
and marriage of Angelo not only unjust, but degrading
to the character of woman. Yet repentance, intercession,
and forgiveness are the stuff of Christianity and of the
old stories of Christendom. In the story which Calderon
used, Cipriano, after selling himself to the Devil in order
to win Justina to his will, repents and dies a martyr at her
side, comforted by her words: "So many stars has not
the Heaven, so many grains of sand the sea, not so many
sparks the fire, not so many motes the sunlight, as the
sins which He forgives."

But the Duke again and again rejects Mariana's plea
for mercy. She turns at last to Isabel:

> Sweet Isabel, take my part;
> Lend me your knees and all my life to come
> I'll lend you all my life to do you service.

Isabel stands silent.

It is many years ago that I saw acted, within this building where we are now met, Calderon's *Life is a Dream,*
in the version of Edward FitzGerald. In that play Basilio,
King of Poland, has learnt from his study of the stars
that his newborn son will end by trampling on his father's
head. So Prince Segismund is kept, from his birth, in a
cruel prison, not knowing who he is. But his father, re-
lenting, determines to test whether he has read the stars
aright: so he brings Segismund drugged to the palace.
There Segismund awakes to find himself heir to the throne
of Poland; but he abuses his one day of power, and is
carried back in sleep again to his prison, to be told that

30. *Study of Shakespeare.*
31. *Characters of Shakespeare's Plays.*

all that he has seen and done that day has been a dream. Yet later the mutinous army releases him. Segismund marches at the head of the army, not knowing whether he dreams or no, and his victories end with the King Basilio kneeling humbled at the feet of his wronged son.

What will Segismund now do? Has he learnt how to forgive, the greatest thing that can be learnt from the Dream which is called Life?

It is not often that one can see a classical masterpiece acted without knowing how it will end. Whether it was the acting of Miss Margaret Halstan, who took the part of the boy prince, or the stage production of Mr. Poel, I have never since felt the suspense of a great scene as I felt that. I like to think that those who first saw Shakespeare's play acted at the Christmas revels of 1604 may perhaps have felt such a suspense. The title, *Measure for Measure,* gave them no clue as to the ending.

A second time Mariana appeals:

> Isabel,
> Sweet Isabel, do yet but kneel by me;
> Hold up your hands, say nothing, I'll speak all.

Still Isabel stands silent, whilst Mariana pleads on pitifully:

> They say, best men are molded out of faults;
> And, for the most, become much more the better
> For being a little bad: so may my husband.

At her third appeal,

> O Isabel, will you not lend a knee?

Isabel kneels at the feet of the Duke.

While Isabel is pleading for his life, Angelo is longing for death. Escalus turns to him, regretting his fall. Angelo only says:

> I am sorry that such sorrow I procure:
> And so deep sticks it in my penitent heart,

> That I crave death more willingly than mercy;
> 'Tis my deserving, and I do entreat it.

The wheel is come full circle.
Only two days before, Angelo had rejected the plea of mercy for Claudio with the words

> When I, that censure him, do so offend,
> Let mine own judgment pattern out my death.

And Isabel had longed for the potency of Angelo that she might "tell what 'twere to be a judge, and what a prisoner." Later we have seen Angelo "unshaped" by his remorse, though still confident that he will escape undetected, whilst Isabel longs to "pluck out his eyes," and is promised revenges to her heart on "this wretch" who has murdered her brother. And now Angelo, publicly shamed, longing for death, faces an Isabel who can bring herself to say, after an agony of silent struggle, "let him not die." It was not in a spirit of "weariness, cynicism, and disgust" that the Master Craftsman made the whirligig of time bring in revenges like these.

Isabel's sufferings are over. The Provost produces the muffled Claudio. Sister meets brother with that "prone and speechless dialect" which moves, or should move, men.

Sir Edmund Chambers asks, Why does the Duke conceal from Isabel in her grief the knowledge that her brother yet lives? Sir Walter Raleigh asked the same question thirty years ago. His answer was that the reason is dramatic; the crisis must be kept for the end. And, as a piece of stagecraft, the ending justifies itself; it is magnificent. But Sir Edmund Chambers is surely right when he says that a play dealing seriously with the problems of life must be taken seriously; the Duke, he thinks, symbolizes the workings of Providence. Is not such treatment of Providence, then, he asks, ironical?

The Duke certainly reminds us of the ways of Providence. And we feel so in the great final scene, where Mariana is imploring the silent Isabel to intercede for

Angelo. Why, then, does the Duke gather up all his authority, as former friar and present monarch, and crash it, with a lie, in the path Isabel must tread?

> Should she kneel down in mercy of this fact,
> Her brother's ghost his paved bed would break,
> And take her hence in horror.

Yet all this time the Duke is keeping her brother in reserve, to produce him when Isabel shall have fulfilled her destiny, by making intercession for the man she most hates.

If we are thinking of the Duke as a character in the play, this is difficult to understand. Equally difficult is it to understand the Hermione of the last scene in *The Winter's Tale*. We cannot imagine the wronged queen of the first three acts shamming death, and tormenting her husband with sixteen years of remorse. There is, of course, the dramatic effect; but is there not also something more? Is there not something symbolic of a mysterious power, when, in the *Alcestis,* Heracles seems to torment Admetus before he restores his wife to him?

> It was the crowning grace of that great heart,
> To keep back joy, procrastinate the truth.[32]

If it be said that this torturing of Isabel,

> To make her heavenly comforts of despair
> When it is least expected,

is unbearably cruel, I can only reply that life undoubtedly is sometimes like that. There are some souls (Isabel is one) for whom it is decreed that no trial, however agonizing, no pain, however atrocious, is to be spared them. Nevertheless, it is also true that there is no trial so agonizing, no pain so atrocious, but that some souls can rise above it, as Isabel does when, despite the Duke's stern warning, she kneels at his feet to intercede for Angelo.

32. Browning, *Balaustion's Adventure.*

Is it then true, as Sir Arthur Quiller-Couch says, that Isabel writes no lesson on the dark walls, and that they teach none to her soul? Or is it true when Sir Edmund Chambers echoes the complaint of Coleridge, and says that *Measure for Measure* "just perplexes and offends," because there is no poetic justice? Is it true that "to no profit of righteousness has Isabella's white soul been dragged through the mire"?

I know that many readers find a stumbling block in this culminating scene, in Isabel's pleading for Angelo. Why should she plead, they ask, for her brother's murderer?

We must be prepared to accept the postulates of Shakespeare's plays, as we do, for example, of Sophocles' *Oedipus Tyrannus*. And, generally, we are so prepared: we accept the caskets and the pound of flesh, King Lear's love test and Prospero's art. It is a postulate of our story that Claudio has committed a capital offense. Angelo has not committed a crime in letting the law take its course upon Claudio; he has not committed a crime in his union with Mariana, to whom he has been publicly betrothed; those are assumptions on which the play is based. Angelo would be despicable if he put forward any such plea for himself, and he does not. But the fact remains that Angelo's sin has been, not in act, but in thought, and human law cannot take cognizance of thought: "thoughts are no subjects." Besides, Isabel is conscious that, however innocently, she herself has been the cause of Angelo's fall:

> I partly think
> A due sincerity govern'd his deeds,
> Till he did look on me; since it is so,
> Let him not die.

And Angelo is penitent. There can be no doubt what the words of the Sermon on the Mount demand: "Judge not, and ye shall not be judged." That had been Isabel's plea for Claudio. It is a test of her sincerity, if she can put forward a plea for mercy for her dearest foe, as well as for him whom she dearly loves.

Criticism of *Measure for Measure,* from Coleridge

downwards, has amounted to this: "There is a limit to
human charity." "There is," says Chesterton's Father
Brown, "and that is the real difference between human
charity and Christian charity." Isabel had said the same:

> O, think on that;
> And mercy then will breathe within your lips
> Like man new made.

Shakespeare has so manipulated the story as to make it
end in Isabel showing more than human charity to Angelo,
whilst at the same time he has avoided, by the introduction of Mariana, the error, which he found in his crude
original, of wedding Isabel to Angelo.

Yet we are told that in *Measure for Measure* "the evidence of Shakespeare's profound disillusionment and discouragement of spirit is plain enough," that "the search-
light of irony is thrown upon the paths of Providence
itself."[33]

The way in which the Duke, an earthly Providence, tor-
tures Isabel till he wrings her agonized forgiveness out
of her, reminds us of the way in which, in Shakespeare's
contemporary tragedies, Providence seems to ordain that
no suffering is spared to Lear or Cordelia, to Othello or
Desdemona. It is very terrible. But it cannot be called,
as it often is called, un-Christian, or "an indictment of
man's maker," or "a definite arraignment of the scheme
of things," or "the final victory of evil."[34] For in that
case the representation would leave us desperate or rebel-
lious. And it does not.[35] Lear and Othello, Cordelia and
Desdemona rise "superior to the world in which they
appear."[36] That wise critic, A. C. Bradley, has said:

> The extremity of the disproportion between prosperity
> and goodness first shocks us, and then flashes on us the
> conviction that our whole attitude in asking or expecting

33. E. K. Chambers, in the *Encyclopaedia Britannica* (1911), XXIV,
785.
34. *Idem, Shakespeare: A Survey*, pp. 215, 220, 231, 247.
35. A. C. Bradley, *Shakespearean Tragedy*, p. 26.
36. *Ibid.*, p. 324.

that goodness should be prosperous is wrong; that, if only we could see things as they are, we should see that the outward is nothing and the inward is all.[37]

It is a thought which is difficult to express, and Bradley felt his own statement to be "exaggerated and too explicit." But the thought that "Whosoever will lose his life shall find it," or, as Kent in the stocks put it, "Nothing almost sees miracles but misery," was, perhaps, more generally understood by the Englishmen of Shakespeare's day than it is now. Mr. Bettenham, Reader of Gray's Inn, was wont to say "that virtuous men were like some herbs and spices, that give not their sweet smell, till they be broken and crushed." And Francis Bacon, of the same Inn, put this doctrine into his essay *Of Adversity,* to show that "Prosperity is the blessing of the Old Testament; adversity is the blessing of the New, which carrieth the greater benediction, and the clearer revelation of God's favor."

And I heard A. E. Housman, who, of all men I have known, was sternest in refusing to break his proud reserve, say in his first lecture:

> Fortitude and continence and honesty are not commended to us on the ground that they conduce, as on the whole they do conduce, to material success, nor yet on the ground that they will be rewarded hereafter: those whose office it is to exhort mankind to virtue are ashamed to degrade the cause they plead by proffering such lures as these.

Forty-one years later, in his last great public utterance, in which he bade us "Farewell forever," he quoted: "Whosoever will save his life shall lose it, and whosoever will lose his life shall find it." "That," he said, "is the most important truth which has ever been uttered, and the greatest discovery ever made in the moral world; but I do not find in it anything which I should call poetical."[38]

37. *Ibid.,* p. 326.
38. *Introductory Lecture,* 1892, p. 36; *Name and Nature of Poetry,* 1933, p. 36.

Now it would take me altogether out of my depth to discuss whether there is anything poetical in those words. But it can surely be contended that Shakespearean tragedy is an expression *in poetry* of that "most important truth which has ever been uttered." And so, equally, is *Measure for Measure* an expression of "the greatest discovery ever made in the moral world": the highly unpleasant discovery that there are things more important, for oneself and for others, than avoiding death and pain.

That, of course, is not a Christian discovery. One of the founders of modern Japan uttered it in two lines of Chinese verse, as he was led to execution, speaking with a loud voice, so that he might take farewell of his friend without implicating him by turning his head:

> It is better to be a crystal and be broken
> Than to remain perfect like a tile upon the housetop.

It is not Christian: but it is a foundation upon which Christianity, in common with every other religion worth the name, is built.

Measure for Measure is a play of forgiveness, more distinctly even than *The Tempest*. Isabel forgives in her moment of direst loss: Prospero only when he has recovered his Dukedom. Isabel urges forgiveness because a Christian must forgive: Prospero forgives because he does not condescend to torment his enemies further. And the contrast applies also to those forgiven. Angelo longs for death, because the Duke, "*like power divine,*" has seen his sinfulness. Sebastian and Antonio learn from Prospero, when he forgives them, that besides their crimes against him, he knows also how they have plotted to kill their king; to the pardoned Sebastian, just as to Angelo, there naturally seems to be something superhuman in such knowledge; but Sebastian expresses his conviction differently from Angelo:

> The devil speaks in him.

"No!" says Prospero; and then he turns to his brother Antonio:

> For you, most wicked Sir, whom to call brother
> Would even infect my mouth, I do forgive
> Thy rankest fault . . .

Antonio makes no answer to this forgiveness. But he and Sebastian, unabashed, continue their joyless jests to the end.

Now, when we mark how evil, and its forgiveness, is depicted in *Measure for Measure* in 1604, can we agree that Shakespeare's philosophy about 1604 was "obviously not a Christian philosophy"? On the contrary, it seems to me more definitely Christian than that of *The Tempest,* though I don't deny that the philosophy of the Romances can also be called Christian. I would not deny that, on the whole, Shakespeare's last plays *are* "happy dreams," "symbols of an optimistic faith in the beneficent dispositions of an ordering Providence."[39] But I see no ground to believe that there is any "complete breach" between the mood of 1604 and that of 1611, or that we must assume a "conversion," caused by "a serious illness which may have been a nervous breakdown, and on the other hand may have been merely the plague."[40]

We are told that the low-comedy characters of *Measure for Measure* are "unwholesome company": that whereas Shakespeare, in Falstaff and his associates, had represented sin as "human," he now represents it as "devilish."[41] But is this really so? Surely the answer was given by Sir Walter Raleigh years ago. These characters in *Measure for Measure* "are live men, pleasant to Shakespeare." Pompey is "one of those humble, cheerful beings, willing to help in anything that is going forward, who are the mainstay of human affairs . . . Froth is an amiable, feather-headed young gentleman—to dislike him would

39. E. K. Chambers, in the *Encyclopaedia Britannica* (1911), XXIV, 785.
40. *Idem, William Shakespeare,* 1930, I, 86, 274.
41. *Idem, Shakespeare: A Survey,* 1925, p. 211.

argue an ill-nature, and a small one . . . This world of Vienna, as Shakespeare paints it, is not a black world; it is a weak world, full of little vanities and stupidities, regardful of custom, fond of pleasure, idle, and abundantly human."[42]

As to Barnardine, his creator came to love him so much that he had not the heart to decapitate him, although Barnardine was only created to be decapitated.

In *Measure for Measure* sin is not represented as "devilish": it is represented as sinful, and that is necessitated by the serious and earnest character of the whole play. Yet the sinners do not altogether forfeit our sympathy. And when the unmasked Duke finally taxes Lucio with his slanders, he is not unequal to the occasion:

> Faith, my lord, I spoke it but according to the trick. If you will hang me for it, you may; but I had rather it would please you I might be whipt.

This, then, is how Shakespeare treats the barbarous old story of *Promos and Cassandra,* removing its morbid details, harmonizing its crudities, giving humanity and humor to its low characters, turning it into a consistent tale of intercession for sin, repentance from and forgiveness of crime. Yet *Measure for Measure* is adduced as the supreme proof that, about 1603, Shakespeare was in a mood of "self-laceration, weariness, discord, cynicism, and disgust."[43] He had been in that mood for the two years since the execution of Essex, and will remain in it for another four or five. This dominant mood of gloom and dejection will bring him on one occasion to the verge of madness, and lead him to write dramas greater than any other man ever wrote save Aeschylus and Sophocles alone. Then in 1608 Sir Edmund Chambers will cure him of his seven years of "profound disillusionment and discouragement of spirit" by giving him either the plague, or (alternatively) a nervous breakdown.

I hear a gentle voice from Stratford murmur

42. *Shakespeare*, p. 166.
43. J. Dover Wilson, *op. cit.*, p. 117.

Good frend, for Jesus sake forbeare.

Yet the critics have one final kick at *Measure for
Measure*. More Papistical than the Pope, they feel outraged that Isabel should "throw her novitiate headdress
over the mill"[44] and marry the Duke. Even the sober
A. C. Bradley thought that here Shakespeare lent himself
to "a scandalous proceeding."[45] Yet Isabel is a novice,
and her business as a novice is to learn her Creator's
intentions for her future. Whether she ought to return to
the cloister from which she has been so urgently summoned rests with her creator—William Shakespeare. And
he leaves her silent, and us guessing. For myself, I am
satisfied that Isabel will do her duty in that state of life
unto which it shall please William Shakespeare to call
her, whether as abbess or duchess.

Yet in Shakespeare's greatest plays, his greatest characters, for all their individuality, have also an imaginative,
a symbolic suggestion. It is so in *The Tempest*, it is so
in *Hamlet*. Thus also in the person of Lear, not only a
helpless old man, but Paternity and Royalty are outraged;
and "Glamis hath murder'd Sleep." No woman in Shakespeare is more individual than Isabel: silent yet eloquent,
sternly righteous yet capable of infinite forgiveness, a
very saint and a very vixen. But, first and last, she
"stands for" mercy.[46] The Duke is first shown to us as
a governor perplexed about justice, puzzled in his search
for righteousness, seeking above all things to know himself; and he becomes the arbiter of the destinies of every-
one in the play. Is it altogether fanciful to remember once
again that *Measure for Measure* was acted before the
court at Christmas, 1604: that when Isabel at the beginning urges her plea for mercy (which she also makes
good at the end) it is on the ground that

> He that might the vantage best have took
> Found out the remedy.

44. New Cambridge Shakespeare, p. xxxi.
45. *Shakespearean Tragedy*, p. 78.
46. This does not make her allegorical, any more than Beowulf is an
allegory because, as W. P. Ker says, he "stands for" valor.

The day before *Measure for Measure* was acted, the finding out of that remedy was being commemorated. All sober criticism must remember the part which the accepted theology played in the thought of Shakespeare's day; that the Feast of the Nativity was—is—the union of Divine Mercy and of Divine Righteousness, and was—is—celebrated in the Christmas psalm:

> Mercy and truth are met together: righteousness and peace have kissed each other.

Shakespeare's audience expected a marriage at the end: and, though it may be an accident, the marriage of Isabel and the Duke makes a good ending to a Christmas play.

But I hear my Japanese student objecting: "I imagine Lady Duchess can not be other than embarrassed, when she welcome Mr. Angel to marriage meal."

We have no business to imagine any such thing. The play is over. But, if we must go by imaginations, I will imagine with you. I imagine that, as they moved off the stage two and two, the Duke and Isabel, Claudio and Juliet, Angelo and Mariana, Abhorson and Barnardine bringing up the rear, Isabel broke silence, and said softly to the Duke, "Give me pardon that I, your vassal, should now beseech that you do intend the Lord Angelo for your swift ambassador to London. England is the place where the poor man will suffer least embarrassment, for in England they are such prudes that they rarely read and more rarely act *Measure for Measure;* although, my Duke"—and here Isabel turns to him with her "heavenly and yielding"[47] smile—"although you and I are agreed that, to us, it is the wisest of all Shakespeare's comedies."

And, to conclude. I have no excuse, save a love of Shakespeare, for trespassing on the specialist field of Shakespeare study. But it was a high adventure to leave Beowulf alone for a while in his contest with Grendel and the Dragon, and to do battle on behalf of pretty Isabel. Further, I have sought to rescue William Shakespeare from his seven years' imprisonment in the pestife-

47. W. W. Lawrence, *op. cit.,* p. 107. And may I here, once again, express my indebtedness to that great American scholar.

rous Cave of Despair, albeit thereby I have had to joust against Sir Arthur and Sir Edmund and the Lady Una Britomartis Ellis-Fermor, backed by all those spells which the Wizard professor of the North, the Prince of the Power of the Air, can weave from his chair amid the mists of high Dunedin. I realize how deeply fixed, by generations of repetition, is the dogma of Shakespeare's disillusioned early Jacobean period, "in the Depths." That is my excuse for venturing to repeat the protest, eloquently made in this place three years ago by Professor Sisson, in his discourse on "The Mythical Sorrows of Shakespeare."

I submit that *Measure for Measure,* whilst it is akin to the tragedies with which it is contemporary, has also a likeness to those "Romances" with which Shakespeare crowned his work. It is, indeed, for the continuity of Shakespeare that I am pleading. "Shakespeare's career is the career of an artist." Let us study his plays as the works of art which we know them to be, rather than weave baseless conjectures concerning details of a biography which we can never know. No one formula can summarize Shakespeare's life for us. Yet instead of always seeing him as suddenly plunged into the Depths, then raised by some convulsion to the Heights, might we not sometimes think of his career as a continuous progress to the Heights? We can trace the steady advance of Shakespeare's art, from *Henry VI* and *Richard III* to *Othello, Lear,* or *Macbeth;* or from the *Two Gentlemen* to *The Tempest*. We can also trace, I believe, the growth of a faith in the power of goodness, the growth of a belief that even in the valley of the shadow of death souls like Cordelia or Desdemona need fear no evil, that the beauty of such souls is Truth. It may be that Shakespeare felt the shadow closing upon him, when he made Prospero return to his Milan where

Every third thought shall be my grave.

Yet no one has rightly felt *The Tempest* to be pessimistic or gloomy.

That is all we know, and all we need to know. The real story is so wonderful that we can only mar it by groundless biographical conjectures. Our knowledge "can only be increased by minute and patient study, by the rejection of surmise about him, and by the constant public playing of his plays, in the Shakespearean manner, by actors who will neither mutilate nor distort what the great mind strove to make just."[48]

I deprecate attempts to define Shakespeare's theological beliefs or unbeliefs. But from his earliest plays to his latest, he shows a belief in forgiveness as the virtue by which human goodness draws nearest to the divine:

> Who by repentance is not satisfied
> Is nor of heaven nor earth, for these are pleased.[49]

And so far from agreeing that when he wrote *Measure for Measure* "he quite obviously believed in nothing," I submit that it is precisely the depth of his belief in forgiveness which has puzzled, in their judgment of that play, so many of his greatest critics, from Coleridge and Hazlitt and Swinburne, down to the present day. *Measure for Measure* shows "the drama of strong characters taking up and transforming the fanciful products of an earlier world, the inventions of minds not deeply or especially interested in character." The great poet (in the words of Aristotle, quoted by W. P. Ker) "gets over the unreason by the grace and skill of his handling."[50] Grace and skill have transformed *Promos and Cassandra* into a noble drama on the theme "Judge not: for with what measure ye mete it shall be measured to you again." It is that which matters, rather than any surviving traces of the original "unreason."

This series of Academy Shakespeare lectures was initiated by the great ambassador of France, Jusserand, who crossed the Atlantic from Washington in 1911 to tell us

---

48. John Masefield, *op. cit.*, p. 251.
49. *Two Gentlemen of Verona*, V.iv.
50. *Epic and Romance*, p. 37.

"What to expect of Shakespeare." He gave me (it is twenty-six years ago) the copy of his inaugural lecture now on the table before me. It is inscribed "To R. W. Chambers, who knows how to fight a good fight." I have tried to fight a good fight this afternoon. I believe that *Measure for Measure* and *The Tempest* are Shakespeare's greatest plays of forgiveness. It is for forgiveness I would ask, if I have hurt the feelings of any of the great English scholars from whom I have ventured to differ. And I shall receive it, for I know their generosity.

> As you from crimes would pardon'd be,
> Let your indulgence set me free.

MARY LASCELLES

from Shakespeare's "Measure for Measure"

. . . The Duke himself does not engage our concern by what he does, or suffers. How, we may fairly ask, does he—or should he—engage it? Criticism has for some while inclined towards the opinion that here is one of those persons in Shakespearean drama who should be regarded as important in respect rather of function than of character, and are to be interpreted as we should interpret the principal persons in allegory.[1] Now, the language of allegory is at least approximately translatable. These persons, therefore, must stand for something that can be expressed in other than allegorical terms, and the concept for which the Duke stands be capable of formulation in such terms as criticism may employ. What is this concept?

This is not an easy question to answer, nor are the answers so far proposed easy to discuss. Since those that suggest a religious allegory, and hint at a divine analogy, are shocking to me, and cannot be anything of the sort to those who have framed them, it must follow that my objections are all too likely to shock in their turn. This offense is apt to be mutual; for, where reverence is concerned, there is even less hope of reaching agreement by

From *Shakespeare's "Measure for Measure"* by Mary Lascelles. London: The Athlone Press, University of London, 1953; New York: John De Graff, Inc., 1954. Reprinted by permission of the Athlone Press.
1. This opinion is shared by those who find in the play an explicitly Christian meaning. See p. 41, above. [The number refers to Miss Lascelles' earlier allusion to G. Wilson Knight and R. W. Chambers.]

argument than in matters of taste. I would not willingly offend; but there is not room for compromise.

Let me recall the burden of the popular tale of the monstrous ransom: the situation in which the woman, the judge, and the ruler confronted one another signified power, exerted to its full capacity against weakness, and weakness (reduced to uttermost misery) gathering itself up to appeal beyond power to authority. Expressed thus, in simple and general terms, it seems indeed analogous with that allegory of divine might invoked to redress abuse of human inequality which is shadowed in Browning's *Instans Tyrannus*. But it should be remembered that such simplification obliterates one particular which, if fairly reckoned with, might forbid religious analogy: in the old tale, the ruler was distant, ignorant, brought to intervene only by uncommon exertion on the part of those whom his absence had exposed to oppression;[2] and none of the amplifications designed to make the tale more acceptable had done anything to shift or reduce this untoward circumstance. Indeed, by magnifying the whole, they made the part more obvious.

Lupton's *Siuqila* beyond the rest develops that element in the story which draws us to think about the maintenance of justice, not merely in the version it gives of this tale but also in the similar tales surrounding it. And it is notable that, whereas this one tale is told by the wretched Siuqila to show that even in his own country one who has no longer anything to lose will tell all and thus bring about retribution, Omen's tales are told to illustrate the happier state of Mauqsun. The theme of three of them is the success of the good ruler who goes about his domain incognito to discover and redress wrong. In one, a judge who waylays and interrogates suitors is able to rescue a woman from oppression. In both of the others, the king himself is shown using disguise and similar subterfuge, not only to obtain truth but also to make it publicly apparent. In one, he learns by means of his "privie Espials," who ride about the country at his com-

2. For this absence, a reason is usually given—seemingly, to forestall censure.

mand in the character of private gentlemen, the plight of a woman who has been ill used by her stepson. He hides her at court and lets it be rumored that she is dead; and, after much handling of witnesses, confronts the offender with his victim, and delivers sentence. The other tells how he "changed his apparell, making himselfe like a Servingmā, and went out at a privie Posterngate, and so enquired in the prisons, what prisoners were there," and was able to confute the cunning oppressor by bringing him face to face with the oppressed.

Now, in all these variations on a single theme, the activity of some magistrate or ruler—going about or sending out his agents, in disguise—*assists* in bringing smothered truth to light. Reflecting on opportune intervention in one,[3] Siuqila sums up the moral of all: "It was only the Lords working, that putte it into his heart" to speak with the woman who was secretly oppressed, and into hers to tell this stranger what she has hitherto forborne to utter; for "God works al this by marvellous means, if we would consider it, for the helping of the innocent and godly." Even under an ideal system of justice, that is, the discovery of wrong might well be impossible were it not for the intervention of divine providence, which, on some particular occasion, puts it into the heart of this or that human agent to make a pertinent inquiry. Now, this is in keeping with popular thought, which comes very near to supposing an element of caprice in divine government,[4] because it does not look ahead, but complacently descries pieces of pattern in particular events, without considering the ugly unreason of the total design which such parts must compose. But, how fearfully the distance between this false start and its logical conclusion diminishes, if the ruler is regarded not as agent but as emblem of divine providence! It is difficult to believe that those who would have us interpret the Duke's part so can have followed the implied train of thought all the way.

3. The story of the ill-used stepmother.
4. This is well exemplified by the speech of Whetstone's compassionate jailer, after he has released Andrugio (In *Promos and Cassandra*, IV.v).

The center of gravity for this interpretation is the passage in which Angelo capitulates to the alliance of knowledge and power in the reinstated Duke:

> Oh, my dread Lord,
> I should be guiltier than my guiltinesse,
> To thinke I can be undiscerneable,
> When I perceive your grace, like powre divine,
> Hath look'd upon my passes.[5]

On this Professor Wilson Knight comments:

> Like Prospero, the Duke tends to assume proportions
> evidently divine. Once he is actually compared to the
> Supreme Power.[6]

So to argue is surely to misunderstand the nature and usage of imagery—which does not liken a thing to itself. Yet this argument has been widely accepted; if not unreservedly, yet with reservations which do not reach the real difficulty. To suggest that the comparison may have been made "unconsciously" by Shakespeare, and to admit that "both the Duke in *Measure for Measure*, and Prospero, are endowed with characteristics which make it impossible for us to regard them as direct representatives of the Deity, such as we find in the miracle plays . . . Prospero, at least, [having] human imperfections"[7]—this is not enough. There will, of course, be human imperfections in any human representation, most plentiful where least desired, for what we ourselves are is most evident when we declare what we would be, in the endeavor to represent ideal beings. But observe where the prime fault occurs, in the character of this ruler: he is to blame in

5. V.i.369–73.
6. *The Wheel of Fire* (1949), p. 79.
7. S. L. Bethell, *Shakespeare and the Popular Dramatic Tradition* (1944), pp. 106–07. See also Leavis, "The Greatness of *Measure for Measure*," and Traversi, "*Measure for Measure*" (*Scrutiny,* January and Summer 1942). V. K. Whitaker ("Philosophy and Romance in Shakespeare's 'Problem' Comedies" in *The Seventeenth Century* by R. F. Jones and others, Stanford University Press, 1951, p. 353) suggests that this passage approaches as nearly to a reference to God "as Shakespeare could come under the law of 1605 against stage profanity"—an explanation which raises many more questions than it answers.

respect of the performance of that very function in virtue
of which he is supposedly to be identified with Divine
Providence. Read the sentence

> . . . I perceive your grace, like powre divine,
> Hath look'd upon my passes

as the figurative expression which its syntax proclaims it—
that is, as a comparison proposed between distinct, even
diverse, subjects in respect of a particular point of resemblance—and it yields nothing at odds with the accepted
idea of a ruler who, despite the utmost exertion of human
good will, must still be indebted to a power beyond his
own for any success in performance of that duty which
is entailed on him as God's vice-regent, and who, when
such success visits his endeavors, will transiently exemplify
the significance of that vice-regency. But, exact from that
same sentence more than figurative expression has to
give, and you are confronted with the notion of a divine
being who arrives (like a comic policeman) at the scene
of the disaster by an outside chance, and only just in time.

Treat the whole story as fairy tale, and you are not
obliged to challenge any of its suppositions. Treat it as
moral apologue, expressed in terms proper to its age, and
it will answer such challenge as may fairly be offered. The
Duke's expedients will then serve to illustrate the energy
and resources of a human agent. But, suppose him other
than human,[8] and the way leads inescapably to that conclusion which Sir Edmund Chambers reaches, when he
reflects on this play: "Surely the treatment of Providence
is ironical."[9] Unless *Measure for Measure* is to be accepted, and dismissed, as simple fairy tale—and what
fairy tale ever troubled so the imagination?—the clue to
this central and enigmatic figure must be sought in repre-
sentations of the good ruler as subjects of a Tudor sovereign conceived him; above all, in those illustrative anec-

---

8. For the extreme form of this supposition, see Battenhouse, *"Measure for Measure* and Christian Doctrine of the Atonement" (*Publications
of the Modern Language Association of America,* December 1946).
9. *Shakespeare: A Survey* (1925), p. 215.

dotes which writers (popular and learned alike) were glad to employ, and content to draw from common sources.

A number of these are to be found associated with the name and reputation of the Emperor Alexander Severus.[10] Developing on a course similar to that taken by Guevara's Marcus Aurelius romance, this curious legend was for a spell popular in England. Its fullest, most circumstantial, and most influential exemplar I take to be Sir Thomas Elyot's *Image of Governance*.[11] Here the salient features of the ideal portrait are these: inheriting a legacy of disorder and corruption, the good emperor is zealous in the reform of manners by means of social legislation and the careful appointment and assiduous supervision of his ministers of justice. To ensure a just outcome he will intervene in a case by subterfuge, not merely employing spies but acting in that capacity himself, and, when he has detected wrongdoing, not content merely to bring the accused to trial, he will handle the witnesses, cause false information to be put about, and trick the culprit into pronouncing his own sentence.[12] One after another, Tudor and Stuart sovereigns were addressed obliquely through anecdotes of Alexander Severus, congratulated on resemblance to him in respect of those virtues which the writer most desired in a ruler, and delicately invited to put to opportune employment those powers and qualities of which the country stood in need.[13] These pseudo-historical anecdotes, of which more than one bears a resemblance to those in Lupton's *Siuqila,* are many of them commonplaces of popular fiction; but, used by writers whose main

10. For an account of this legend, its development in England and range of application, see my article: "Sir Thomas Elyot and the Legend of Alexander Severus" (*Review of English Studies,* October 1951).
11. *The Image of Governance Compiled of the Actes and Sentences notable, of the moste noble Emperour Alexander Severus* (1541). This purports to be a translation from a Greek work by the Emperor's secretary, supplemented from other sources.
12. See particularly Chapters VIII to XIX, XXIV, XXXVIII, and XXXIX.
13. For an illustration of the adaptability of Elyot's anecdotes, see Whetstone's *Mirour for Magestrates of Cyties,* apparently a free version of those that Whetstone found congenial to his own times, and temper.

intention was not to tell a story (either historical or fictitious), they illustrate an idea of the business of government which could then be seriously canvassed by men involved in that very business, or eager to advise those so involved. They chart the tides and currents that a writer for an Elizabethan audience must have reckoned with, and remind us how far the direction of these habitual sympathies and antipathies has since altered: thus removing some of the obstacles to a fair estimate of the Duke's conduct. . . .

Isabel is the chief of those characters who are themselves engaged, and engage us, by the opportunity and capacity they are given for suffering; of whose sentient core we are keenly aware. And yet our consciousness of it is not constant. From the moment when she presents herself before Angelo to that of the Duke's intervention between her and Claudio, she holds our imagination subject by her alternations of hope and fear. Then she seems to abdicate. Her reaction to the one subsequent event which should reinstate her, the news of Claudio's death, is, as the text stands, hardly more than squirrel's chatter, "anger insignificantly fierce." From the moment of her submission to the Duke, until that in which she pleads for Angelo against his express injunction, she *is* insignificant. We may usefully recall, here, the comparison afforded by *The Heart of Midlothian*: whereas Jeanie takes matters into her own hands and, at severe cost to herself, wins her sister's pardon, Isabel appears to relinquish initiative and, under another's direction, to follow a course at once easier and less admirable. Out of her seeming subservience the opinion has arisen that Shakespeare wearied of her; had never (perhaps) intended that she should fill so big a place, or else, had designed her to perform a particular task and had now no further use for her. And yet, in the estimation of many, a full tide of significance flows back into her even in that instant of recovered independence. Here is an extreme, if not a singular, instance of a character fluctuating between two and three dimensions.

I believe that the explanation must be sought through

scrutiny of a greater anomaly, within the character. Isabel's chief activity in the play springs from the passions generated by a personal relationship—and yet this *source of all she does* is very strangely treated. The conventions of poetic drama bear hard on minor personal relationships; but *this* is of major importance. It is, besides, almost the only such relationship explicit in the play. Escalus' recollection of Claudio's father hardly alters this strangely *un-familied* world; and, though he is seen entering the prison, we do not see him with the prisoner. As for Claudio and Juliet, the extant text leaves me in doubt whether they are ever seen together. More surprising still, Claudio seems never to speak of Juliet, after that single reference in talk with Lucio. Shakespeare's *improvers,* mindful of those proprieties which are rather social than literary, attempt a remedy: Davenant making Claudio commit Juliet to Isabella's care, and introducing a letter to him from Juliet; Gildon adding a scene between these two.[14] Their officiousness is at least understandable: Claudio's silence must appear an oversight, unless we suppose that Shakespeare was deliberately flattening this part of his composition in order to throw into relief another relationship—and what should this be but the relationship between brother and sister? It is as Claudio's sister that Isabel comes into the play: as the woman who is drawn by a personal attachment into a dire predicament. And yet in her pleading on his behalf this personal relationship is faintly expressed. Many times, in her most moving passages, it would be possible to substitute "neighbor" for "brother," and hardly wake a ripple. Not that her pleading is passionless—to suppose so is to fall into Lucio's error. The very incandescence of her fiery compassion transcends the personal occasion, carrying her to a height at which, if she would plead for one man, she must plead for all. By contrast, the sense of personal relationship is sharply, even intolerably, explicit in the

14. Juliet committed to Isabella's care: Davenant, *The Law against Lovers*, p. 161; Gildon, *Measure for Measure, or Beauty the Best Advocate*, p. 24. Juliet's letter, Davenant, *op. cit.*, p. 185; Gildon's scene between Claudio and Juliet, *op. cit.*, pp. 34–36.

scene of her conflict with Claudio—the only scene in which they speak together. It puts an edge on her anger and fear; and it is in terms of their common heritage, and what it entails of participation in shame, that she denounces him. Thus this personal connection, which is the pivot of the play's action, is presented in its full significance only at the instant of its apparent dislocation.

Suppose we should find a single explanation valid for these, and all those other apparent anomalies in this character which have emerged from the foregoing examination of the play: it would surely be a master key. Let me briefly recapitulate the perplexities that have to be taken into account. When Isabel first hears of Claudio's predicament, her thought follows that course taken by Epitia's and Cassandra's: "Oh, let him marry her."[15] But, when she intercedes with Angelo, she does not urge, as they had done, and as all Vienna is ready to do, that the law is at fault if it demands the life of an offender who is able and willing to repair the wrong he has done. Nevertheless, when the Duke proposes to her a course of action whose justification is that it will commit Angelo to an act for which he may be compelled to make similar reparation, she acquiesces; and this, although she has reiterated to him her abhorrence of Claudio's act. And, if we explain this compliance in terms of her anxiety on her brother's behalf, we are reminded of strange fluctuations in her relationship with that very brother—and even, in the *density* of her own substance.

To understand what has happened, we must take into consideration something that emerges from a comparison between Giraldi's various developments of this theme, of a woman confronted with an abominable choice. Where this woman is sister to the condemned man and herself unmarried, it is assumed that any wrong done and suffered, in her surrender to his adversary, can be repaired by marriage.[16] But the situation that this assumption yields is fundamentally undramatic: there is no real con-

15. I.iv.49.
16. Whetstone, despite national and religious differences, is in accord with Giraldi here.

flict between characters, nor within any character; merely
such a show of opposition as suffices for a slight story.
The sister has only to say on her brother's behalf: "Since
he can, and will, make good the wrong done, your sentence is too severe." And to say this costs her nothing.
Likewise, when her opponent—bearing down this acknowledged right by might—tempts her to obtain what
she asks by consenting to an offense the counterpart of
her brother's, the two of them agree that she has but to
stipulate for the same reparation, marriage. Thus, the
whole cause of her distress is the advantage which strength
takes of weakness: the double breach of faith by a man
whose will is—for the time being—law. It is a piteous
tale. It does not yield the stuff of a play. In those other
versions of this theme, however, which make the woman
wife to the condemned man, dramatic tension is developed
through her abhorrence of the act required of her as injurious to that very relationship by force of which she
is brought to consent: she must buy his life at the price
of an infamy in which he is to be sharer. This is a dilemma such as we associate with tragedy, because it
presents a choice of courses from which there can be no
good issue. (Hence, such versions as those of Roilletus,
Lupton and Belleforest.) Now, in Giraldi's variations on
this theme, still in his favorite mood of tragicomedy, his
tales of Dorothea and Gratiosa, romance and comedy are
respectively invoked and given power to challenge the
assumption that a choice must be made between
two bad ways. And, in both, this favorable intervention
forestalls any possible distress, and so prevents painful
engagement of our sympathies: for, no sooner is the
wicked proposal made than something points to the existence of a third door.

Shakespeare accepted the version in which the woman
is the condemned man's sister, and unmarried. As an ex-
perienced dramatist, however, he could not but recognize
the dramatic insufficiency of this situation. It offered him
an unhitched rope, one of which the slack would never

be taken up; and the only means of making it taut was to give Isabel a motive for reluctance equivalent to that which forbade the wife's surrender. He gave her the convent.[17] So much may be common knowledge; but, like a troublesome debtor, I must still ask more patience of the reader, before I can show any return on what I have already borrowed. In making this one alteration, Shakespeare found himself committed to a number of others. As to plot, he must prevent the violation of her person; or else a happy ending would be repugnant to moral sentiment. As to character, she is marked at the outset by her sense of separateness: she cannot plead in the terms others use; and no shadow of comparison between Juliet or Mariana and herself ever crosses her mind. What, then, has become of her isolation when, with no apparent consciousness of doing anything questionable, she publishes her fictitious shame, and incurs suspicion of which she cannot count on being cleared?

I suggest that the dramatic center of the play, until the Duke intervenes, is an abhorrence of unchastity which carries the force of the original situation in which a wife faces a tragic dilemma. The form is changed, Shakespeare having taken (deliberately or no) that one of Giraldi's two channels for carrying the story away from tragedy which necessitates a change of relationship between the woman and the condemned man; but it is the old current which flows between these new banks. The pressure which we feel comes, as in a stream dammed up, from such a reluctance on the woman's part as neither Epitia nor Cassandra had fully known. But this dam does not hold. Once the responsibility for choosing has been lifted from Isabel's shoulders, the obstacle to choice begins to lose its significance. In the situation as it is refashioned by the Duke, it is no longer a factor. Presently it vanishes from recollection. In a world rapidly becoming secular; on a stage which was (by force of tacit agreement as well as censorship) the most secular institution in that world; and in the hands of a dramatist who

17. By the same means, he fastens guilt upon Angelo's inclination, barring the way to love and marriage.

in matters of conscience adhered to two rules,
To advise with no bigots, and jest with no fools,

it did not offer itself to free and familiar expression. An Elizabethan dramatist of far less than Shakespeare's power could far more easily have conveyed to an Elizabethan audience, within the conventions both understood, the reluctance, say, of Lucrece.

When a storyteller has to devise an equivalent for something in his story, as he originally knew or conceived it, which has proved intractable to his purpose, this new constituent is liable to remain imperfectly substantiated, perhaps because he unconsciously reckons on its retaining the potency which his imagination still associates with that which it replaces. Here it may signify all that he requires, and there, dwindle into insignificance. An echo of this story as it may first have visited Shakespeare's imagination seems to reverberate in that antagonism which develops between brother and sister, when she perceives that he does not participate in her sense of the infamy of consent. But that very sense, and its justification, are so little evident in the part of the play which follows that Isabel's account of herself as one "in probation of a sisterhood,"[18] seems but a reminder of something lost by the way. It is only when she stands alone again, opposed even to the Duke, that her former separateness seems for an instant to recover its importance.

18. V.i.72.

Suggested References

The number of possible references is vast and grows alarmingly. (The *Shakespeare Quarterly* devotes a substantial part of one issue each year to a list of the previous year's work, and *Shakespeare Survey*—an annual publication—includes a substantial review of recent scholarship, as well as an occasional essay surveying a few decades of scholarship on a chosen topic.) Though no works are indispensable, those listed below have been found helpful.

1. Shakespeare's Times

Byrne, M. St. Clare. *Elizabethan Life in Town and Country*. Rev. ed. New York: Barnes & Noble, Inc., 1961. Chapters on manners, beliefs, education, etc., with illustrations.

Craig, Hardin. *The Enchanted Glass: the Elizabethan Mind in Literature*. New York and London: Oxford University Press, 1936. The Elizabethan intellectual climate.

Joseph, B. L. *Shakespeare's Eden: The Commonwealth of England 1558–1629*. New York: Barnes & Noble, Inc., 1971. An account of the social, political, economic, and cultural life of England.

Nicoll, Allardyce (ed.). *The Elizabethans*. London: Cambridge University Press, 1957. An anthology of Elizabethan writings, especially valuable for its illustrations from paintings, title pages, etc.

Shakespeare's England. 2 vols. Oxford: The Clarendon Press, 1916. A large collection of scholarly essays on a wide variety of topics (e.g., astrology, costume, gardening, horsemanship), with special attention to Shakespeare's references to these topics.

Tillyard, E. M. W. *The Elizabethan World Picture*. London: Chatto & Windus, 1943; New York: The Macmillan Company, 1944. A brief account of some Elizabethan ideas of the universe.

Wilson, John Dover (ed.). *Life in Shakespeare's England*. 2nd ed. New York: The Macmillan Company, 1913. An anthology of Elizabethan writings on the countryside, superstition, education, the court, etc.

2. Shakespeare

Barnet, Sylvan. *A Short Guide to Shakespeare*. New York: Harcourt Brace Jovanovich, Inc., 1974. An introduction to all of the works and to the traditions behind them.

Bentley, Gerald E. *Shakespeare: A Biographical Handbook.* New Haven, Conn.: Yale University Press, 1961. The facts about Shakespeare, with virtually no conjecture intermingled.

Bradby, Anne (ed.). *Shakespeare Criticism, 1919–1935.* London: Oxford University Press, 1936. A small anthology of excellent essays on the plays.

Bush, Geoffrey Douglas. *Shakespeare and the Natural Condition.* Cambridge, Mass.: Harvard University Press; London: Oxford University Press, 1956. A short, sensitive account of Shakespeare's view of "Nature," touching most of the works.

Chambers, E. K. *William Shakespeare: A Study of Facts and Problems.* 2 vols. London: Oxford University Press, 1930. An invaluable, detailed reference work; not for the casual reader.

Chute, Marchette. *Shakespeare of London.* New York: E. P. Dutton & Co., Inc., 1949. A readable biography fused with portraits of Stratford and London life.

Clemen, Wolfgang H. *The Development of Shakespeare's Imagery.* Cambridge, Mass.: Harvard University Press, 1951. (Originally published in German, 1936.) A temperate account of a subject often abused.

Craig, Hardin. *An Interpretation of Shakespeare.* Columbia, Missouri: Lucas Brothers, 1948. A scholar's book designed for the layman. Comments on all the works.

Dean, Leonard F. (ed.). *Shakespeare: Modern Essays in Criticism.* New York: Oxford University Press, 1957. Mostly mid-twentieth-century critical studies, covering Shakespeare's artistry.

Granville-Barker, Harley. *Prefaces to Shakespeare.* 2 vols. Princeton, N.J.: Princeton University Press, 1946–47. Essays on ten plays by a scholarly man of the theater.

Harbage, Alfred. *As They Liked It.* New York: The Macmillan Company, 1947. A sensitive, long essay on Shakespeare, morality, and the audience's expectations.

———. *William Shakespeare: A Reader's Guide.* New York: Farrar, Straus, 1963. Extensive comments, scene by scene, on fourteen plays.

Ridler, Anne Bradby (ed.). *Shakespeare Criticism, 1935–1960.* New York and London: Oxford University Press, 1963. An excellent continuation of the anthology edited earlier by Miss Bradby (see above).

Schoenbaum, S. *Shakespeare's Lives.* Oxford: Clarendon Press, 1970. A review of the evidence, and an examination of many biographies, including those by Baconians and other heretics.

————. *William Shakespeare: A Compact Documentary Life*. New York: Oxford University Press, 1977. A readable presentation of all that the documents tell us about Shakespeare.

Smith, D. Nichol (ed.). *Shakespeare Criticism*. New York: Oxford University Press, 1916. A selection of criticism from 1623 to 1840, ranging from Ben Jonson to Thomas Carlyle.

Spencer, Theodore. *Shakespeare and the Nature of Man*. New York: The Macmillan Company, 1942. Shakespeare's plays in relation to Elizabethan thought.

Stoll, Elmer Edgar. *Shakespeare and Other Masters*. Cambridge, Mass.: Harvard University Press; London: Oxford University Press, 1940. Essays on tragedy, comedy, and aspects of dramaturgy, with special reference to some of Shakespeare's plays.

Traversi, D. A. *An Approach to Shakespeare*. Rev. ed. New York: Doubleday & Co., Inc., 1956. An analysis of the plays, beginning with words, images, and themes, rather than with characters.

Van Doren, Mark. *Shakespeare*. New York: Henry Holt & Company, Inc., 1939. Brief, perceptive readings of all of the plays.

Whitaker, Virgil K. *Shakespeare's Use of Learning*. San Marino, Calif.: Huntington Library, 1953. A study of the relation of Shakespeare's reading to his development as a dramatist.

3. Shakespeare's Theater

Adams, John Cranford. *The Globe Playhouse*. Rev. ed. New York: Barnes & Noble, Inc., 1961. A detailed conjecture about the physical characteristics of the theater Shakespeare often wrote for.

Beckerman, Bernard. *Shakespeare at the Globe, 1599–1609*. New York: The Macmillan Company, 1962. On the playhouse and on Elizabethan dramaturgy, acting, and staging.

Chambers, E. K. *The Elizabethan Stage*. 4 vols. New York: Oxford University Press, 1923. Reprinted with corrections, 1945. A valuable reference work on theaters, theatrical companies, and staging at court.

Gurr, Andrew. *The Shakespearean Stage 1574–1642*. Cambridge: Cambridge University Press, 1970. On the acting companies, the actors, the playhouses, the stages, and the audiences.

Harbage, Alfred. *Shakespeare's Audience*. New York: Columbia University Press; London: Oxford University Press, 1941. A study of the size and nature of the theatrical public.

Hodges, C. Walter. *The Globe Restored*. London: Ernest Benn, Ltd., 1953; New York: Coward-McCann, Inc., 1954. A well-illustrated and readable attempt to reconstruct the Globe Theatre.

Kernodle, George R. *From Art to Theatre: Form and Convention in the Renaissance*. Chicago: University of Chicago Press, 1944. Pioneering and stimulating work on the symbolic and cultural meanings of theater construction.

Nagler, A. M. *Shakespeare's Stage*. Tr. by Ralph Manheim. New Haven, Conn.: Yale University Press, 1958. An excellent brief introduction to the physical aspect of the playhouse.

Smith, Irwin. *Shakespeare's Globe Playhouse*. New York: Charles Scribner's Sons, 1957. Chiefly indebted to J. C. Adams' controversial book, with additional material and scale drawings for model-builders.

Venezky, Alice S. *Pageantry on the Shakespearean Stage*. New York: Twayne Publishers, Inc., 1951. An examination of spectacle in Elizabethan drama.

4. Miscellaneous Reference Works

Abbott, E. A. *A Shakespearean Grammar*. New edition. New York. The Macmillan Company, 1877. An examination of differences between Elizabethan and modern grammar.

Berman, Ronald. *A Reader's Guide to Shakespeare's Plays*, rev. ed. Glenview, Ill.: Scott, Foresman and Company, 1973. A short bibliography of the chief articles and books on each play.

Bullough, Geoffrey. *Narrative and Dramatic Sources of Shakespeare*. 4 vols. Vols. 5 and 6 in preparation. New York: Columbia University Press; London: Routledge & Kegan Paul Ltd., 1957–. A collection of many of the books Shakespeare drew upon.

Campbell, Oscar James, and Edward G. Quinn. *The Reader's Encyclopedia of Shakespeare*. New York: Thomas Y. Crowell Co., 1966. More than 2,700 entries, from a few sentences to a few pages on everything related to Shakespeare.

Greg, W. W. *The Shakespeare First Folio*. New York and London: Oxford University Press, 1955. A detailed yet readable history of the first collection (1623) of Shakespeare's plays.

Kökeritz, Helge. *Shakespeare's Names*. New Haven, Conn.: Yale University Press, 1959; London: Oxford University Press, 1960. A guide to the pronunciation of some 1,800 names appearing in Shakespeare.

———. *Shakespeare's Pronunciation*. New Haven, Conn.: Yale University Press; London: Oxford University Press,

1953. Contains much information about puns and rhymes.

Linthicum, Marie C. *Costume in the Drama of Shakespeare and His Contemporaries.* New York and London: Oxford University Press, 1936. On the fabrics and dress of the age, and references to them in the plays.

Muir, Kenneth. *Shakespeare's Sources.* London: Methuen & Co., Ltd., 1957. The first volume, on the comedies and tragedies, attempts to ascertain what books were Shakespeare's sources, and what use he made of them.

Onions, C. T. *A Shakespeare Glossary.* London: Oxford University Press, 1911; 2nd ed., rev., with enlarged addenda, 1953. Definitions of words (or senses of words) now obsolete.

Partridge, Eric. *Shakespeare's Bawdy.* Rev. ed. New York: E. P. Dutton & Co., Inc.; London: Routledge & Kegan Paul, Ltd., 1955. A glossary of bawdy words and phrases.

Shakespeare Quarterly. See headnote to Suggested References.

Shakespeare Survey. See headnote to Suggested References.

Smith, Gordon Ross. *A Classified Shakespeare Bibliography 1936–1958.* University Park, Pa.: Pennsylvania State University Press, 1963. A list of some 20,000 items on Shakespeare.

Spevack, Marvin. *The Harvard Concordance to Shakespeare.* Cambridge, Mass.: Harvard University Press, 1973. An index to Shakespeare's words.

Wells, Stanley, ed. *Shakespeare: Select Bibliographies.* London: Oxford University Press, 1973. Seventeen essays surveying scholarship and criticism of Shakespeare's life, work, and theater.

5. *Measure for Measure*

Bradbrook, M. C. "Authority, Truth and Justice in *Measure for Measure*," *Review of English Studies,* 17 (1941), 385–99.

Coghill, Nevill. "Comic Form in *Measure for Measure*," *Shakespeare Survey 8,* ed. Allardyce Nicoll (1955), pp. 14–26.

Doran, Madeleine. *Endeavors of Art: A Study of Form in Elizabethan Drama.* Madison: University of Wisconsin Press, 1954.

Empson, William. *The Structure of Complex Words.* New York: New Directions; London: Chatto & Windus Ltd., 1951.

Fergusson, Francis. *The Human Image in Dramatic Literature.* New York: Doubleday & Co., Inc. (Anchor Books), 1957.

Foakes, R. A. *Shakespeare: The Dark Comedies to the Last Plays.* Charlottesville: University Press of Virginia, 1971.

Geckle, George L. (ed.). *Twentieth Century Interpretations of "Measure for Measure."* Englewood Cliffs, New Jersey: Prentice-Hall, 1970.

Hunter, Robert Grams. *Shakespeare and the Comedy of Forgiveness.* New York: Columbia University Press, 1965.

Knight, G. Wilson. *The Wheel of Fire,* 5th rev. ed. New York: Meridian Books, 1957.

Lascelles, Mary. *Shakespeare's Measure for Measure.* London: Athlone Press, 1953.

Lawrence, W. W. *Shakespeare's Problem Comedies.* New York and London: The Macmillan Company, 1931.

————. "Measure for Measure and Lucio," *Shakespeare Quarterly,* 9 (1958), 443–453.

Leavis, F. R. *The Common Pursuit.* London: Chatto & Windus Ltd., 1952.

Leech, Clifford. "The Meaning of *Measure for Measure,*" *Shakespeare Survey 3,* ed. Allardyce Nicoll (1950), pp. 66–73.

Maxwell, J. C. "*Measure for Measure:* A Footnote to Recent Criticism," *The Downside Review,* 65 (1947), 45–59.

Merchant, W. Moelwyn. *Shakespeare and the Artist.* New York and London: Oxford University Press, 1959.

Miles, Rosalind. *The Problem of Measure for Measure.* New York: Barnes & Noble, 1976.

Nagarajan, S. "*Measure for Measure* and Elizabethan Betrothals," *Shakespeare Quarterly,* 19 (1963), 115–119.

Pope, Elizabeth M. "The Renaissance Background of *Measure for Measure,*" *Shakespeare Survey 2,* ed. Allardyce Nicoll (1949), pp. 66–82.

Rossiter, A. P. "*Angel with Horns*" and Other Shakespeare Lectures, ed. Graham Storey. New York: Theatre Arts Books; London: Longmans, Green & Co., Ltd., 1961.

Schanzer, Ernest. *The Problem Plays of Shakespeare: A Study of "Julius Caesar," "Measure for Measure," and "Antony and Cleopatra."* London: Routledge & Kegan Paul Ltd., 1963.

Sewell, Arthur. *Character and Society in Shakespeare.* Oxford: The Clarendon Press, 1951.

Sisson, C. J. *The Mythical Sorrows of Shakespeare.* New York and London: Oxford University Press, 1934.

Stevenson, David L. *The Achievement of "Measure for Measure."* Ithaca: Cornell University Press, 1966.

Tillyard, E. M. W. *Shakespeare's Problem Plays.* Toronto: University of Toronto Press, 1949; London: Chatto & Windus Ltd., 1950.